Also by Linda Greenlaw

JANE BUNKER MYSTERIES
Slipknot
Fisherman's Bend
Shiver Hitch

NONFICTION
The Hungry Ocean
The Lobster Chronicles
All Fishermen Are Liars
Seaworthy
Lifesaving Lessons

WITH MARTHA GREENLAW
Recipes from a Very Small Island
The Maine Summers Cookbook

BIMINI
TWIST

Linda Greenlaw

St. Martin's Paperbacks

This is a work of fiction. All of the characters, organizations, and events portrayed in this novel are either products of the author's imagination or are used fictitiously.

BIMINI TWIST

Copyright © 2018 by Linda Greenlaw.

For information address St. Martin's Press, 175 Fifth Avenue, New York, NY 10010.

ISBN: 978-1-250-21432-4

Our books may be purchased in bulk for promotional, educational, or business use. Please contact your local bookseller or the Macmillan Corporate and Premium Sales Department at 1-800-221-7945, ext. 5442, or by e-mail at MacmillanSpecialMarkets@macmillan.com.

Printed in the United States of America

St. Martin's Press hardcover edition / June 2018
St. Martin's Paperbacks edition / June 2019

St. Martin's Paperbacks are published by St. Martin's Press, 175 Fifth Avenue, New York, NY 10010.

10 9 8 7 6 5 4 3 2 1

Acknowledgments

Through the course of eleven books, I have become acutely aware of one basic commonality between my lives of writing and fishing: the strength of the outcome is in direct correlation to the strength of the people with whom I surround myself. I no longer consider writing a solitary exercise.

Many thanks to my literary agent, Stuart Krichevsky. The Stuart Krichevsky Agency's A-Team of Ameilia Phillips, Laura Usselman, and Hannah Schwartz is second to none. I am so fortunate and grateful for their representation.

Thanks and appreciation go to the crew at Minotaur, the best in mystery publishing. Kelley Ragland, Hannah Braaten, and assistant Nettie Finn of the editing department are responsible for coaching, cheering, and supporting *Bimini Twist* to the finish line. Special thanks to Allison Ziegler for her talents in publicity. Of course, I would be remiss not to give a salute in thanks, respect, and admiration to Will Schwalbe—my editor for life.

The support of friends and family is enormous and much appreciated. The people I see and speak with on a regular basis are sources of both inspiration and material. I am most grateful to my parents, Jim and Martha Greenlaw, and my husband, Stephen Wessel. Friends Don and Annie Ervin have become part of my Surry, Maine, family and their love and generosity serve as examples of what I strive for. My sister, Beth, is my sounding board, voice of reason, and best friend. If we accomplish even a fraction of what we plan to, there are many books in our future.

ONE

"Any get-together described as a *social, fete, gala,* or *soiree*— you can count me out," I said as I stood, brushing tiny scraps of blueberry muffin from my jeans into the palm of my hand. I deposited the muffin crumbs onto the place mat that marked my usual spot at the breakfast bar at the Harbor Café. The place mat that advertised every commercial enterprise between my home in tiny Green Haven and Ellsworth, Maine, and still allowed room for the café's menu was all that was needed to explain the size and rural-ness of the area where I had decided to hang my hat following a knee-jerk move from Miami. "I'm just more casual than that. Think *shindig.*"

"But you *have* to go," urged Audrey from the working side of the counter. "The Alfonds' Summer Solstice Soiree is like the annual who's who of Green Haven."

"And all the more reason for me to not attend. I detest that sort of thing. And why was I invited? I am the epitome of nobody."

I stood and bent over the stool, resting both elbows on the counter. I was anxious to hear the sassy young waitress talk her way around the fact that my invitation was clearly a case of mistaken identity or at the very least a serious lapse in the Alfonds' judgment. "Are *you* going?"

This literally stopped what I had come to know as Audrey's perpetual motion in its proverbial tracks. I had met Audrey right here nearly a year ago to the day. And in that time I had never been less than amazed at her ability to multitask, running the show at the café while carrying on a conversation (or three!). Now, in this brief moment, Audrey wasn't clearing a place setting, pouring coffee, taking orders from customers or barking orders to the kitchen, scraping plates, serving food, or answering the phone. She looked at me in astonishment through her paradoxical, contradictory combination of maturity beyond and naivety before her nearly twenty years of age. "You are kidding, right?" She sucked a gold lip ring into her mouth thoughtfully, then allowed it to pop back out. "Yours truly is not even on the B-list. Someone like me would never be invited." This was matter-of-fact, and not at all a lament or complaint. "That's why it's so important for you to go and report back to me! The only time *real* people get invited to the soiree is when a selectman or code enforcement officer is included. And that only happens when some hobnobber needs a variance for a project that does not comply with zoning rules."

"And once again, why am *I* invited?"

"News flash for you, girlfriend . . ." Audrey now switched gears back into full speed ahead. She quickly cleared and reset the counter where I had been, and turned to load the coffee maker while talking over her shoulder with her back to me. "You are Green Haven's most eligible bachelorette."

"Ha! Prospects aren't good for the single men in this town if I top the list of possibilities."

"Not to downplay any appeal you might have, but have you looked around lately?" Audrey disappeared through the swinging doors to the kitchen and returned with a tray loaded with plates full of eggs and pancakes before the insult sunk in. "You are it, period. The only other single ladies in town are gay, widowed seniors, or socially unfit for a soiree—like me!" Audrey served the breakfast plates like she was dealing from a deck of playing cards: smoothly and precisely. She breezed by me as I pulled on my jacket to leave and added, "You are going to the Alfonds, and that, as they say, is that."

I laughed knowing that there was no way that I would go. In fact, I had the RSVP in my bag, and was planning to check the "I can't attend" box and stick it in the mail this morning on my way to work. Cowbells clanged when the café's door opened revealing Green Haven's equivalent to the village idiot, Clydie Leeman. Glad to avoid the usual nonsensical conversation with him by excusing myself and leaving, I made my way through the door, which Clydie held open with more flourish than was necessary. Before the door closed behind me, Audrey called out playfully, "And now enters your plus-one!"

"Plus what?" I heard Clyde ask while I quickly made my way down Main Street as the sounds and smells of the café dulled to nothing. I always enjoyed the light banter I shared with Audrey,

3

as well as her insights into the community that had fostered her in the absence of nurturing biological parents. That same community, which was so different from that of low-income, migrant-and-immigrant Miami from where I had come, was beginning to feel like home, I thought as I walked briskly along Green Haven's Main Street toward my apartment perched on Burnt Hill.

Well, this somewhat native Floridian had survived her first Maine winter. Not exactly my first. But the only one that I had any recollection of. I had left Maine at the age of five in an old station wagon with my mother at the helm and my infant brother, Wally, in the back seat with me. Stopping only for fuel and catnaps, we ran out of road and money in Miami, where we set the anchor. I suppose most people would consider my childhood a little rough, or unorthodox at the very least. But one thing's for sure, it was indeed *mine*. And I had come to realize that my childhood was one of very few things that I truly possessed and that could never be lost or taken away. In my early teens, I am embarrassed to admit, I was envious of my brother's Down syndrome. Wally's affliction seemed more a blessing than what I had been dealt—Nothing special—No great beauty or intellect—No God-given talent—No charm or sex appeal—No reason to be noticed. Plain Jane. Jane Bunker. Milk toast. Uninteresting. Except, I reminded myself as I started up the hill, in my career. There had been no lack of luster on the job.

I had clawed my way to the top grade of detective in crime-ridden, drug-laden Miami in the days when women were addressed mostly as Mrs., Mom, or both. My life at work was far from boring. My career eventually defined me. Detective Jane

Bunker became feared by the outlaws who smuggled drugs onto the shores of my territory, so ripe for such activity with mangrove swamps and everglades. Thankfully, law enforcement is a career that translates well geographically. Cops are needed everywhere. It hadn't taken long for my initial Down East gig of insurance investigator to cede way to the growing duties at the sheriff's office of Hancock County, where I had been named deputy.

Since my arrival in Green Haven, I had waged what amounted to a single-handed war on drugs in Down East Maine, and had won many battles, the numbers of which were on a frighteningly steep rise. I had made busts up and down the supply chain, knowing that each time I severed a link, it interrupted flow. Interrupted flow saved lives. I had also managed to investigate three non-drug-related murder cases, all of which ended in lengthy prison sentences for the convicted. Not that prison equals justice for all victims and families. But it is the best we can do short of practicing eye for an eye (not that I always oppose it) which I suspect was a standard mode of operation prior to my presence. The fabric of remote, coastal, small-town Maine is lumpy with so much having been swept under the rug through the years.

My apartment, which I now approached, was an efficiency over a seasonal gift shop called The Lobster Trappe. My landlords lived in the main house, and graciously rented their guest bedroom to my brother Wally, who moved to Maine from Miami four months ago when his assisted-living situation closed due to loss of federal funding. I had been skeptical of how the

5

arrangements would work out. And I initially reasoned that Wally would be under the same roof only temporarily. Our landlords, Henry and Alice Vickerson, or Mr. and Mrs. V, were so much more than that. Both in their mid-eighties, Alice and Henry were quirky and cool, and very much like the grandparents that I never knew. They had grown fond of Wally quickly, and this endeared them to me even more than their generosity and kindness to me had. Stepping around unopened boxes of inventory for the gift shop, I made my way to the main entrance to check in with Wally before heading off to work at the Hancock County Sheriff's Department.

I rapped twice on the door with the back of my hand, opened it, and called out, "Good morning."

"Good morning, Janey," was the cheerful reply from the chorus of three voices that I had come to expect. This was our daily morning routine. I found everyone in their usual places around the breakfast table. Mr. V was the only one fully dressed, and he looked as dapper as he always did, with perfectly creased chinos and a blue-and-white plaid dress shirt tucked in neatly and accented with a canvas belt embroidered with lobsters. Mrs. V wore her long cotton summer nightgown under a white-and-red lobster-print terrycloth robe. Her slippers were a matching red and a little floppier than what I thought safe for an elderly woman to shuffle around in. Wally sported his favorite Batman jammies, which had been part of a welcome package from Alice and Henry.

"Motley crew," I said as I pulled out the fourth chair and

plunked into it. "Wally, you are working bankers' hours! It is nearly eight thirty, and you're not dressed," I teased.

"I like split swing shift. It's more civilized," he responded with what I knew was a direct quote he had picked up from the Vs. Wally could be somewhat of a parrot, which is why I am so concerned about who he spends time with. Back when he was a teenager, the local kids used to take strange joy in teaching him to swear, and then I was stuck teaching him to apologize to whomever he had offended. Now, I heard the landlords' influence every time he spoke. That, and Audrey's. Wally's "split swing shift" was spent at the café where Audrey kept him busy and entertained. The job was great. It gave Wally a little independence and a lot of pride and self-respect. Employment gave Wally a bit of swag, and Audrey gave him too much sass for my liking. But I knew to take the good with the bad. Besides, I realized that the shifts had been created specifically for my brother. The first two hours of the split shift landed directly between the breakfast rush and the lunch onslaught, and the second was right after lunch. I didn't know what the "swing" portion of his hours referred to, but assumed I would find out when Wally's shift swung.

I sipped a cup of black coffee that Mrs. V poured from a lobster carafe and listened contentedly to everyone's plans for the day. The landlords would be busy stocking shelves in the gift shop with new merchandise—all of which had something to do with lobster traps, buoys, boats, or the critters themselves. Tourist season had just begun with a little light traffic in the way of shoppers. "But," Mrs. V reminded, "we'd better hold on to our hats." The season would be in full bloom by July Fourth. They had just three short months to "make hay." And then it would be another nine months of "tough sledding."

Wally drank hot chocolate and slurped the last of the milk from his now empty cereal bowl. Mr. V drummed his fingers on the table until I made eye contact with him. "So, we understand that you'll be attending the Alfonds' annual Summer Solstice Soiree. That's wonderful!" It was now clear that my landlords, who consider my business (personal or professional) their business, had gleaned this particular insight from sifting through my mail, which was always delivered to their box as I had not secured one of my own.

Three wide-eyed expressions waited anxiously for my affirmative reply. They sat with elbows on the table, leaning forward encouragingly and welcoming what they hoped would be an excited acquiescence to what they all understood was not at all something I would desire or enjoy. "Nope," was all I could muster. All three sank back in their chairs, crossed arms at their chests, and exhaled in disgust. "I am not interested in socializing with summer people."

"From what we see and hear, you're not interested in socializing with anyone." Mrs. V sounded sad and sort of whined as she continued. "Janey, you must be lonely. If you don't put yourself out there, you'll never meet anyone."

"I am fine, really. But thank you for caring. I have work. And I have all of you!"

"Audrey says Janey is a squayah," Wally interjected in a

8

pretty good Down East accent. As the Vs and I realized that Wally didn't know what it meant to be square, we chuckled and lightened what was heading toward awkward for me.

Before they could badger me further, a sharp dinging rang out from a kitchen timer—of course the timer was a plastic lobster—alerting us that it was now time for Wally to get ready for work. This was always my cue to leave, and I did so quickly, thanking my landlords for the coffee and kissing my brother on his forehead. "Time for me to break camp," I announced happily and started toward the door.

"You are breaking rank," teased Mr. V, beginning what had become a game of play on words that we engaged in frequently. In this case, Mr. V had chosen "break."

"Them's the breaks," I quipped.

"You should break new ground," Mr. V advised.

"You sound like a broken record."

"Break the ice!" Mr. V pounded a fist on the table for emphasis.

"I'll break out in a sweat."

"After you, they broke the mold." He shook his head.

"If it ain't broke, don't fix it."

"But you can't make an omelet without breaking a few eggs."

"Break it up!" yelled Mrs. V as she placed her right hand on top of her left forming a T, calling for a time-out. Although I still had a few arrows in my quiver, when the boss lady speaks, we listen. Before I reached the door, Alice once again pleaded her case, giving reasons why I should start socializing, and added, "At least promise you'll think about going to the soiree. Won't you, dear?"

"Will do," I said in concession as I stepped over the threshold and closed the door behind me. I couldn't imagine why my landlords worried so about my personal life. I was content and fulfilled in my work. Although Audrey had defined my extracurricular activities as "lame," I never paid heed as I knew that I had no time for men, which is where any such conversation always took us. Sure, I had been through my fair share of relationships, I thought as I bobbed and weaved through lobster birdhouses and wind chimes that dangled from the gift shop's exposed beams. I had even been engaged once. And the memory of how that had ended so badly, and the fact that my ex-fiancé was solely responsible for my move to Maine at the top of my career, sealed the deal on the RSVP to the soiree.

I climbed behind the wheel of my Plymouth Duster, stomped on the gas pedal three times, and cranked up the motor. My car was another conversation starter. Although I refer to it as a Duster, it is in actuality a 1987 Plymouth Turismo with 186,000 original miles. The Turismo's original sales brochure boasted what spoke directly to my Scottish heritage—"The American Way to Get Your Money's Worth." Budget wheels and a taste for Scotch whiskey are perhaps the only connections I have to my roots. Of course I never celebrate them in unison, as drinking and driving would be a blemish I could not live down. I bought my car used, and it is the only car I have ever owned. In its day, the beige crystal coat and sable brown were probably pretty sexy. But thirty years in, even this "Florida car" had faded to a dull, nondescript hue—like me, I realized with a laugh. I forced all thoughts of men and cars out of my head and allowed myself to appreciate the scenery as I drove the narrow, twisting road that connected Green Haven to the rest of Maine, including my destination—Hancock County Sheriff's Department in Ellsworth.

Daffodils that had pushed proudly through brownish banks and roadside ditches just days ago were now looking limp as fresh greenery spread and budded nearly everywhere I looked. Coastal Maine in spring was far different from what it had been in winter, I thought. The only remnants of winter's retreat were crusty, white rings of snow at the bases of trees that shaded them from direct sun, and what remained of fishermen's trap piles that shrunk daily in preparation for the first shedders to strike. Spring brought bustling activity and renewed spirit to Green Haven, I thought. Freshly painted buoys were strung to dry in nearly every yard in town. The florescent Day-Glo buoy paint splattered bright spritzes of color onto backdrops of yellow or green trap wire. Boats loaded high and wide with gear disappeared from the harbor and returned empty to docks to reload and set again. Dawn was greeted with the roar and purr of diesel engines. By daylight the calm of the harbor was chopped by boats and skiffs dashing about for fuel and bait. And all quelled at dusk as boats returned to moorings and fishermen with empty dinner pails headed home in pickup trucks that drained from parking areas in steady streams.

The seasonal shops that lined Main Street were getting their annual sprucing up. Shutters were opened and windows were cleaned. Porches and railings were painted and repaired as needed. Signs were freshened and flags were displayed. Food shacks boasted "The Best Lobster Roll in Maine" and "Fresh Blueberry Pie," surely the staples of the Maine food scene during tourist season. "Help Wanted" was a common theme among the seasonal signage. Picnic tables appeared where snowmobile trailers had been. Mailboxes that had taken the brunt of careless plow drivers were shored up. The inventory at the General Store had changed from ice fishing gear, rock salt, and shovels to mackerel jigs, sun block, and T-shirts touting all of the glories of Vacationland. As I left Green Haven proper and swerved my way across the snakelike causeway to the mainland, I thought how nicely I had settled in here. I am happy, I thought to myself as I drove the final ten minutes to work.

As July Fourth approached, the traffic in Ellsworth would become heavy and parking spaces hard to find. Fortunately, I had a place reserved with a sign that read "Hancock County Deputy Sheriff" right in front of the station. I swung the Duster into my dedicated slot and hustled to and through the front door where I was greeted by Deloris, the dispatcher. Actually, to refer to Deloris as a dispatcher was doing her a disservice, I knew. Deloris had proven herself invaluable in electronic forensics and reconstruction and was adept in researching and navigating all of the Federal and State websites and systems for any and all investigative information needed to assist me in my pursuit of justice. (Hacker is a term that I save for those on the wrong side of the law).

Deloris had just recently returned to work from a long stint at home where she convalesced from broken heels suffered in the line of duty. Although she longed to be more hands-on, we wouldn't have that conversation until she was fully healed (no pun intended). And until that time, she would remain at a desk and assist where I was weakest. Yin and yang. Deloris was the perfect partner, I thought as I stopped at her desk to get the early scoop on what was on the docket for this morning. "I see you made the front page, again." Deloris smiled and handed me a newspaper that she had neatly folded to display a single headline and article. "Hancock County Sheriff's Department Strikes Again," she read as I focused on the subheading: "Two New York City men arrested on charges of trafficking heroin and crack cocaine."

"They never get it right," I said as I placed the paper on top of a pile of folders in front of Deloris. "I arrested three people. Two men and one woman."

"You're averaging a bust a week!" Deloris held up a hand for a high five, which I was happy to reciprocate, and I accepted the congratulations. "You're killing it."

"Unfortunately, the frequency of arrests made is a statement of how rampant the drugs and thugs are, rather than a true testament to my police work. But I *am* killing it, aren't I?" Stamping out illegal drugs that were chalking up deaths due to overdose at a history-making rate had been my mission since taking on the position of deputy sheriff. It was what I had done in my past life in Miami, and was perhaps the one thing that I was passionate about.

"Yes, indeed. Now, if you can squeeze your swelled head through the door, the sheriff is waiting for us in his office," Deloris said with a grin as she stood and tucked the doctor-prescribed

13

crutches under her arms. I allowed Deloris to lead the way, limping down the corridor and into the sheriff's office. This had become our morning routine. I would modestly accept accolades for this most recent bust, and listen to what the sheriff had in mind for an agenda. Most commonly, he would defer to my judgment on how best to spend my time on the clock. Deloris was always enthusiastic about assisting, and I was quick to praise her publicly for her expertise.

"Morning, ladies," the sheriff said as he motioned for us to take seats opposite him at a large, handsome desk. "This comes from the powers that be," he started as he scanned what appeared to be an email he had printed out. I sat up straight and proud, waiting for more high praise from Green Haven's town fathers, or another pat on the back from the Maine Drug Enforcement Agency. The sheriff scanned the mail, sat back, and sighed. He shrugged his shoulders, cocked his head to one side while looking me in the eye, and said, "They're asking me to put the binders on you."

This was not at all what I had anticipated. I was confused. Deloris wiggled uncomfortably in her seat while I tried to collect my thoughts enough to ask a question. Before I could do so, the sheriff continued. "It seems that the number and amplitude of your drug-related arrests are making Green Haven's authorities uneasy." This did nothing to unravel my scrambled thoughts. I turned and looked at Deloris for clarity or some explanation, but her jaw had dropped and her complexion had become ashen.

The sheriff offered the sheet of paper to me as I struggled to make sense of what he had said. I realized that Down East

Maine had its own colloquialisms, some of which I had yet to decipher. But putting binders on was somewhat universal. The sheriff had been asked to hit the brakes of the vehicle on which I had been riding so high and fast, facilitating taking down dealers and smugglers of any illicit substances that made their way into Hancock County. I refused the paper as I had no need to see this ridiculous order in writing. "Why?" I asked.

"Tourism. Maine is Vacationland. People leave the cities to get *away* from crime. The Town Fathers are of the opinion that the publicity surrounding your . . . well, achievements, will have an adverse effect on the local economy, which they remind us is hospitality based until after Labor Day." A long silence followed. I couldn't believe what I was hearing. Uneasy with my silent stare, the sheriff turned to Deloris and asked, "What will the summer people think? You get it, right?"

"Loud and clear." Deloris snapped to. "Nothing says Welcome to Maine like the meth lab next door. Sort of puts the ain't in quaint." I mulled, frustrated, while Deloris and the sheriff quickly went on to another, relatively benign subject. How could I possibly put my ambition and main purpose in life on hold until the elite vacate Vacationland? As my boss and Deloris discussed how the summer community and tourists bleed money that is so badly needed after the drying winds of winter, I pulled something from the recesses of my memory that made me smile.

Could it have been that long ago, I wondered, that I cracked the case that put me on the map? It was 1993. News of my tri-county drug bust made headlines in every national and daily

15

publication. And it was one tongue-in-cheek article that I clipped and saved—something I have not done since. A US Customs official had been quoted referring to the arrestees as "the most technologically sophisticated drug-transport group ever captured," a statement that the writer of the article deemed an unsolicited testimonial that should be turned into pure gold. The journalist went so far as to suggest that drug smugglers all over the world might like to travel to Dade County to check out gadgets including "metal cylinders with infrared lights and radio transmitters for tracking packets of cocaine all over the North Atlantic Ocean." Laundered money would boost the local economy when the drug lords came to town—a particularly large benefit would be realized by the gold neckchain industry. I would dig out the clipping and share it with Deloris, I thought as I rejoined the meeting.

I considered suggesting that the sheriff man up and stand up to the town authorities. Then I realized that money trumps principles every time. And if the folks with the deepest pockets want to live with their heads buried in the clam flats, who was I to disenchant them? But given the appropriate opportunity, I knew that I could be very convincing in explaining why my work in drug enforcement was critical in preserving the summer world the elite possessed. Realistically, I thought, there was no sense bucking the system or arguing with the sheriff. His hands were tied, I was sure. As badly as I would like to burst the bubble in which the delusion of pristine paradise thrived, it was not my place to do so. The sheriff was the one who had to answer to the mucky-mucks, not me. And, I rationalized, it wasn't a bad thing to give the war on drugs a breather. Let the dealers, push-ers, and mules get a false sense of security. Then this fall, when the bad guys are overconfident and getting careless, I'll pounce and round them up like cattle, I thought. I knew this attitude was what I needed to get through the next three months with-out being miserable. I sighed audibly in concession, drawing the attention of the sheriff and Deloris. "So, now what? Should I set up a speed trap or write parking tickets?" I asked sarcastically.

"I have a report of a missing person that needs attention. Just came in this morning," said the sheriff. "That, and there is a file cabinet full of cold cases that you can start on anytime."

Oh no, I thought. The endless cold case assignment was one that I had always dreaded. It seems to be the last stop for cops on their way out of employment. "Have anything lukewarm?" I asked.

"Hey, I'm sorry, Jane. I am not in favor of cramping your style. But let's make the best of it, and know that you can dive back into the junkie circuit when we get our town back." The sheriff picked up a sheet of paper on which he had scribbled some notes. He handed it to me and said, "Here's what I have on the missing girl." I grabbed the paper and stood to leave, waiting for Deloris to struggle out of her chair and collect her crutches. "Thanks, ladies. And Jane, I am happy to hear that you will be representing the department at the Alfonds' this year."

Before I could respond in the negative, Deloris spoke up. "You got invited to the annual soiree? Yay! Who's your plus-one?"

When I hesitated with a response, I must have expressed

something of a balk in my body language as the sheriff chimed in again: "I don't care who you take, as long as you go."

"Yes, sir." I was relieved to now be able to justify my attendance at the Summer Solstice Soiree as a direct order from my boss. I had made such a big deal about *not* going that I felt weird about the flip-flop, and needed to save face. Fortunately, I have always been slow to RSVP. And now that I *had* to go, I would slip the envelope into the outgoing mail here at the department. And who knows, I thought as Deloris and I exited the office and headed down the corridor from where we had come, I may get an opportunity to bend a highfalutin ear or two in the name of fighting real crime. As much as I detest social functions, I would put a positive spin on this one in hopes of lessening my despair in the time leading to the party. Mr. and Mrs. V and Audrey would approve. Now that I knew I would go, I thought at the very least, going would allow me to form my own opinion of some of Green Haven's affluent summer residents. I would keep an open mind.

"What will you wear?" Deloris asked as she plunked herself behind the front desk.

"I haven't thought about it yet."

"Well, you better start. Isn't the party Friday evening? Today is Wednesday."

"I must have something in my closet," I said, hoping to dismiss any helpful hints that Deloris, who was a virtual fashion plate, might otherwise be compelled to drop.

"Oh, I'm positive that you have a lot of *somethings* in your closet. I am also fairly certain that you'll stick out like a sore thumb at the soiree unless you go shopping."

I couldn't help but laugh at this. "You don't like my wardrobe?"

"You dress like a librarian. But drab. Like a prison librarian. But dated. Like an out-of-style prison librarian."

"Ouch," I said. "Wow, I didn't realize you'd given my clothes that much thought."

"You don't wear clothes. You wear garments. All very practical, but not at all suitable for the Alfonds'. Hey, I'm just trying to help."

"Oh, in that case, thanks," I said and put on the biggest, cheesiest smile I could stretch my lips into. "I am so happy for your help. I won't be at all self-conscious now. With my new clothing, and my social graces, I'll be the belle of the fucking ball." I didn't normally use foul language. But I knew Deloris well enough to get away with the F-bomb without falling from grace with her.

I gave the missing persons report a stiff, noisy shake, then held it to focus. "Nineteen-year-old, Bianca Chiriac," I read aloud. "Doesn't sound like a local." As I continued to read the sheriff's notes, Deloris entered pertinent information into her computer. "Reported missing by her roommates. Last seen Tuesday evening."

"Yesterday," echoed Deloris as she typed.

"Bianca shares an apartment with three other young women—all foreign names. And she is employed at the Bar

Harbor Inn and Resort." There wasn't much information on the handwritten sheet the sheriff had supplied. I imagined that he took the call and only jotted down the bare essentials I needed to get going.

"Address of her shared apartment?" Deloris asked.

"Nothing here."

"Contact number for the roommate who reports her missing?"

"No. That's all I have. Nineteen-year-old girl missing since last night. By the time I get to Bar Harbor, she will probably have surfaced—sheepish and embarrassed," I said. "I'll start with her place of employment."

"Good. I'll start a file in the event that she is still AWOL," Deloris said as I headed for the exit. "Most of the seasonal employees in the local hospitality industry are here on J-1 student visas."

"That accounts for the name," I said as I waved and added, "See ya." The majority of the thirty-minute ride to Mount Desert Island (the large, mountainous landmass connected by bridge to Ellsworth and physical address of Bar Harbor and a handful of other, less notorious communities) was all about windshield time. Deloris was probably right, I thought. The young woman who had been reported missing by her roomies had likely been a case of poor communication coupled with possible intoxication. Kids that age are less than thoughtful, I thought as I crossed the line into the town of Bar Harbor.

As I drove, looking for a sign that marked the Inn and Resort, I couldn't help but notice the outward, panoramic dichotomy of life on either side of the bridge linking MDI to the mainland.

Working-class homes bordering on ramshackle gave way to palatial estates bounded by meticulously manicured hedges interrupted only by handsome gates that said Keep Out without actually spelling out the words. Most outlets from the road were marked with beautiful "Private Drive" signs. Glimpses I caught through the barricades revealed professionally kept grounds, bursting with flower gardens, ornate shrubs, and climbing vines, against a cobalt-blue ocean that glistened as brightly as newly polished silver. I imagined I would enjoy the same from the other side of the gate at the Alfonds' Solstice Soiree. Green Haven's wealth was less conspicuous, in my opinion. Not that I had much first-hand knowledge. My impression of the much-noted Bar Harbor was forming quickly. The effect of what I could see and feel could be summed up in a single word: ostentatious.

I approached a four-way intersection with a red flashing light and a stop sign. I stopped and read a series of wooden signs presented list style on a hewn post that was visible from all directions. "BHIR" underscored with an arrow pointing to the left was, I assumed, all I would get in the way of directions to the Bar Harbor Inn and Resort. I obediently turned left and continued until I found the resort property marked with a bigger, but still unobtrusive, wooden sign: "BHIR—Guests Only." I turned sharply into the drive and followed the blacktop to what appeared to be the main check-in area. I pulled into a spot under an awning and among parked golf carts where I was immediately intercepted by a young man in uniform. He stooped to my window as I cranked it down. "Hello, ma'am," he said with a thick accent. A pin on his breast pocket indicated that he was from Latvia. "May I park your car?"

"Oh, no thank you," I replied. "I am looking for the resort manager, and won't be here long. Can I leave my car here for a few minutes?"

"No, ma'am. We are strictly valet. I can park your vehicle around back and retrieve it for you at your request. Just dial ten from any phone in the resort." I glanced around the short-term parking area and realized that this kid had been parking luxury vehicles, and was probably given orders to hide anything less.

I reluctantly climbed out, leaving the Duster running, and asked the valet to leave my keys over the rear, driver-side tire, to which he gasped. "Leave the doors unlocked. I'll find it when I'm done," I said as I headed toward the main entrance of a grand building. There was no way I was tipping a valet, I thought as a bellhop from Hungary opened a door and asked if I had bags. "No, I am looking for the manager. I'll check at the registration desk," I said in defiance of the feeling that I might need to slip the bellhop a few bucks for information. I knew from past experience that as soon as I dipped my hand into my pocket, I would be swarmed by uniformed employees wanting to assist me. Worse than panhandlers, I thought as I snubbed the concierge, whose pin read "Maine," before he could ask to help me in some way.

A perky young woman from Turkey manned the reception desk. She smiled and said, "Hello, and welcome to the Bar Harbor Inn. Name, please?"

"Jane Bunker," I said. "But you won't find my name on your

computer screen. I am the Hancock County deputy sheriff, and I need to speak with the manager, please."

"Oh, yes ma'am. Right away," she said as she scurried over to a house phone and pressed a button. "The manager will be with you momentarily. May I get you a cup of tea while you wait?" Tea sounded good, I thought, and wondered how long the average wait was if tea was an option. I reached into the hip pocket of my chinos feeling for some money. "Oh no, ma'am. The tea is complimentary, and we do not accept tips. May I show you to the lounge? You'll be more comfortable there." I followed the gal to an overstuffed chair where I waited for tea, which was delivered by a young woman from Croatia, according to her pin.

Although I enjoyed the hospitality, the bowing and scraping was making me uncomfortable, I thought as I selected a mint tea from a tray of assorted bags that the server held for me. When I was just about on polite overload, a slightly overweight middle-aged man in an ill-fitting suit burst upon the scene and hustled toward me. "You the cop?" he asked, clearly in a hurry and annoyed by my presence.

I stood and offered my hand. "Deputy Sheriff Jane Bunker." His hand was sweaty, as was his round, pink face. He did not introduce himself, and instead opened his eyes wide as if asking what my business was and urging me to make it snappy. The manager wore no nationality-identifying pin, but I assumed from his demeanor and accent that he was a local. "I am following up on a missing persons report. Bianca Chiriac? She works here," I said, realizing that the manager had many seasonal and part-time employees, and that it was likely he knew few or none of their names.

"Yeah, I'm on a bit of a scavenger hunt myself today. Do you have any idea how many of these kids jump ship? I'm missing some persons, too. I was hoping you were here looking for work."

"Is Bianca here today? Do you have a copy of her schedule? Do you have a home address on file? How about a phone number?" This guy's attitude was irritating me. Knowing that I was probably on a wild-goose chase anyway, I wanted to make short work of this and get back to something more important.

"Jesus Christ, you're kidding me. Right?" He pulled a cell phone from his pocket and pretended to scroll through contacts. "No, I guess I don't have her info." Then he patted his jacket pockets and said, "And I must have misplaced her business card. Sorry."

This would go nowhere, I knew. I assumed that the manager was aware of and nervous about a few infractions regarding the premises and employees that could result in fines, or worse. He must be confused about my role, I thought, and he just wanted to get rid of me. Rather than convince him that I couldn't care less about whatever was making him nervous, I simply thanked him for his time and said that I would ask around to see if Bianca was here, admitting that this was probably a false alarm. Before he could protest, I headed for the lobby, leaving him to stew.

I figured the best way to get information would be to find the inn's laundry room and kitchen. Those would certainly be manned by young college kids here on visas, I thought. I jumped in an elevator and pushed the button to go down one floor to the basement. Sure enough, the laundry was bustling with what appeared to be immigrant workers. The noise of several languages spoken over the washers and dryers stopped abruptly when I announced my entrance. "Hi. I am from the Hancock County Sheriff's Department. We received a call about a missing person—Bianca Chiriac. Does anyone know her or where she might be?" I asked.

A brief silence was followed by a throat clearing. I acknowledged the young woman who was now raising her hand for permission to speak. "I called the police," she said tentatively. "Bianca is my roommate. She is gone. I am scared." I asked the girl to step into the hallway so that the rest of the laundry team could get back to work, and also to have a bit of privacy.

"What is your name?" I asked as I pulled a small notepad and pen from my back pocket.

"I am Anika. My English is so-so. I am sorry." She pushed long bangs away from a very thin, plain face and tucked them behind her ears. Pimples on her forehead indicated youthfulness.

"Your English is fine," I said. "Tell me what you know about Bianca. Where do you live? When did you last see her? Does she have a cell phone? Does she have a boyfriend? Anything you can tell me might be helpful."

"We live in the UN. That is what it is called by everyone for United Nations because all of us are from not here," she explained quickly and quietly. "Me and Bianca, we share a unit. It's not very bad. Same as my dorm room at university."

"Can you give me the street address for the UN?" I asked, poised to jot it down.

"No address. Right back there," she said as she pointed at the end of a long hallway. "In the forest behind the resort. We

25

can walk to work, so we don't none of us have cars. I have called Bianca's cell a thousand times. I left messages, then it go-ed right to voicemail."

"What is her number?" I asked.

She recited it as she peeked at my notepad to ensure that I got it right. "And Bianca has some boyfriends. She is so beautiful. Not like me."

"Any serious boyfriend? Do you have any names? Any problems with boys?"

"No. Bianca is too so smart for that. Just nice boys and good friends. She never stays out late because we have to work early and we need money for university. We only have three months to save our money, then we go back home to Romania."

"Where do you go to school?" I asked, thinking that this was a waste of time, but not wanting to shortchange this girl's concern for her friend.

"University of Bucharest," she said proudly as she threw her shoulders back.

"When did you see Bianca last?"

"Yesterday after work, Bianca was very excited to go to town to meet a friend from the university. Her friend has job in the kitchen on a cruise ship that was coming in to this harbor. Bianca left in a taxi, and did not come home at all." Oh, I thought, that makes sense. Cruise ships are notorious for shenanigans, especially young crewmembers making landfall after many days at sea. Knowing that they will be ashore for a brief time before weighing anchor again, most of the crew tends to let their hair

26

down, and Bianca may have been swept up in the frenzy of activities that is best described as those of drunken sailors.

"Name of the friend?"

"No."

"Name of the ship?"

"No."

"Okay. Thank you for your help," I said as I dug for a card. "Please call me when Bianca shows up, or if you think of anything that might help me find her? And text me a picture of Bianca."

"Thank you so much. Last time nobody came."

"Last time?" I asked. "Has Bianca gone missing before?" Now I was getting to where I assumed I would end up. The sheriff had sent me all the way to Bar Harbor for this. He probably wanted to take my mind off of drug busting, I thought. What a complete waste of time. Even pawing through cold cases was time better spent.

"Last year. No, not Bianca. It was another girl who lived in the UN and worked here. Her roommate called the police, and they never came. They never looked for her."

"Well, did she show up on her own?"

"No. Never. Her roommate was very upset. We all were scared. But then I guess everyone forgot now until Bianca."

"Maybe I can speak to her roommate. What is her name, and where can I find her?"

"She is in Turkey. She graduated from university and has a job so no need to get the visa and come here anymore."

"Do you know the name of the girl who went missing?" I asked.

"No. But the call was placed to you. Middle of last June. So you must have it in records." Rather than defend myself and explain that the calls do not come to me directly, I chose to nod and take notes. I could sift through last June's call log and verify this, just to close the loop. The call probably went to the Ellsworth police, and not the Hancock County Sheriff's Department, I thought. If we jumped every time a twentysomething girl didn't come home at night, we'd be in perpetual motion, I thought skeptically. I thanked Anika for her help, and promised to do what I could to locate Bianca. Anika went back to her job of folding fresh white linens while I watched and wondered about her accusation of a neglected missing person report last year. I assumed whoever took the call had better sense than to send an officer to investigate. College-aged girl hasn't seen her beautiful roommate since last evening . . . Those dots almost connected *themselves*.

I found a basement-level exit that opened in the direction that Anika indicated was where I might find employee housing, or the UN. On the far side of a parking lot, there was a well-beaten path wide enough for two people to walk abreast. I followed the path until I happened upon what looked like tenement housing. A string of small, single units with white siding was joined by porches like a giant strand of pearls dropped haphazardly on uneven ground. I did what amounted to a drive-by, maybe out of curiosity, but also covering bases. I had no idea which unit or even which group of units Anika and

Bianca lived in. And it didn't matter unless Bianca was home and sleeping off a night of fun. And if that were the case, Anika would call and inform me at the end of her shift.

I hustled back to the parking lot and found the Duster. As long as I was here, I should at least check out the waterfront, I thought. And my stomach was growling. I needed lunch, and Bar Harbor had a reputation for many options as it boasted a thriving tourist, merchant shipping, and cruising sailor trade. I loved looking at boats, and realized that I might never be back in Bar Harbor. As I reached for the key over the tire, my phone dinged, indicating that I had a text message. I climbed behind the wheel, started the engine, and rolled down a window before checking the text. It was, I assumed, from Anika, as it consisted of a link to Bianca Chiriac's Facebook page. Her profile picture added credence to Anika's description of her. She was indeed a beauty. I had neither interest nor intention of slogging through Bianca's (or anyone's, for that matter) social media accounts. So I swiped my phone closed and tucked it into my hip pocket. Just as I did, the phone rang. I pulled it back out. The caller ID showed HANCOCK COUNTY, which I knew was the sheriff or Deloris. "What's up?" I asked cheerily.

"We've got another missing person," said the sheriff.

"Oh, come on! This is silly," I pleaded. "If you plan to have me running around looking for teenagers until fall, I'll go nuts."

"I just got a call from the president of Dirigo Maritime Academy. One of his cadets didn't make it back to campus for spring semester. His parents are distraught."

TWO

I am not above any job. And it's nearly impossible to insult me (a personal attribute about which I have been quite vocal, causing many to accept it as a challenge). But now it had become clear that I had been reduced to an entry-level detective. Rather than whine about it, I would cover my disappointment with sarcasm (mainly because I have been fairly emphatic about my dislike for complainers). In fact, I am certain that I coined "Just Do It" long before Nike trademarked the slogan. I took a deep breath and listened to the sheriff as he recited directions to Dirigo Maritime Academy and suggested that I get there today to record and file an official missing persons report. He would text me a number for the president of the school.

"Okay, boss," I said. "And you be sure to let me know of any old ladies needing help crossing the road or any cats in trees looking for rescue." The silence on the other end indicated no appreciation for my wit. Rather than letting it go, I persisted. "Are the local Boy Scouts all busy today?" Another pause led me to pull the phone from my ear and examine the screen. No service. The call had been dropped. Probably a good thing, I thought as I drove around to the front of the building and parked in the valet zone, waving a finger at the valet indicating no need for his service as I would be only a minute. Before I could get out of the Duster, he was right in my window.

"You can't park here. Please, it's my job."

"Okay, okay. I need contact information for all of the taxi services in town," I said, suddenly realizing that he would be the best source.

He reached into his inside pocket, producing a business card. "Only one company. Two cars owned and operated by a married couple." He handed me the card and smiled, seemingly happy to be able to assist.

"Would employees of the resort use this company?" I asked as I read the card. "Tag Team Taxi? Would you use them if you needed a ride?"

"Yes, ma'am. They have an exclusive here. All guests use them, too, unless they rent a car at the airport." The valet leaned with a hand on the edge of my window and looked over the top of the Duster toward the driveway. I pulled my phone out and started to dial the number on the card. Before I finished, the valet said, "Here comes half of the tag team now. He has guests. Can you please pull over there?" He pointed to the parking lot.

"You bet," I answered and pulled out of the greeting and unloading area. This would save me some time, I thought as I parked and jumped out of the car. I waited on the fringe as an elderly couple was helped from the Subaru wagon by a bellboy, and all of their bags were loaded onto a roller cart. As they made their way to the front door, I approached the cabbie, who had not left his vehicle and sat with a wallet in his lap sorting small bills. "Excuse me," I said, interrupting his count.

"I'm open for business! Where you going?" The sixtyish, pleasant-looking man peeked out from under the visor of a sweat-stained ball cap embroidered with his company logo—"TAG TEAM TAXI."

"Hi, I'm Jane Bunker from Hancock County Sheriff's Department. I'm not looking for a ride, just information." I couldn't help but smile at the cabbie whose demeanor was nothing short of jovial.

"I'm your man. The name's Dudley. Everyone calls me Dud." This really floored me. In my experience, cab drivers are notoriously tight-lipped until a palm is greased. "What can I do you for, Deputy?" I waited, expecting his hand to shoot out for me to slap with something green. I reached into my hip pocket for my phone. "No thanks," he said, putting a hand up in a stopping motion. "I don't take money unless you need a ride."

I laughed. "No, I'm not trying to buy information," I said, relieved that I didn't have to cough up any cash. "I want to show you a picture of a young woman I am trying to locate." I pressed the text icon on my phone and found the link. I opened Bianca's Facebook page and held it for the cabbie to check out. I was slowly getting accustomed to the smartphone the department had provided, dragging me reluctantly away from my trusted flip phone and into present-day technology.

"Wow, ain't she cunnin'!" he exclaimed as he pulled my wrist closer so that he could get a better look. He pulled reading glasses from a shirt pocket and placed them on his nose. "She don't look familiar, sorry. What did she do?"

"She works here at the resort. Her roommate reported her missing and says that she took a cab into town last evening. I was hoping you'd remember her and where you dropped her."

"That would be the wife," he said as he grabbed a handheld device that looked like a walkie-talkie. "Hey Doll, what's your twenty?"

"Hi Babe," a perky voice said, seeping through the handheld's speaker. "Just passed the loop, and headed to the resort with a lovely family from Michigan. Twin boys, not much older than Dean and Everett. First trip to Maine, and they are *some* excited." The voice went up a decibel and an octave. As she explained where in Michigan the folks were from and what they planned to do this week while on vacation, the cabbie chuckled.

"She loves this job. She loves the *people*." He stared at nothing and listened in total adoration to his wife's voice. "She loves hearing about their lives and where they come from. Dreams of visiting every place she hears about . . ."

We waited patiently through her enthusiastic bio of the couple who, she boasted, were both oncologists, adding, "Too bad they weren't here last month. Geez, poor Nell." Her voice cracked a bit. Then she picked back up with some specifics on her customers' musical talents. "Remember when we bought Georgie the drum set? Lord, what a racket." She had pure joy in her voice now as she recounted quite a list of trials and tribulations their

33

own children had experienced with a variety of instruments. I wasn't sure whether she was reminiscing with her husband or entertaining her clients, but she did have a gift.

As she rattled on, the cabbie turned to me. "She'll spend half the night surfing the Internet soaking up Michigan unless her next fare is from somewhere more exotic." When the walkie-talkie fell silent, the cabbie keyed his mic and said, "That's great, Doll. Very interesting, indeed. When you get here, there's a deputy looking for a girl—thinks you might have given her a ride last night." His wife stated that she was five minutes out. "Then I'll pass you at the gate, sweetheart," he said, signing off with a double click on the mic key.

I thanked the cabbie for his help, which he passed off as having not done anything. He was confident that if his wife had ever had the missing girl in her van, she would remember in great detail. "She drags these kids home like stray cats," he said. "Once a week, we have resort employees at the house for a nice, home-cooked meal. She's a good cook and a good woman. We work hard, and don't have much to show for it. But what we do have, she wants to share. Hey, I gotta go. Good luck."

"Start packing for Michigan!" I smiled.

"Oh, we never *go* anywhere. A customer gave me two tickets to a Sox game last season. The wife wouldn't budge. Never been out of the state, and not about to go," he said as he pulled away slowly and shrugged a c'est la vie gesture.

As the Subaru disappeared around a corner, I stood and thought about the affection he showed his wife within the tone of his voice. And the nice things he shared with me about her really endeared him. I now had another stunning example of happiness. Wow, if I had a guy like that . . . Oh no, let's not go down that well-worn road now, I thought as I pushed the angst surrounding my everlasting solo status out of my head with great thrust. My day would come. Or at least that's what my landlords preached.

Sure enough, just at the five-minute mark, a maroon-colored van pulled up to the unloading zone. I walked slowly, allowing the bellhop time to unload the mountain of luggage from the back and the people within to climb out. A stout woman appeared from behind the steering wheel and gave each of the four passengers a hug. After she collected her fare, she looked around, I assumed searching for me. I approached, introduced myself, and thanked her in advance for her time. "I'm Dolly," she said brightly.

After shaking my hand, the other half of the cabbie couple pushed aviator-style sunglasses onto her head, holding back some fairly wild bangs and exposing a rosy, flawless complexion. Dolly appeared to be in her fifties, but could easily pass for forty, I thought as she tucked spears of dark hair behind ears whose lobes sported dangly earrings that jingled when she moved. I explained that a young woman employed at the resort had been reported missing. "Bianca Chiriac," I said as I showed her Bianca's profile picture that was once again displayed on my phone.

"Oh dear! I drove Bianca to the waterfront park last night!

The college kids who work here are all great. Really good kids, and very serious about making money for school. No monkey business. Not like the local crowd."

Dolly had already answered my next line of questions with her first reply. "Do you recall what time you left her at the park?" I asked. "And did she mention anything about who she was meeting?"

"Let's see . . . I left her at the southwest entrance at about five thirty," she said. "Bianca was meeting a girlfriend from home she goes to school with. She didn't mention her friend's name, though. They are both entering their fourth year at the University of Bucharest."

"Did Bianca mention the name of the cruise ship, or what their plans were for the night?" I asked, still convinced that I was following up on a false alarm, and therefore wasting time.

"No, but there are only two ships in yesterday—*Princess of the Seas* and *Carnival Allure*. I didn't get any details for her plans with her friend because I was really more interested in her homeland. She comes from Romania."

"Okay, thank you," I said hoping to curtail the incoming recitation of the Travel Channel. "If you think of anything that might help me locate Bianca, please give me a call," I said as I handed Dolly my contact information. "I am hopeful that she is simply MIA, and will return to her job soon. Maybe she and her girlfriend partied too hard, and are sleeping it off somewhere. Maybe aboard the ship," I suggested.

Dolly's handheld came to life with her husband's voice asking her to help with an airport pickup. She excused herself to get back to work, and I did the same. I figured that as long as I was this close, I should check out the cruise ships. Maybe someone had seen the two women or knew of their whereabouts, I thought as I followed signs to the waterfront.

Bar Harbor was bustling. Storefronts were full of brightly colored displays, parking spots were full, and pedestrians wandered sidewalks with heads on swivels admiring all that Bar Harbor had to offer. Traffic moved slowly and stopped frequently to allow tourists to cross Main Street from side to side where they poked in and out of restaurants and gift shops. Even the trees and flowers were ahead of Green Haven's, I thought as I admired how meticulously manicured this downtown section was. The kids weren't even out of school, and tourist season was well underway.

I swung into a town lot and miraculously grabbed the last free spot (free both of occupancy and charge). As I walked toward the water that I could now see in the narrow gaps between buildings that lined the east side of Main Street, I took a deep breath and enjoyed the sun-warmed salt air. Yup, summer was indeed upon us! I would force myself to enjoy the season, even in the absence of any *real* crime fighting. Hey, maybe the break in scouring Down East Maine of drugs would do me some good, I thought as I made my way toward the waterfront park, made clear with signs marking the number of steps that remained to the entrance. When was the last time I strolled through a park on the clock? Sure beats most of the locales that compose my usual stomping grounds in the line of duty, I thought as I stopped to admire the view from a grassy knoll just inside the park's entrance.

From this vantage point, the harbor itself appeared as a punch bowl at the end of a long, narrow sound hemmed on either side by landmasses that began as steep ledges jutting from thick stands of spruce trees that gave way to mountainous terrain that explained the Mount in Mount Desert Island. I scanned the harbor from east to west. Two cruise ships were anchored out on the perimeter of the harbor and away from the docks. *The Princess of the Seas* and *Carnival Allure* both appeared to be mid-range cruise liners in terms of size, probably around seven hundred feet in length and with approximately 1,200 passenger capacity, according to my estimate from the distance. The area closer to the docks was speckled with moorings occupied by work skiffs and dinghies. There were a few sailboats anchored out, and a couple of commercial lobster boats remaining on moorings.

I could see two very distinct piers. One was clearly for commercial use only; the wooden planks on its deck were lined with empty lobster crates, fish boxes, bait bins, and a set of electronic scales. The ramp leading to some rickety floats looked a little wobbly and well-worn. The parking area adjacent to this wharf was filled with an assortment of pickup trucks. The other pier was likely off-limits to the fishermen, I thought. A pristine concrete surface lined with kiosks selling trinkets, tickets to local tours, and information seemed rather deserted in light of the foot traffic everywhere else. Two shiny aluminum gangways led to large floats where I assumed cruise ship passengers landed to come ashore from ships when anchored out. Three beautiful launches cleated at bow and stern were protected by oversized fenders that kept the boats from chafing against the floats. I gathered that these sea-going shuttles were owned and operated by the Town of Bar Harbor, and a service to cruise ships that scheduled stops here, accommodating passengers from ship to shore and back to ship.

I wandered down to the top of a shared area where both piers shot off from the land, forming a forty-five degree angle, and watched a lobster boat approach from the mooring field. Well, I might get a bit of information about where to find launch captains who *might* remember a pretty young woman, I thought as I started down the shaky commercial ramp, anticipating the boat to land at the fishermen's floats. Partway down, it looked as though I had been mistaken. The lobster boat was closing in on the pleasure boaters' territory. So I climbed back up and headed down the aluminum gangway to greet the incoming vessel and perhaps catch a line.

I hustled and beat the boat to the float. As the bow turned its cheek, narrowly missing the float, bold red lettering announced *Ragged But Right*. The captain backed her down hard, swinging the boat's stern gently against the chafing gear lining the float and coming to a complete stop. "Ahoy," said the captain, his black eyes and white teeth both gleaming under a long visor.

"Hi," I answered, returning his smile. "I thought I'd help, but it doesn't appear that you need any." With this, the man handed me the bitter end of a short line that was secured with a clove hitch to the base of the boat's davit.

"Never turn down help from a pretty lady," he said casually

as he watched me quickly lace a cleat with the line. "Looks like you've done that before."

"Yeah, a couple of times," I said. The cleanliness of the boat did not escape me, nor did the good looks and confidence of its captain. "You don't strike me as a Deadhead," I said, acknowledging the boat's name, which I knew only as a Grateful Dead song.

"I have been known to wear tie-dyes," he said with a chuckle.

Was I flirting? I didn't think so. I really could not go any further with this particular exchange as the closest I had been to being a Deadhead was in choice of ice cream—Cherry Garcia. But I did know boats enough to hold up my end of that conversation, so I jumped into my comfort zone. "Nice boat. Really clean. You fish?"

"Yup. Haul a few lobster traps and fish for halibut. My other gig is pilot boat, which is why I'm here. I am waiting for the ship's pilot to come. I need to put him aboard *The Princess*," he said, pointing over his shoulder at the cruise ships. "She's weighing anchor in thirty minutes. And the *Allure* just dropped anchor." Well, that was helpful, I thought. If the *Allure* had just arrived this morning, she could be eliminated as a possibility. But Dolly had stated that there were two ships in port when she left Bianca here last evening.

This seemed like the right time to introduce myself and my reason for being here, I thought. "I'm Jane Bunker, Hancock County deputy sheriff." I extended for a handshake, and was delighted when he took my hand in both of his and held gently rather than doing the macho squeeze. "I am chasing down a missing person report, and that has led me here—to the cruise ships. I was hoping to speak with the launch captains. Do you know them?"

He released my hand slowly and said, "Hello, Deputy Sheriff Jane Bunker. Pete, the pilot boat captain, fisherman extraordinaire at your service. Yes, I know the launch guys. But they won't be back here until the *Allure* passengers want to be shuttled back and forth. All of the *Princess* passengers are aboard now, otherwise the departures would be delayed. It's not good for business to leave behind paying customers!"

I wanted to kick myself for checking his ring finger. And held back a secret swoon when I saw that it was unoccupied. This guy was indeed exceptional, I thought. Age appropriate, polite, confident . . . Stick to business! "No, not a passenger. I am looking for an employee of the Bar Harbor Resort. A young woman from Romania," I said and quickly ran through the few details I had including the taxi ride here to meet a friend who reportedly worked in the galley of one of the cruise ships. "Did a cruise ship depart earlier today? I was told that there were two here yesterday, and if the *Allure* just got here, I can cross her off of the search list." I resisted the urge to defend my status by telling him that I am a decorated detective on light duty for the sake of tourism. I bit my tongue rather than admit that this was likely a wild-goose chase, as I was unwilling to leave his presence that quickly.

"That's good detective work," he said. "Yes, the *Radiance* departed late last night. I'm not sure what time because I was not on duty. I share the pilot boat job with another guy. The

41

Radiance is a quantum-class ship—fifty-four hundred passengers! That line has top-notch security and is super organized. I guess they all are, but I can't imagine keeping track of all of those people plus employees."

My heart sunk with the possibility that Bianca might have been aboard the *Radiance* when it left. That would certainly explain how a good, dependable girl went missing. Maybe she had a better opportunity aboard the ship, I wondered. But Bianca would have called her roomie so that she wouldn't worry or report her missing, wouldn't she? "What's her next port of call?" I asked, hoping Pete would know.

"I believe she was southbound. Next stop Cuba." I filed this information in my head and knew that verifying this was a job for Deloris. I hoped that Deloris could also find employee lists for the *Radiance* and *The Princess*.

"Here comes the pilot," Pete said, nodding to someone approaching from behind me. "If you'd like, you can ride out and spend a few minutes at the boarding door of *The Princess* while they prepare to get underway. We are always greeted by the head steward of the ship. They know everything and everyone aboard their vessel."

While I considered this invitation, Pete welcomed the pilot aboard, introduced me to him, and explained my mission. The pilot seemed impatient. Definitely all business, I thought, which was all the persuasion I needed to climb aboard. And I did so with help from a hand of the captain. I stood at the starboard rail and watched Pete unweave the line from the cleat, put the boat in gear, and steer away from the pier.

This was about all I could do, I thought. I didn't have much to go on in tracking Bianca down. I had a picture on my phone, though. How very fortuitous to happen upon Pete! He could get me aboard *The Princess*, eliminating that possibility, and allow me to feel as though I had put in appropriate effort. And I would at least have an opportunity to ask a question or two before going back ashore and looking into my other missing person. Not exactly exhausting every avenue, I knew. But at least enough to justify the trip to Bar Harbor.

In less than a minute, we were in the shade of *The Princess*. Pete pulled right up to a boarding door near the stern, leaving the boat in gear, and pressed against the ship's hull to allow the pilot easy transfer. A man in a white uniform welcomed the pilot in a manner that indicated familiarity. As they chatted, I turned to Pete and asked, "What's with the pilot? Is he always so unfriendly?" Pete smiled and held his reply until the pilot disappeared up a long set of stairs, I assumed to find the bridge.

"The pilots have quite a racket going. They get paid cash, which I assume goes unclaimed. And they receive gifts— mostly top-shelf liquor. The presence of the law probably made him nervous." Pete waved at the man in uniform to come close, and spoke loudly to be heard over the various noises associated with a large ship. After an abbreviated explanation, I handed my phone, which was open to Bianca's Facebook portrait, to him and waited.

The steward took a long and thoughtful look, shrugged, and handed the phone back to me. "Sorry, detective," he said. "I don't recall seeing her. We don't allow employees to bring guests to the ship unless it's an open-house situation, which hasn't happened this trip. Do you know the name of the friend employed here? I am happy to find her for you."

"All I know is that she is from Romania," I answered.

"Yup. That fits about fifty percent of the kids in housekeeping and scullery. Frankly, I am shocked that you are looking for a *foreign* worker," he said. "And if push came to shove, you wouldn't be allowed aboard to investigate due to the fact that *The Princess* is flagged in Bimini."

"What? What does that have to do with anything?" I asked as I pushed my phone back into my hip pocket.

"Most cruise lines register their ships in Bermuda or Africa for tax advantages. And with the foreign flag comes other rules. No US law enforcement, not even the FBI, has jurisdiction aboard this vessel unless investigating a crime involving a US citizen," he said as if from rote memorization. Something suggested that he had had this conversation before, which caused me to bristle a bit. "And seeing as you are looking for someone other than a US citizen, you're out of luck. And so is she, I guess."

"Wow, that's cold," I said. I pulled a business card from my bag and handed it to him. "If you find a stowaway, I'd appreciate a call."

"I can do that," he said with a smile. "I don't mean to sound callous. But a missing college girl in Bar Harbor, Maine? This isn't exactly a den of iniquity. Maybe she ate too many fried clams." He tucked my card into his shirt pocket. "Some of our other ports of call are another story. That's why we don't allow anyone other than paying passengers aboard. The students who come from Eastern Europe on visas are good kids. My guess is that your girl will surface before the end of the work day."

A voice barked over a loudspeaker announcing the ship's departure and ordering all crew to man stations for weighing anchor. This was our cue to exit. I grabbed a handrail and braced myself as Pete pulled away from the ship. Although the ride out to the ship had proven fruitless, I had at least been able to cross a t and dot an i by following up on the only information I had regarding Bianca's no-show. I loved getting out on a boat for any reason. And Pete was a bonus. "Thanks for getting me out to *The Princess*," I said. "I guess the only thing more I can do here is speak with the launch boat captains. Maybe one of them recalls Bianca. Maybe she *is* headed to Cuba!"

"Maybe." Pete nodded. "Even with the good reputation, kids that age can be so impulsive and pretty thoughtless. It's not unusual for the J-1s—that's the student visa—to job hop. They secure any position to get a visa, then once they arrive, they get better offers. There's a limited number of visas issued, and lots of jobs to fill. The foreign kids will do work for a lot less money than the locals. Doesn't make them very popular with anyone except the business owners."

"Understood," I said. "Can you tell me how and where to find the launch captains?"

Before Pete could answer, the VHF radio blared—"Mayday, Mayday! This is the *Elizabeth*. I am taking on water. Just east of Porcupine."

Pete turned the wheel hard to starboard and pushed the

45

throttle ahead to full. He grabbed the VHF's mic and said, "Hey Ron, this is Pete on *Ragged But Right*. Headed your way."

"She's going down! Going down fast!" The voice was loud and urgent, but not hysterical at all. "About a half mile off the Thunder Ledge."

The Coast Guard came on next. *"Elizabeth, Elizabeth,* this is US Coast Guard Southwest Harbor, Maine group. Channel one six, come in please." There was no reply. *"Elizabeth, Elizabeth,* this is US Coast Guard Southwest Harbor, Maine group. What is the nature of your emergency?" Silence. The Coast Guard called the vessel in distress many times, asking how many people were on board, if they had donned life jackets, if they were taking on water, and what their latitude and longitude was. Each question was followed by an eerie silence.

"Sorry about this. But I'll get to Ron before the Coast Guard leaves the dock," he yelled over the roar of the diesel engine. "I fish around Ron. I know where he is, and we can be there in fifteen minutes." Pete clenched his teeth, which caused a muscle to twitch in his jaw, pulsing in and out as he scanned the horizon with his black eyes. The GPS displayed our speed at twenty-six knots. I grabbed a handrail and hung on tight as we crossed wakes of working boats in their endless circles around traps and short sprints to the next buoy. The Coast Guard continued to try to raise the captain of the sinking boat on the radio, to no avail, which made the back of my neck prickle.

A black ledge jutted from the surface off to our starboard bow. I looked at the chart plotter and saw that it was indeed Thunder Ledge, so I assumed we were within a couple minutes of the *Elizabeth*. Visibility was excellent. But the only vessel within range ahead of us was steaming north at a good clip, coming from the south as if they too were responding to the Mayday call. Pete slowly pulled the throttle back and kept his eyes moving, desperately searching. "How many people are we looking for?" I asked.

"Just one. He fishes solo," Pete said as he nervously shifted his weight from foot to foot.

I jumped up onto the wash rail for a better vantage point. There was a long, slow swell running, but otherwise calm. As *Ragged But Right* mounted a swell, something caught my peripheral vision. My eyes darted to the right. "Right there!" I yelled, and pointed. "Two o'clock!"

Pete thrust the throttle lever ahead so hard I thought it would snap. He hadn't seen what I did, but responded to my direction. Coming around forty-five degrees, he straightened her out and kept her steady on a southeasterly course. "Can you still see him?" Pete yelled over the noise of the engine.

I kept my eyes riveted on the area where I had seen something. A swell ahead of our bow pushed what looked like a man clinging to a submerged object into my field of vision. "Dead ahead! It's him," I bellowed, never releasing my eyes from what appeared as a tiny pin and quickly grew as we approached. The other boat raced to the scene from the opposite direction. I started to feel relieved as I knew we would pluck Ron from the ocean just as his boat went out from under him and into the briny deep. "I'll swing by and back down to him. Throw him the life ring when I get close enough. I don't want to foul the wheel if there's floating line around. Keep an eye out for me." Pete barked orders which I followed.

The other boat was still coming fast and furious. As Pete swung hard to port, then backed down toward Ron, who was now waving an arm, I stood with my thighs braced against the transom, waiting to throw the ring. The approaching boat was now dangerously close and bearing down on us at full speed. We weren't close enough to get the life ring to Ron. I threw it as far as I could. It landed short of him. "He can't swim. I'll get closer," yelled Pete as he lined the stern up with his friend and backed down hard again. I pulled in the slackline, retrieved the ring, and got ready to heave it out. The bow of the oncoming boat now appeared as if it would split us in half if we didn't take evasive action. I read "INSIGHT" on the boat's bow. Pete yelled, "Hold on!" He went ahead at full throttle. All I saw was a blur of white as the boat just missed our stern quarter.

The wake of *Insight* nearly put me on my butt as it crested up and over the wash rail, filling the cockpit with water. I held on for dear life as the water that was up to my waist slowly drained through stern scuppers. The wake had also brushed Ron from whatever he had been hanging on to. He now thrashed wildly. I knew he wouldn't stay on the surface for long. "Jesus Christ!" I screamed. "That guy never saw us!" I thought that the boat's name had been misspelled—"INCITE" was more like it.

Pete went full steam ahead again to help drain the water we had shipped aboard. Unfortunately that meant getting farther away from Ron, who was flailing and bobbing up and down. When it was safe to do so, Pete swung around and put the bow right on his friend, who was now underwater more than he was on top. "We are running out of time. I'll run right up to him and grab him here on the starboard side. Be ready with the gaff in case he's under the surface." I glanced to port to see the menacing boat do a 180 and head right back at us. I realized that the captain had intended to hit us and was coming back for another try.

"You get Ron, I'll take care of this idiot," I said as I laid the gaff on the wash rail and felt my gun in its holster. I stood at the port rail bracing myself for impact. I drew my gun and put a bead on the ball cap–covered head that I could see at the helm behind the windshield. I fired a round into the hull as a warning that I was not afraid to use my weapon. The next round would be deadly. At the last possible second, the boat swerved hard to starboard, missing us again by inches. Through my sights, I noticed dark green streaks and deep gouges along the boot stripe, just above the waterline of *Insight*. I assumed that Ron's boat was dark green and that it had been rammed.

Pete now had the engine in reverse. I watched *Insight* fade in the distance, holstered my gun, and hustled forward to help Pete. There was no time for conversation. Orange foul-weather gear was slowly sinking out of sight. I peeled off my jacket and gun belt, ready to dive in if I had to. Pete reached down and thrust the gaff hook toward the color. He snagged something solid and pulled with both hands until Ron's head broke the surface, the gaff hook at the end of the pole fortunately twisted in Ron's hood.

Adrenaline peaked as Pete reached down and grasped Ron

by the shoulders of his jacket and hauled him over the rail with one mighty yank. Ron landed on the deck with a thud. He was lifeless. Pete sat on the rail and put his head in his hands. I rolled Ron onto his side, knelt beside him and noted that he was not breathing. I checked for a pulse, and found nothing. I rolled Ron onto his back, preparing to perform CPR. Just as I placed my hands on his chest, he sputtered and spat. I quickly rolled him back onto his side. A jagged cough spewed salt water and bile onto the deck. When Ron settled down a bit, Pete patted him on the back and said, "I draw the line at mouth-to-mouth resuscitation. I thought you were a goner."

"Me too. I may as well be. My boat is," Ron said sadly. Pete helped his friend onto his feet and steadied him as he stood bent at the waist with his hands on his knees. After a minute, Ron straightened up and staggered forward and into the wheelhouse where he took a seat on a built-in bench.

"Let's take a look around for *Elizabeth*. She may be here, just under the surface. Jane, would you mind climbing onto the roof to take a look around?" Pete asked.

"Not at all," I said as made my way around the house to the bow where I found a foothold to crawl up over the windshield and onto the top. I had a notion that Pete wanted to speak with Ron privately. I looked below the surface for any sign of color as Pete did slow, lazy turns until he had scoured the area. Finally, Pete motioned for me to come down.

I joined Ron at the starboard console where he stared blankly. Pete once again took the wheel and swung the bow toward land. "I guess I had better get you both ashore," he said without looking at us. "You want to call the Coast Guard and cancel the Mayday?" Pete asked Ron and held a cell phone out to him.

"Sure. Thanks." With that, Ron took the phone and went back to the transom to make the call. I wished I could hear, but knew I might learn more by staying with Pete.

Before I could ask what the hell had happened, Pete spoke up. "Well, Detective Jane Bunker, that was a little more excitement than I expected today. Thanks for your help."

"All in a day's work, right?" I said lightly. "Is the hull color of *Elizabeth* dark green?"

"Uh huh," Pete said in the affirmative.

"What do you know about *Insight*? Why would her captain try to kill Ron?"

"Just territorial fishing stuff," Pete answered nonchalantly. "Some guys play rough."

"Play? I call it attempted murder."

"Best if you just let it go. That's what Ron wants, and he's the victim here," Pete reminded me. "Besides, you've got yourself a missing girl to find."

"Somehow the missing girl pales in comparison. A man's boat was rammed and sunk. He almost died. We could have been killed. How are you able to shrug that off?"

"You're not from around here, are you?"

"Actually, I am," I said proudly. "I live in Green Haven. And I come from Acadia Island." I was more surprised at this admission than Pete was.

"Well then, you should understand that Ron will not press

51

charges. Things could get worse if the law gets involved." Pete looked me square in the eye, opening my mind and allowing his words to penetrate.

"Worse than almost dead? Yeah, I get it. Dead would be worse, wouldn't it? But how can he be okay with letting that jerk get away scot-free?"

Pete broke his concentrated stare and gazed over the bow. "Oh, nobody said anything about letting that asshole go unpunished. He'll get what's coming to him, believe me."

I did believe him. And that belief did nothing to assuage my anxiety.

THREE

Pete landed on the commercial fishing floats a little faster than was necessary. He backed the engine down hard, slamming the starboard side of his boat against pilings, nearly toppling a young man from his seat on a cooler where he sat with a fishing rod. This was the first and only sign that he had been shaken by the near miss of collision and nigh death of his fishing buddy, Ron. As *Ragged But Right* rode up and down in her own wake, Pete tied her off and let out a loud sigh. He sat on the rail and relaxed. I could see stress dissolve from his shoulders as he seemed to collect his thoughts. The guy who had been fishing, annoyed about the wake, reeled the jig from the water to the tip of his rod and approached. "What the fuck, man?" His eyes widened in surprise, I assumed a combination of my presence and Ron's, who was still dripping.

"Mind your business, Rat," Pete advised.

"This is my business. You are on my waterfront," the man

snapped back as he flipped a cigarette butt into the water. He then turned and walked slowly up the ramp and sat on a park bench where he stared in defiance at us.

"That's The Wharf Rat," Pete explained to me. "No need to introduce you. He's just a bum who lurks around the docks. Sells a little weed." Pete did not wait for any reply from me, and started shutting down the boat's electronics.

Ron looked stronger as he stepped over the rail and onto the float. "Thank you both," he said sadly. "My wife will be up in the parking lot soon. She insists on getting me checked out at the ER."

"Listen to your wife," Pete admonished. "And give me a call tonight."

"Yup. I'm sure the insurance company will need to get your statement," Ron reminded Pete. I considered interjecting with the fact that I was the only insurance investigator in the area. But I thought better of it. I would follow the advice of Pete and let this go. For now. Besides, there was no boat to inspect for cause of sinking. And Ron had clearly not scuttled his boat for the insurance payout. I certainly didn't want or need to get involved in the ongoing gear wars waged in Down East Maine. From what I had heard since arriving in Green Haven, there was no beginning and no end to the tit for tat among a large percentage of the local lobster fishermen. And even guys who kept their noses clean eventually got sucked into retaliating for losses suffered at the hands of competitors. Traps cut off or stolen were simply replaced—a line item on annual ledgers that kept the trap builders employed. But a lost boat? I wondered what had transpired between the two men to have escalated to attempted murder. I had certainly been aware of boats that had been burned, sabotaged, or sunk while on moorings, with neither witnesses nor risk of personal injury or death. And I knew of rage-induced drive-by shootings. This was different. This was aimed not only at putting a man out of business, but out of life.

Ron made his way up the ramp and disappeared among the fleet of pickup trucks waiting in the parking lot. Pete walked over to the helm. He shut the boat's engine down with the push of a button. Stepping over the rail and onto the float, he offered me his hand and said, "Can I walk you to your car?" This was obviously my invitation to leave. I accepted his arm as a steadying piece as I joined him on the float. "I know it's asking a lot. But it really is best if you forget about what you saw out there. This is just another page in the bullshit book."

"Is that a long book? Or a short story?" I asked.

"Endless, unfortunately."

"Well, this isn't the first time I have been asked to ignore my duties today. So I guess I will go about my business of searching for missing kids. But if I get dragged into this by my boss at the insurance company, I won't lie."

"I would never ask you to lie. The truth is, we responded to a Mayday and pulled a guy out of the water when his boat sunk from underneath him, right?"

"True enough," I said as we walked side by side through the park and toward the Duster, acutely aware of The Rat's watchful gaze. "And there isn't a boat to inspect for evidence of foul play, is there? I didn't happen to notice the depth of water where we pulled Ron out. Any chance of recovering *Elizabeth*?"

"Zero chance." Pete shook his head. "Right in the middle of a deep hole—she's sitting in about fifty fathoms of water. If she could be brought up, there'd be nothing left to save. Probably cheaper to start over rather than paying for salvage and repairs. The insurance companies are all about the path of least expense."

"There is the complication of explaining shots fired," I said. "Anytime I discharge my gun, for any reason, I need to file a report."

"Target practice?" Pete suggested with a smile.

"One round?"

"Maybe you'll empty your gun before the end of the day."

"God, I hope not," I said. I knew that I was exaggerating a bit. I could easily explain away the single shot fired. But I wanted Pete to know that I was on the up-and-up, and not 100 percent on board with his request that I suffer short-term memory loss. Yes, I understood that sometimes it is in the best interest of victims to *not* pursue assailants. But I needed to know more before I determined that this was one of those cases.

We arrived at the side of the Duster. I dug out my key and said, "This is my ride." Pete took the key from my hand, unlocked the driver's door, and held it open for me. "Well, thank you," I said as I held my hand open for the key before I climbed in. I had grown accustomed to being alone, and really appreciated this small act of chivalry.

"My pleasure," he said. "This may be awkward, but what the

hell. Can I see you again? I mean under different circumstances, of course."

"I would like that," I said, surprising myself again.

"How about Friday night? I need a date for a party at my aunt and uncle's. It's a celebration of the spring solstice."

"You're kidding," I chuckled. "You're related to the Alfonds? I sent my RSVP in this morning."

"Well, do you have a date?"

"Nope."

"You do now. Can I pick you up? Where do you live?" I hesitated. There was no way I wanted to be picked up at my apartment. Too weird, I thought, to have the Vickersons and Wally all present and in my business. Before I could make an excuse, Pete said, "I don't mean to be forward. How about we meet there?"

"Sounds good. Now I am off to Dirigo to see what's up with another missing person. See you Friday." And I jumped into the Duster and started the engine before I could say something stupid. I glanced in my rearview mirror as I pulled away and was happy to see Pete watching me go. Not even The Wharf Rat's silhouette in the background hindered the rush of excitement that flooded in with the attention of a desirable man. It had been so long, I thought, since I'd felt that little flutter of emotion brought on by reciprocated interest. I assumed that Pete was 100 percent available. Otherwise he would not have asked me to join him at a party where he no doubt was known by most attendees. At his age, he must certainly have a past carried in assorted baggage, I thought as I stopped to allow pedestrians to access a crosswalk. But who doesn't? Starting a new life in Green Haven was not limited to work. A tragic personal life was what had propelled me to leave Miami. Comparing relationship notes with Pete was something that would come way down the road, when and if we got that far.

As soon as I cleared the congestion of Bar Harbor, I pulled off into a spot designated for enjoying the scenic view. I dialed Deloris. "Hello. Hancock County Sheriff's Department. How may I help you?"

"Hi Deloris. Jane here. Checking in from Bar Harbor. Has our missing girl surfaced?" I asked.

"Hi Jane. Nothing on Bianca yet. I did find a copy of her J-1 visa, though. Everything appears to be in order. Nothing unusual. The Bar Harbor Inn and Resort sponsors lots of foreign college kids. Looks like most of their seasonal help comes from that pool."

"How about Facebook and cell phone records for Bianca? Can you do your magic and let me know if there's anything I should know about? Recent activity? People that age usually post or text their every move."

"Can do. That's easy."

"Okay, thanks. I have chased down the only leads I had, and have come up with nothing. Everyone assumes that Bianca partied too hard and will reappear. I do have some other, possibly unrelated things for you to check out, though."

"Bring 'em on," Deloris said. "I am absolutely bored!"

"I need you to research a missing persons report that we may have received last year at this time. It supposedly came from an employee of the inn, and I understand that it was never responded to."

"Okay. And?"

"And I need employee and passenger lists for a cruise ship called *The Princess of the Seas*. And the same for *Radiance*. And an itinerary might be helpful. And I need any information you can get on some commercial lobster boats based in Bar Harbor. *Elizabeth*, *Ragged But Right*, and *Insight*. I am really interested in knowing what you can find on the owners of these boats."

"You mean, rap sheets?"

"*Anything*."

"Is this related to Bianca? Or is this other business?" Deloris sounded more interested than skeptical. She wanted to be in the know. "It would be helpful to know what I am digging for and why."

"I'm not sure yet if there is a connection. There is so little to go on. Can I call you after I get the scoop at Dirigo?" I knew that asking for information on Pete was strictly out of curiosity and for my personal interest. But hell, cops do this sort of thing all the time, I thought, trying to assuage my guilty conscience. And if push came to shove, I could easily justify wanting to know more about Pete. But that would require reporting all of the details of my boat ride with him. And that might be a can of worms best left sealed.

"Aye aye," Deloris quipped sarcastically. I thanked her, hung up, and pulled back onto the road.

I brought the sheriff's verbal directions back from memory, recalling that he had instructed that I would be heading north on one peninsula and back south on the next peninsula. The visual image of his directions showed two necks poking out into the ocean separated by very few miles. Between the two peninsulas there was the large and beautiful Jericho Bay. Until now, I had only observed the area on a paper navigational chart. And I had heard stories about what lies east of Bar Harbor that might make someone of lesser courage (or higher intelligence) cringe. This area was notoriously lawless with the exception of Dirigo, or "the Academy," to which I was now going. The school must certainly be a diamond in the rough, and quite an anomaly, I thought. I imagined the dichotomy of straitlaced and unlaced as I turned right onto Route 1 in Ellsworth.

Five minutes later, I saw the sign for Route 176. I turned right and immediately noticed the poor condition of the road. Potholes the size of craters were too numerous to avoid by straddling. I drove slowly, fearing loss of hubcaps as the Duster crept along the bumpy road. I laughed out loud at the number of dilapidated mailboxes. This collection of rundown receptacles was much worse than the ones that had been abused by snowplows in Green Haven, I thought. Some of the boxes were merely mangled, while others were missing from posts altogether. There were obvious attempts to repair in true Down East fashion. Broken posts bolstered by five-gallon buckets filled with cement and boxes wrapped with duct tape entertained me. When I dared take my eyes from the road, I enjoyed the view to my right.

Jericho Bay was littered with tiny, uninhabited islands that I imagined were ringed with bountiful lobster bottom, as buoys marking lobster traps speckled the surface of the water as far as I could see. A number of boats worked in circular patterns hauling and resetting traps. Visibility was excellent. I wondered how fishermen got away with molesting competitors' gear without being seen. I had heard that the Maine Marine Patrol had no teeth when it came to prosecution for fishing crimes. So I imagined that had led to the free-for-all that this sliver of ocean was noted for. I understood that gear wars were out of control here. And if this morning's events had been an indication of how things were handled at sea, I figured the Marine Patrol as an agency of enforcement was a joke.

Before long, I slipped into a daydream starring Pete. It had been such a long time since I had encountered a man who caught my eye and my breath that I had nearly forgotten how to fantasize. I imagined meeting him at his family's party. He would offer me his arm, which I would graciously accept. He would whisk me around, politely introducing me to everyone and anyone. What would I wear? What would I drink? Would there be dancing? Would there be a good night kiss? I inhaled deeply and could almost smell his aftershave.

A pickup truck approached too swiftly from behind, filling my rearview mirror and distracting my thoughts. The driver swerved out around me and passed on a dangerous curve in the road. Darting back to the right lane, nearly cutting me off, the pickup bounced along until it disappeared around another corner. Glancing at my speedometer, I shrugged when I saw that I was well below the speed limit. I imagined that the locals who drove this stretch of road daily had become accustomed to the deep and massive fissures that peppered Route 176, and perhaps didn't baby their vehicles as I did mine. And it was likely that they were not preoccupied with dreams of romantic possibilities.

By the time I found the entrance to Dirigo Maritime Academy, I had been passed by three trucks and a tractor. The parade of more patient drivers that had accumulated behind me seemed relieved as they rushed by when I turned off at the school. A single honk of a horn seemed more a thank-you than it did a gesture of good riddance. But that could have been a reflection of my mood made buoyant by my mounting intrigue with Pete (not to be confused with any intrigue in mounting Pete. I am, after all, a relative prude when it comes to such things).

I was happy to find that Dirigo maintained their drive meticulously. In fact, the entire campus was groomed to perfection. While most of Maine's scenic land and seascapes were rugged and handsome in a natural way, Dirigo's campus seemed more artificial. The beauty was contrived, I thought. Flowering shrubs lining walkways were exotic and gorgeous. But I preferred indigenous to alien, I thought as I followed signs to the visitors' parking.

I found a spot, parked, and jumped out of the Duster. I ran my hands down both thighs to straighten my now wrinkled khakis, and tugged the back of my jacket down from where it had ridden up while I was seated. Freshly painted wooden signs directed foot traffic along various walkways. I started in the direction of "Administration," following signs at intersections until I stood in the shadow cast by a large brick building propped up on pristine white columns. I checked my phone for a text from the sheriff, and found contact information for the Academy's president, Earl Smith. Now I knew who I was looking for.

I bolted up the stairs of the administration building, knowing that I would go through the formalities of filing the missing person report for the wayward cadet, and get back on the road toward home ASAP. By the time I got to the sheriff's department, Deloris would have any and all pertinent details on Pete. And the rest of her assignment? Well, yes, I would be interested in learning about whatever Deloris could dig up on the menacing captain of *Insight*, as I would no doubt eventually be assigned to investigate the sinking of *Elizabeth*. My second job as insurance gal was less exciting than my deputy gig. But it helped pay the bills, I thought as I looked through a list of the building's occupants by office number.

Earl Smith, according to the list, was in office number one. Appropriate, I thought as I walked a long, cool corridor looking for the academy's president. The office numbers were in descending order. I found number one at the very end of the corridor, knocked once, and entered. I was greeted by a very pleasant, chubby, elderly woman who stood from her desk as I entered. "You must be Deputy Bunker," she said quietly.

"Yes. I'm here to see President Smith."

"We have been expecting you. Thanks for coming. He's with the parents. Everyone is very concerned." She was almost whispering as she made her way from behind her desk to shake my hand. "Right this way," she said as she led me to another door where she knocked lightly until a voice beckoned us to enter.

The secretary opened the door and motioned for me to enter, which I did. She introduced me to her boss and the couple that remained seated in comfortable, easy chairs. The woman wept quietly while her husband wrung his hands. Overreacting, I thought to myself as I took a seat and pulled a small notepad and pen from my jacket's inside pocket. I couldn't help but think of the dramatic difference in the two missing persons cases. No tears were being shed for Bianca. And help from the inn was scarce. My presence at the inn had been a nuisance. Here, I sensed relief that I had arrived. There, nobody seemed alarmed that a young woman hadn't come home. Here, emotions were running on high.

President Smith pulled reading glasses from his face and wiped a bead of sweat with a neat handkerchief pulled from a trouser pocket. I couldn't remember the last time I saw a man use a handkerchief. Old-school, I thought as I waited for someone to start the conversation. "Thank you for coming, Deputy Bunker," Earl said as he placed the glasses on the top of his head. "In the interest of time, what do you know so far? No sense rehashing the upsetting facts."

"Well, I haven't been told much," I said. "I know that one of your students is missing following an at-sea training period. Cadet shipping, I think is what you call it."

"Yes, all Dirigo students spend three summers in our cadet shipping program. Two summers are spent on our school's training ship, and the third is aboard a commercial vessel—real hands-on experience that often leads to employment with the same company." This sounded a bit like a school brochure, I thought as I jotted notes. The woman, who was the mother of the missing cadet, wailed loudly as her husband tried to console her. Earl Smith continued, "In this case, Second Classman Franklin Avery had been placed aboard a cruise ship two months ago. He was due back in port and back to school yesterday. When he missed muster this morning, we called his parents."

I looked up from my notebook. The Averys stared at me. This wasn't much to go on, I thought. What did they expect me to say? "I understand your concern," I lied. "When was Franklin last heard from?"

The cadet's father answered. "We received an email from him on Monday. He emailed from the ship daily. We didn't think much of not hearing from him yesterday, as we expected him to call wanting us to pick him up when he got ashore. We had planned to catch up over lunch, and then deliver him back to school in time for dinner last night. When he hadn't called for a ride, we just assumed that he got held up aboard the ship and that he would call as soon as he was relieved of all duties."

"What about friends or roommates?" I asked. "Has anyone checked?"

"His girlfriend," the father answered. "We assumed that Franklin would want to see her first, and rightly so. But she hasn't heard from him since yesterday either."

The realist in me had a notion that Franklin had met another woman. Happens all the time, I thought. He may have been led astray. He was probably shacked up somewhere in a local hotel. But that wasn't a theory I would share with his doting parents. Not yet, anyway. "And assuming he has a cell phone,

I know that you have been dialing that. And you have left multiple messages, correct?"

"Of course," Mr. Avery confirmed.

"What about social media? Can you share any Facebook account information? Twitter? Anything that might help track recent activity would be good for me to have. What about credit cards?" I asked, knowing that a credit card is a must for checking into any hotel. "My associate back at the sheriff's department is highly skilled at electronic forensics and just plain digging." I regretted using the word forensics as soon as it slipped out, as it brought on a fresh round of howling from Mrs. Avery. If she only knew how ridiculous she'd feel when her son showed up like nothing had happened. Some people have a penchant for drama, I thought.

Even Mr. Avery seemed a bit put off by his wife's theatrics as he answered my inquiries. "Yes, we will give you everything you need to track Franklin down."

"He's only been missing since last night, right? There's a very good chance that your son is in no danger at all. How old is Franklin? And do you have a recent picture of him?" I asked, trying to sound as optimistic as I was without sounding as annoyed as I was.

"Our Frankie is turning twenty next month," Mrs. Avery stopped sobbing long enough to interject. "And he is not one to disappear! He is a good boy, isn't he, President Smith?"

"Yes. Franklin is the last cadet I would suspect of misbehaving or being irresponsible. He is a model student and one we are very proud of here at Dirigo."

"I'm sure that is true," I said truthfully. "And the majority of nice young men who fall out of communication with parents and girlfriends and have never been in any trouble before show up unscathed."

"Well, we are all hoping and praying for that," said President Smith. "But I'm sure you didn't come all the way to Dirigo to tell us to sit tight. What can we do in the meantime? Are you filing a formal missing person report? Is there a waiting period that needs to be met?"

"In Maine, we have no formal missing person report. It's simply a police report, and that was filed when you placed the call to the sheriff," I said. "I am here to follow up, and collect all pertinent information that will assist in locating Franklin." I handed my notepad to Mrs. Avery and asked her to write down everything she knew regarding social media that her son used, cell phone number, girlfriend's contact info, credit card numbers, social security number, and the like. "What is the name of the ship he was training aboard? Do you have any contact information for his employer? When and where was Franklin scheduled to be relieved of his duties?"

President Smith opened a file folder and produced a nice headshot of Franklin Avery. I took the picture and admired how handsome and wholesome he looked in his uniform. The president shuffled through a few pages and read, "Franklin was training aboard a cruise ship called *The Princess of the Seas*." I cringed as he continued. "The ship landed in Bar Harbor as scheduled yesterday morning. The Averys waited to welcome Franklin home, but he never came ashore."

"We waited for hours," exclaimed Mrs. Avery. "The launch went back and forth from the dock to the ship at least twenty times. The last trip of the day carried all of the ship's officers except our Franklin. We assumed that he had been required to stay aboard for some reason. We left phone messages for him to call when he needed a ride, and we went home to wait. He never called."

I suddenly had more interest in this case. *The Princess of the Seas* was the last known destination of my missing girl, Bianca. I would have Deloris check for a connection between Franklin and Bianca. And if Franklin was involved in a clandestine relationship, it made sense that he would not come ashore to the waiting arms of his mother and his girlfriend. If they had rendezvoused, there would be plenty of evidence in the form of texts, emails, or phone calls. Just as I was formulating a tactful way to tell the parents that I had a hunch regarding their son that might cast a shadow on his sterling reputation, a phone dinged loudly. Mr. Avery apologized as he pulled his phone from a pocket. "It's Frankie!" Mr. Avery pushed the phone to open the text with great force, and read, "Stuck aboard—sorry. Will get ashore in Rockland Saturday. TTYL."

"Thank God!" Mrs. Avery wiped a tear from her cheek. "Ask him when we should be there." Mr. Avery obediently texted back and forth with his son while we all waited for his report. I wanted badly to ask Mr. Avery to inquire about a young Romanian girl, but resisted. I made a note to have Deloris check the ETA for *The Princess* into Rockland. My sense of local geography was not great. But I thought Rockland, Maine, was just a few ports down the coast from Bar Harbor. I didn't understand why Franklin would not be ashore until Saturday when I had watched *The Princess* weigh anchor hours ago. I noticed a nautical chart on the wall of President Smith's office, and got up to examine it. I half listened to Mrs. Avery bark orders to her husband while he texted. "Why don't you just call him? Why hasn't he answered our messages?"

"He says that his phone had no service in Bar Harbor and that he just got our messages," explained Mr. Avery. I could tell from his tone that he was trying to cover for his son. And that he didn't believe the lame excuse for no contact. "He was required to stay aboard ship because he is low man on the totem pole, and the other engineers all wanted shore leave in Bar Harbor."

"That's our Frankie," praised Mrs. Avery. "He is very responsible and thoughtful of others. But what about school? He is missing classes."

Earl Smith chimed in. "He can be excused from a few classes in the line of duty aboard ship. The hands-on experience he is getting is invaluable." Another plug for Dirigo, I thought as I found Rockland on the chart. "I am relieved, but not surprised, to learn that all is well." I stretched my hand from port to port—planting my thumb on Bucksport, the tip of my middle finger landing in Bar Harbor. I then moved my hand to the lines of latitude at the vertical edge of the chart and measured minutes. "I guess we should let the sheriff know that the lost has been found." I felt this was my invitation to leave, but was still figuring out how long it would take *The Princess* to steam from

Bar Harbor to Rockland. And I was still looking for a way to mention Bianca. Cops don't tend to believe in coincidence.

"The trip from Bar Harbor to Rockland is less than one hundred miles," I said as I stared at the chart. "And most cruise ships steam at a minimum of twenty knots. So, he should be in Rockland by this evening."

"You know that from waving your hand over the map?" asked Mrs. Avery skeptically.

"Well, it's not entirely accurate. But as the crow flies—it's good enough. Every minute of latitude equals one nautical mile," I explained.

"Whatever." She was clearly not impressed with my navigational skills. "Dear," Mrs. Avery said as she patted her husband's back, "we should pick up Melissa and go to Rockland. I can't wait to see him!" I assumed that Melissa was the girlfriend.

"But Frankie says he can't get off the ship until Saturday," replied her husband. Somehow I suspected that Mr. Avery hadn't relayed all of the text messages. "We should wait until then to go to Rockland. Let's do as he has asked."

"But what about Melissa? That is unfair of the cruise line to expect Frankie to stay aboard while in port—especially seeing that he was supposed to be relieved yesterday." Mrs. Avery was nearly pouting. "Come on. Let's get out of President Smith's hair. We have wasted enough of his time."

The three shook hands and thanked one another and all shared sighs of relief. The parents thanked me and apologized for wasting my time. "Not at all," I said. "I am glad to know your son is in no danger." I waited behind as President Smith

70

walked the Averys to the door. When he returned to his desk, I filled him in on my missing girl. I confided my suspicions to him regarding Frankie and Bianca. I realized that he might see the connection as a stretch. But with young people, where there's a will there's a way. And mere acquaintances were fair game among millennials to hook up with sexually, especially for those born at the very end of Generation Y, I thought. "I am not judging. But it seems likely that these two may have hooked up aboard the ship. My partner is looking at activity on Bianca's phone. Now that I have Frankie's number, I may be able to establish a connection."

"But Frankie is no longer missing. There is no need to investigate, is there?"

"Well, I still have a missing girl to locate. And the only lead I have is a friend she was meeting aboard a cruise ship that was in Bar Harbor last night. See where I am going with this?"

"Yes, I understand what you're driving at. Not Franklin Avery. No way. He is very devoted to his girlfriend and not at all susceptible to being led astray."

I knew that Earl was protecting the reputation of the Academy by defending one of its highest potentials. I knew the military-school mindset—officers and gentlemen. But I also knew that I could not ignore the fact that two young people had been reported missing, and that they may have *The Princess* in common. I had a gut feeling that Bianca was enjoying her cruise from Franklin's stateroom. The delay in Franklin's homecoming was easily explained. He had volunteered to stay on port duty to get more time with Bianca. Not that there was any harm done.

But I would like to follow this through until Bianca was no longer of the missing status.

I would call the sheriff and explain that I needed to go to Rockland. I had no intention of being the buzz killer for the two kids. But I did take seriously the accusations of Bianca's roommate who had stated that when another foreign, visa-ed girl was reported missing, nobody responded. She did have a point. President Smith and the Averys were all-consumed with Franklin's tardiness. They would insist on leaving no stone un-turned if he hadn't texted. Everyone in Bianca's world was back to work by now. And I assumed they had not heard from her. When she found her way ashore and back to Bar Harbor, she would confess all. And it would sound like fun and an adven-ture. And her friends would scold her while asking for more details of her stowing away with the handsome cadet engineer. "Will there be anything else?" President Smith asked. "I really appreciate your quick response to my call. Please thank the sheriff for me, won't you?"

"Okay. Will do."

"Allow me to walk you to your car," he said politely.

"Of course." I waited for President Smith to lead the way from his office and down the corridor lined with pictures of past Dirigo presidents: some in suits and ties and others in mil-itary garb boasting medals of significance unknown to me. "This is quite a school, President Smith. I have heard great things about the opportunities afforded to your graduates."

"Please, call me Earl," he said as he opened and held the exit door for me. "Yes, I have been here for three years, and am still pinching myself. We are so fortunate to have an amazing faculty. And our reputation for placing graduates in the shipping industry has made our application process highly competitive."

We walked side by side on stone pavers that weaved around and through the campus toward the visitor parking area. I stopped to admire one particularly lush garden. I know a rose from a daisy from a tulip—but I am far from a horticulturist. This section of the campus gardens was bright yellow. As if sensing my curiosity, President Smith pointed out specifics by name. "Those trumpet-shaped flowers are *Allamanda*. Can you smell their fruitiness? And those are Yellow Elders, the national flower of the Bahamas." I smiled and nodded with interest and appreciation as we continued along the pavers. "And this area honors Eastern Europe," he said as we stopped to take in the dense purple-and-blue, delicate-looking flowers. "Siberian Iris. Aren't they perfect? And the white clusters are baby's breath."

"I am impressed," I said honestly. "My compliments to the groundskeeping team."

"We have a healthy percentage of foreign students here. We do our best to make them feel less estranged." I thought that was a nice sentiment, but a strange choice of words. "You can well imagine what it might be like for kids from Malaysia, Turkey, Romania, or the Bahamas to be in small-town Maine for four years when the rest of our student body is from less than one hundred miles from campus."

"Yes, I can understand the importance of making everyone feel welcome and less homesick," I said.

73

"Not to mention the money that comes to Dirigo from these relationships. Many countries have a navy, but no maritime academy," he said as he looked at his watch and picked up the pace. "And as most merchant shipping is foreign flagged, we enjoy the ability to place cadets, such as Franklin Avery, aboard for invaluable training. This is stuff that can't be taught in the classroom."

"Well, there's my car," I said when we reached the fringe of the parking lot. "Thanks for the tour. Please let me know when Franklin returns to school, won't you?" I handed him a card with my name and cell number and watched as he turned and headed back toward campus.

A soon as I was seated in the Duster, I pulled out my phone and called the station to update Franklin's status to no-longer-missing. Deloris answered, clearly having checked caller ID. "Okay, what's your theory?"

"Hi, Deloris," I said and chuckled at her blunt greeting. "My theory on what?" I asked.

"Your theory on Bianca. You need to tell me *everything* if you expect me to do my job to the best of my ability—which is substantial."

"Let's start with this," I said. "The missing Dirigo student, Franklin Avery, has been found aboard *The Princess of the Seas*, where his training cruise was extended. *The Princess* is the last known destination of Bianca. She was meeting a *friend*. I think she and Franklin are shacked up in his stateroom."

"Oh, yeah. That makes sense. So, where does Peter Alfond fit in?"

"Red herring, I guess," I said, hoping Deloris would dish up a bit of Pete's personal history to bolster my interest. "Why? What did you learn?"

"Well, I just found it interesting that Peter Alfond's name was handwritten in the margin of the police report you asked me to find for the missing girl last year."

Mrs. Fletcher, do you have any more information? What is it that you need?"

"Well, I just found it interesting that Pete, the one I gave the number to, the person in question, should show up in your casebook. Is it likely he would just happen to—"

FOUR

I stopped breathing for a second as I digested what Deloris had said. "So I thought you were on to something. But if you have solved the mystery of the missing Romanian, we will close this case. Quite a coincidence, though."

"Bianca hasn't been located yet," I said as I tried to make sense of why Pete had not mentioned last year's missing girl, assuming that he had been questioned. How else could the appearance of his name on the report be explained? I wondered. "Fill me in on the report from last year," I said, hoping that Deloris would not detect the slight shade of angst in my voice.

"It states her name, and that she was in Bar Harbor working on the same student visa as Bianca. She was a student at the University of Turkey. That's the whole report." Deloris slapped her desk, the sound reverberating through the phone line, then continued. "Azra Demir, A-Z-R-A, D-E-M-I-R. There is no file other than the police report, so I assume that Azra was located before anyone investigated or followed up."

Suddenly, I had more concern for Bianca. Or, I checked myself, maybe my concern was related to the reason for Pete's name to have been involved. "Dig a little deeper on Azra," I said. "And please find an itinerary for *The Princess of the Seas*. She left Bar Harbor this morning and is heading to Rockland. She should arrive there soon. But according to the no-longer-missing cadet, he will not make landfall until Saturday."

"Okay, that sounds fishy," Deloris said as I heard her jotting notes through the phone. "And if you're correct, the Avery kid is buying time with the girl, right?"

"Yes, that makes the most sense. Were you able to get a passenger list?" I asked.

"Yup. And I have a comprehensive crew list that includes names from master to ordinary seamen. And I have a long list of other personnel that runs the gamut from ship's steward to housekeeping—many names I can't pronounce. But I can confirm that the majority of the scullery team are students from Eastern Europe. I found copies of all visas. And I can also confirm that Franklin Avery was employed as an apprentice engineer, and that his sea time terminated yesterday. And just to ease your mind about Bianca's possible trip to Cuba, the *Radiance* employs folks from Central and South America pretty much exclusively in the galley and housekeeping."

Oh, I thought. There was almost no chance that Bianca's friend was employed aboard *Radiance*. That was important to eliminate as a possibility, I knew. It was now clear that my efforts would be focused on *The Princess*, whose housekeeping duties were all performed by kids from Eastern Europe. "What did you find in your research on the owners of the boats I asked about? *Elizabeth* and *Insight*—anything that might be of interest to a somewhat bored detective on restrictive duty?" I asked playfully, intentionally leaving Pete out of the list, which I was certain did not go unnoticed by the very sharp and perceptive Deloris.

"Nothing significant," Deloris replied. "Unless you are curious about the fact that the Coast Guard received a Mayday call from *Elizabeth* just a few hours ago. The call was cancelled and the boat has been reported as a total loss. Coincidence?" I held my tongue when it wanted to ask, "Already?" Instead of interjecting, I waited patiently for Deloris to divulge anything else she might have learned. "The owner of *Insight* is an unsavory character. Name's Larry Vigue. He's been arrested on domestic assault charges, public intoxication, and has outstanding warrants for unpaid fines for indecent exposure," Deloris added a bit of commentary, "which is usually associated with relieving oneself in public when intoxicated. His record goes back to the seventies when he was suspected of running drugs, but was never convicted."

I took this all in, and was not at all surprised by Deloris's findings. Again, we both waited for the other to say something. I outlasted my associate again. She continued. "There's nothing on Ronald Thomas, the owner of the unfortunate *Elizabeth*. Nothing of an arrest record. Looks to be a straight shooter," Deloris said. "And other than his name on the police report last year,

Peter Alfond is the nephew of *the* Alfonds. Now if you don't find *that* intriguing, I'll have to check you for a pulse."

I realized that I needed to be forthright with Deloris if I expected her to know what she was digging for and why. She had already made connections, so there was no sense keeping anything from her. Besides, I knew I had nothing other than loose ends that could easily be explained as coincidence. And, I reminded myself, Deloris and I were on the same team. "As hard as this may be to believe, I met Pete Alfond this morning on the Bar Harbor waterfront. He offered me a ride out to *The Princess* as he was acting as pilot boat and transporting the ship's pilot out. I learned nothing from the ship's steward that might help with locating Bianca. Pete heard and responded to the Mayday from *Elizabeth* with me on board. By the time we reached the scene, it was too late to do anything other than pick a nearly drowned captain out of the drink."

"Well, that explains why you needed info on two of the boats' captains. But what about Larry Vigue? And the *Insight*?" Deloris was quick to note that I had left something out of my brief explanation.

Should I let it go, as advised by Pete and Ron? Or do I confide in my counterpart, asking her to keep it under the radar for now? Of course I did the right thing, and filled in the blanks for my loyal coworker, whom I trusted implicitly. "I am fairly certain that Larry Vigue rammed and sank the *Elizabeth*."

"Motive? Evidence?"

"The evidence is in tight-lipped eyewitnesses who are more interested in retaliation than they are justice. And there's hard evidence on the bottom of the ocean," I said. "Motive? Well, Pete and Ron passed it off as just another chapter in the gear wars that are unending. But that does not ring true with me."

"It's common knowledge that the guys who fish this part of the Maine coast are brutal," Deloris said. "How credible was Pete Alfond?"

I fought the urge to reply with "Incredible," with regards to my first impression of Captain Alfond. Instead, I decided that full transparency was necessary if I expected my working relationship with Deloris to continue to be successful. I took a deep breath and said, "I'll let you know after our date on Friday. I'm meeting him at his family's party."

"Wow! So I am now surfing every source—beyond a criminal search," Deloris remarked as I imagined her fingers flying around her computer's keyboard. "Nice picture. Looks to be single. *Never* married at age forty-seven—some might see that as a red flag." Deloris was enjoying this, I knew. I was hesitant to stop her, as I was indeed curious to know all she could find prior to my date. But when Deloris hacked into his college transcript, I had to interject.

"Okay, enough. I don't think this is pertinent to the case."

"What case?" Deloris asked. "The case of the missing Bianca? Missing Franklin Avery? Boat sinking?"

Again, I was tempted to mention the only case at hand, which was a head case—mine—and created by Pete Alfond's name and how it related to the missing girl from last year. "None of the above. Poor choice of word. There is no case. Besides, unless someone is pressing charges, the boat sinking was an accident that I will no doubt be assigned to investigate wearing my *other* hat," I said, referring to my part-time work as a marine insurance investigator. "And the case of the missing lovers will be cracked as soon as the lovebirds run out of energy."

"Speaking of lovebirds," Deloris said teasingly.

"Stop!" I cut her off. "Can you get details on *The Princess*'s itinerary? It seems strange that Franklin Avery will not be coming ashore until Saturday. I watched the ship leave Bar Harbor today when I was there."

"Done. Way ahead of you, girlfriend." Deloris was back to business, which was a relief. "The official itinerary that is registered with Cruise Lines International Association has *The Princess of the Seas* weighing anchor in Bar Harbor today at noon, which you witnessed. Correct?" I answered "yes" and waited for more. "And this indicates arrival in Rockland Saturday morning at oh six hundred."

"Well that makes no sense," I said. "I could paddle between Bar Harbor and Rockland in sixty hours."

"I wasn't finished," Deloris scolded. "The online brochure for this particular cruise circuit, which promises a full week on the Maine Coast, includes puffin and whale watching, and a full-blown clambake on a small, remote island. In this case, the puffins are found on Sheep Island Ledges, whales will be found on the Schoodic Ridges, and the clambake will be on the south shore of Great Duck Island."

"So it isn't all about buying trinkets and T-shirts, I guess," I said.

"Nope! This cruise is really more family-oriented. Not the

floating meat market and food fest I had always imagined," Deloris said, her voice trailing off as I pictured her surrounded by computer monitors and keyboards. Deloris had really settled in to her position since her accident, I thought. Prior to breaking her heels in the line of duty, she was disgruntled, always complaining that her abilities were being wasted at the desk end of the job.

"I had hoped to wrap up the missing kids sooner. But that's not possible until Saturday. I'll plan to be in Rockland by daylight. I want to see Franklin as he is greeted by his parents and girlfriend. And Bianca! Do young people still refer to the morning after as the walk of shame?"

"Are you kidding? This generation has no shame. They wear their indiscretions like badges. I can't believe I haven't found anything on Bianca's Facebook account," Deloris exclaimed. "I'm not a prude, but am shocked at what some people share with the world. Whatever happened to kissing and *not* telling?" My silence brought another chuckle from Deloris as she added, "Oh yeah. Then there's the throwback, Jane Bunker, who neither kisses nor tells. Want me to go to Rockland with you Saturday? You can tell me all about your date with Pete Alfond, and the Solstice Soiree."

"No, thank you," I answered politely. "And it's not a date."

"Really? What is it?"

"Just part of my job. You heard the sheriff. He expects me to go to represent the department. And the appearance of Pete's name on that missing girl's report . . . That is now part of an active investigation."

"Right."

I wasn't about to discuss the details of my growing interest in Pete Alfond with Deloris. I had to get on the road and back to Green Haven. Tomorrow was another day. And I was not excited about the direction my job had taken me in. I felt rather useless chasing missing people, and much preferred chasing drug traffickers. "Thanks, Deloris. See you tomorrow morning," I said as I prepared to buckle my seat belt and start the Duster.

"Have you decided what you'll wear?"

"Have a good night." And with that, I hung up and pulled out of the Academy's guest parking area and headed toward home. I bounced and rattled the length of the gauntlet-like Route 176, relieved to not hold up other vehicles this time. The sun was thinking about setting as I pulled onto Route 1 and mixed easily with other late commuters on this busy section of road that ran the length of the eastern seaboard. This day had flown by, I thought, as I realized my stomach was growling in anticipation of dinner.

I quickly exited Route 1, taking a sharp right turn onto the peninsula whose sign promised "Green Haven—Voted Most Scenic Fishing Port." And of the beautiful ports that I had seen to date, I had to agree that I lived in the most breath-taking. Shadows cast by thick stands of healthy spruce trees eased the squints in my eyes, and I pushed the Duster's visor up. The breeze was cooled in its transit across the bay that flashed glints of white light, a massive paparazzi lining a red carpet event. My right arm was a bit too short to roll up the passenger side window when the air was too cool. So I put on a little heat instead, and found that to be the best of all worlds. The back of my neck was whipped lightly by windblown hair as my sunglasses, now on my head, tacked down long bangs and protected my eyes from the same lashing. My toes were perfectly toasty in open sandals with the Duster's fan on its lowest setting. This is indeed "The Way Life Should Be," I thought as I mentally scheduled tomorrow.

I was always behind on paperwork. As painful as it was for me to spend a day at the desk, it was necessary. I needed to formalize all documentation of what I had done today. The documentation would be more impressive than the results of the activities recorded in the ongoing reports required. Let's see, I thought, I started by driving to the Bar Harbor Inn and Resort where I questioned the manager about Bianca Chiriac. He was less than helpful, but not offensive or blatantly uncooperative. The manager was neither concerned nor surprised that an employee was MIA.

I had found Bianca's roommate, Anika, in the inn's laundry facility. Anika was very concerned, and grateful for the attention put forth on behalf of the missing roomie. I learned of a second reported missing girl that seemingly was never resolved—and may not have been thoroughly investigated. I met and questioned the owner/operators of Tag Team Taxi, Dud and Dolly. I learned that Dolly had driven Bianca to the waterfront where she had stated she was meeting a friend from Romania who worked aboard a cruise ship. I had since learned that *The Princess of the Seas* was the only possibility of the two cruise ships that were in port when I arrived at the waterfront myself, as the

Allure had arrived this morning. The other ship that I learned had been in Bar Harbor—*Radiance*—had weighed anchor for Cuba the night before and had no Eastern Europeans on its passenger or employee lists, probably ruling that out as a possibility.

Pete Alfond transported me to *The Princess* with his lobster/pilot boat, *Ragged But Right*. I spoke briefly with the ship's steward at the boarding door. The steward had looked at Bianca's picture, and did not recognize her. He also claimed that there had been no visitors allowed aboard in Bar Harbor, so was confident that Bianca had not been there. I noted that this was questionable. I could not board and ask around, because the ship was getting ready to leave. And, as the steward had mentioned, the foreign flag enabled the ship to not allow me access to investigate unless the missing person had been a US citizen.

The trip to Dirigo was easier in terms of paperwork, I thought as I drove the length of Green Haven's Main Street. I had met the school's president, Earl Smith. I had met the parents of the missing student, Franklin Avery. And by the time I left the school, the case of the missing cadet was seemingly resolved as he had texted that he was still aboard *The Princess* as part of his cadet shipping experience, and would disembark in Rockland Saturday morning.

With the exception of Bianca's roommate, Anika, everyone else I had questioned believed that she was in no danger and that she would show up to work soon. And all of the evidence certainly supported that theory. I would know for sure on Saturday when I planned to be in Rockland to close this case. I would not be accused of dropping the ball, as someone had with the missing girl from last year, I vowed as I pulled into my parking spot in the Vickersons' yard. And that concluded my day's activities, I thought as I locked up and made my way to my apartment. The case of the lobster boat ramming and sinking would be on hold until I was asked to investigate for the insurance company. And if Pete Alfond's insights on that were accurate, it might never be reported. So I could focus on police business for now, I thought. Maybe I would crack open a cold case after all.

I knew that I had time to freshen up before joining Henry, Alice, and Wally for dinner, as my landlords fancied themselves late diners, which I had come to know meant plenty of time for a Scotch or two. They had even taken to mixing Wally a mocktail every night! I was certainly ready for the real thing by the time I knocked and entered the tidy kitchen.

Well, look what the tide left!" Mr. V greeted me with a smile and arms open for a quick hug. "Glad you made it home for dinner. Alice has a real treat for us—Mediterranean mussels over angel-hair pasta." The brief embrace was warm, and I noted how bony the old man's back had become. I could feel individual ribs, and realized that in his mid-eighties, Mr. V was doing quite well in spite of his thinness.

Mrs. V waved a wooden spoon from her station at the stove, reminding me of a stereotypical grandmother. Her white hair was pulled back into a neat bun that filled the nook between the base of her skull and slight hunch in her back. "Hello, dear!

Get comfortable in the living room while Henry tends bar. Your brother should be home from work soon."

I plopped into my favorite armchair and immediately started my inspection of the nautical knickknacks lining every horizontal space. The glass sailboats holding unlit tea lights continued competing in the endless regatta along the fireplace mantle. Although all eight frosted glass boats were identical, they were a catalyst for the Vickersons' frequent discussions on sailing and boats. Sloops, ketches, yawls, gaffers . . . If it has a sail, it's a sailboat, in my opinion. But my landlords were virtual naval architects, and not always from the same school. This made for interesting and often heated debates about hull speeds, sail styles and sizes, etc. Hoping to avoid Sailing 101 this evening, I forced my stare to the large sill at the bay window. "What happened to the mermaids?" I asked.

"She moved them to the bathroom," answered Mr. V as he filled the ice bucket from a drawer-style freezer. "Do you like the wheel?" I couldn't help but notice the full-sized ship's wheel—wooden and spoked—that diminished the top of the table. "It's from *Queen Anne's Revenge*. You know? Blackbeard?"

"Really? Where did you find it?"

"It's a replica."

"Oh. Of course," I said feeling a little stupid. Mr. V handed me a Scotch with two ice cubes. He placed his wife's drink on an anchor coaster on an end table next to the chair she liked, and made his way to the "south end of the couch" as he liked to call it, leaving the north end for Wally. Slowly, Mr. V lowered himself onto the overstuffed cushion, bracing with his right hand on the arm of the couch and his left fist in the cushion. He groaned and exhaled as his buttocks finally landed and took the weight off of his extremities. I had recently noticed that Mr. V was showing his age. It made me sad that I was not comfortable with mentioning this or even asking how he was feeling. I had never dealt with the joys of aging parents. I jumped up to grab his drink that he had forgotten on the bar. "So where did you get the replica?"

"Uncle Henry's," he said, referring to the Maine-based swap, sell, and trade publication that was fodder for a large percentage of local small talk. "Drove clear to Gouldsboro to pick it up. Twenty-six miles, round-trip. Still a deal, though. I got that beauty for fifteen bucks!"

"Plus lunch," Mrs. V chimed in as she joined us. "Henry always neglects to mention all expenses when he boasts of the deals he gets."

"Good thing you're such a cheap date," Henry laughed. "Wasses Hot Dogs. Two with everything for five bucks. And a bottle of water from home. We used to eat two dogs apiece. Not anymore. We're getting old, my love."

We sipped Scotch and chatted about a number of things as we waited for Wally to come home from the café. Mr. V gave me a lecture on Blackbeard and his ship, which I found interesting. Who doesn't love pirate intrigue? We agreed that the ship's wheel would sell quickly in the Lobster Trappe, as soon he found something suitable to replace it on the coffee table. By suitable, I knew the item would need to be found in Uncle Henry's, and involve a road trip, and be worthy of little conversation.

As Mr. V struggled to his feet to mix another round, I filled my landlords in on my missing people. The working theory that Bianca and Franklin were enjoying a tryst aboard a cruise ship delighted Mr. and Mrs. V. "Young love is wonderful!" Mrs. V exclaimed. "You're not going to *bust* them, are you?" It always cracked me up when the octogenarians used contemporary vernacular.

"No, they haven't done anything illegal. But it is my job to follow up and ensure that they are accounted for. There was a girl reported missing last year at this time, and we have no idea whether it was resolved. Not on my watch," I said.

"Yes, young love . . . And old love ain't too bad." Mr. V was trailing us in the conversation, which was happening more and more. "Alice and I met at the Blue Hill Fair. Sixty. . . ." Henry turned toward us from the bar, stopped to think and appeared to be confused.

"Sixty-two years ago this September." Mrs. V rescued her husband, as usual. "And I know we went *missing* on occasion." She winked at her adoring husband.

"Yep. I met my wife at the Blue Hill Fair. She was working at the girlie show."

"Henry! Stop that! I'm glad Wally isn't home to hear that nonsense."

Almost on cue, the door flew open and Wally made a grand entrance. Not grand in a grandiose way—just grand in that his quiet, positive presence lit up the room without effort or intention on his part. All smiles, Wally hugged me while I remained seated. Happiness breeds happiness, I thought as Wally took a seat at *his* end of the couch. "What are you drinking, Walter?" asked Mr. V, using the full name as requested by my brother after being told by Audrey that *Wally* was not mature enough.

"Yes please, Mister V," Wally said politely.

"Okay, double Scotch, neat. Coming right up." Henry answered my questioning scowl with a playful grin, and popped the top on a can of root beer. As he poured it over ice in a highball glass, he said, "I was just explaining to your sister how I met Mrs. V."

"Dinner is served! Bring your drinks to the table," Mrs. V said loudly. "I want you to eat this masterpiece while it's hot," Mrs. V announced as she bounced to her feet and hustled toward the kitchen just as a timer dinged. We all obliged obediently, as we were acutely aware that the cook is the boss—even when she isn't cooking.

Mrs. V oohed and aahed and smacked her lips as she served up four plates of piping hot angel-hair pasta topped with her newest creation for the *All Mussel Cookbook* she had been working on since I had landed on her doorstep over a year ago. We ate mussels in some form every night. And she never repeated a recipe.

After a quick joining of hands for grace delivered by Henry, we dug in. I hadn't realized how hungry I was until I took the first bite. The mussels were just the right size and were cooked to perfection—shells were open and meats nearly fell out. They were moist and smooth, not dry and grainy like when they are overcooked. The broth was slightly briny, and had a hint of fresh tarragon and Pernod. Capers, sundried tomatoes, and Kalamata olives added color, texture, and flavor. I willed myself to slow down when I realized I was gulping.

Wally and I cleared the table, rinsing and placing the dishes in the sink for Henry and Alice to deal with later. (I appreciated the fact that Alice never allowed us to actually *wash* the dishes, because I was usually yawning by the time that was necessary). As soon as there was room on the table, Mrs. V presented a beautifully plated dessert. Wally literally clapped his hands in applause of the mini tower of sweetness dusted in powdered sugar and capped with a dollop of lemon-flavored cream. "Wow, Mrs. V, you have outdone yourself. What is this?" I asked while still admiring my plate.

"Reinette apple dessert," she answered proudly. "It's to die for. Believe me. But I had to substitute golden delicious for the Reinettes. Welcome to Down East Maine . . ."

"A taste of the forbidden fruit! This is how Eve entrapped Adam, my dear," said Henry as he pushed a fork down through four layers of his stacked dessert.

"Forbidden?" Wally asked, laying down his fork.

"In the biblical sense only, my friend." Mr. V turned to me and asked, "Didn't you kids attend Sunday school?"

"When it comes to poison apples, the Evil Queen and Snow White is more my speed," I answered as I nearly licked my plate.

"Well, that's a case of comparing apples to oranges," Mrs. V added, knowing she was starting one of our word battles.

"An apple a day keeps the doctor away," I said.

"How do you like *them* apples?" Wally surprised me by jumping in appropriately.

"The apple doesn't fall far from the tree," Mr. V noted.

"But one bad apple don't spoil the whole bunch," I reminded him.

"Don't be a wise apple," Mrs. V teasingly scolded her husband.

"You're the apple of my eye!"

"You are an apple polisher!"

"Don't upset the apple cart."

"American as apple pie," I shouted. We all sat silently thinking. I couldn't come up with another apple reference, and it was clear that nobody else could either. "I win!"

"I concede. It is time for everyone to get away from the table so we can police-up the kitchen and get ready for bed," Mrs. V said as she started clearing the dessert plates. "Walter, you go get cleaned up now, sweetheart."

"Thank you for dinner," Wally said as he pushed his chair in. He then gave me another hug and retreated to his room. I, too, thanked my landlords for dinner, and was happy to retire to my apartment. I was not sleepy, but would always log in a few extra hours of sleep when I could.

It was just eight thirty when I was in my nightshirt and ready to tuck into bed. The sun was disappearing, leaving behind traces of citrus that mingled then dissolved into the western bay. I heaved a contented sigh and pulled the shade on the day. Although I was not excited about my duties right now, I had to admit that chasing down missing people was like a vacation. I wouldn't be shot at or threatened in any way, I thought as I turned down the top sheet. And after all, it was summer. And summer was a great time to spend more time with friends and family. I wasn't sure whether the Vickersons were friends or family, but I did enjoy and appreciate all they did and were doing for Wally and me. As I reflected, I had to acknowledge the fact that I was indeed looking forward to Friday night. Wouldn't it be great, I thought, to investigate possibilities with Pete Alfond?

Just as I drifted, nearly sleeping, my cell phone rang. Nobody ever calls me unless it's work-related, I knew. I cleared my head and jumped up to grab my phone. It was my boss at the marine insurance company, Mr. Dubois. "Hi, Jane. Sorry for the late call. I have a job that needs to be done tomorrow if you're not busy fighting crime," he said.

"Hello, Mr. Dubois," I answered. "I am on fairly light duty now, so I can give you a day. What's up?" When I wasn't in the throes of a major investigation, the sheriff appreciated my moonlighting as the insurance adjustor/investigator, as it was easier on payroll to not have hours tallying up without real purpose and progress. And it was an easy back and forth between law and insurance, I thought. And I didn't have anything on my deputy sheriff slate until Rockland on Saturday.

"Not the most pleasant assignment, I'm afraid," he said. "One of our commercial lobstermen passed away this afternoon. Looks like a heart attack brought on by his boat sinking." I was stunned and remained silent. I waited and was not surprised to hear, "Ron Thomas. Nice family man. His widow needs some attention and assurance that we are on it."

93

FIVE

I was at first stunned, and then saddened, to hear of the death of a man whom I had helped save from drowning. I wondered briefly about Pete Alfond. He and Ron Thomas seemed to be close friends. Was Pete aware of the death yet? If the truth were to come out, would there be manslaughter charges brought against the captain of *Insight*? Murder one was more appropriate, I thought. But chances of that ever happening were slim, I knew. "Where and when do I meet the widow?" I asked.

"Her name is, let's see . . . Liza Thomas. I'll text you the address listed on the policies. She's in Northeast Harbor, and expects you in the morning—first thing. They carried a lot of insurance, both property and life, with us. The boat was paid for, which is unusual." Mr. Dubois's voice cracked and squeaked with emotion. I didn't know if he was overwrought with sadness about the death, or if doling out large sums elicited his grief. "If you can console her and give her confidence, I'll start the paperwork for the claims and reach out to her personally as well."

"Will do. Let her know that I will be at her door at eight a.m. And I'll look for the text with her address from you," I said. We hung up, and I crawled back under the covers of my bed and lay awake staring at the ceiling. I realized that I would have to fill my boss in about what I had witnessed today. Would it be considered a conflict of interest for me to conduct any duties on behalf of the insurance company or the sheriff's department? Judging from what I had learned about the unlawful way of Down East Maine in general, I doubted anyone would raise an eyebrow if I were to testify as a witness as well as being an arresting officer should charges be filed. Didn't I owe it to the insurance company to hold Larry Vigue accountable? *Insight* must certainly be fully insured, I reasoned. But nearly every commercial fisherman in the region was covered by the same underwriters. So, I reasoned, the claims would eventually come from the same till.

I wondered how much the widow knew of how *Elizabeth* came to sink today. Did her now late husband tell her it had been an accident? Did he confide in his wife the degree of hostility that had been reached in the ongoing territorial war that I had learned was part and parcel of the inshore lobster fishery? How would Ron's death affect the battles? Would the aggressive activity escalate? Or would Ron's death act to curtail it? I knew of boat sinkings that had occurred while boats were on moorings, scuttlings that had been self-inflicted for high insurance payouts, and boat burnings that occurred when nobody was aboard. I was aware of boats that had been cast adrift and of shootings that amounted to warning shots across bows. There were daily reports of gear molestation and theft. But what I had witnessed today was an intention to kill, attempted murder that could easily be seen as involuntary manslaughter at the very least.

I needed to turn my mind off and get some sleep. Tomorrow morning could be long and emotional. I heard my phone ding with an incoming text just as I was teetering on the edge of sleep. In my cloudy state, I fantasized that the text that I knew was from Mr. Dubois was from Pete, saying good night. I have always reveled in that half-in, half-out stage of consciousness where I can manipulate reality to suit me.

Sleep came quickly, and morning too early. First light slipped around the window shades and through my eyelids, waking me gently. I stretched and yawned, not daring to turn over and risk falling back to sleep. I hopped up and into a warm shower and pulled on light clothes, ready for a hot day in my un-air-conditioned Duster. Khakis, blouses, and sensible shoes were what I lived in. One of the things I enjoyed about living and working in Maine was the absence of a dress code. As long as I was covered appropriately, I could get away with most anything in my modest wardrobe. Clean was the only guideline I had been given, and was what I followed whether performing duties for the insurance company or the sheriff's department. I liked not wearing a uniform. Those days were way behind me, I thought as I buttoned up. I hadn't worn a uniform since being a beat cop in Miami. Once I had been promoted to detective, the Dade County taupe became a thing of the past. (Taupe was never becoming on me, a mousy blonde with a low-color complexion. I would have much preferred a dark blue or green—but they were too hot in the summer.) Before I closed my closet door, I glanced through my hanging clothes for something to wear to the Alfonds' party. Maybe I would have to buy something new, but not tell Deloris.

The text on my phone was indeed the address I needed from Mr. Dubois. I opened my *Road Atlas to Maine* and found the only route from Green Haven to Northeast Harbor. It looked to be a forty-five-minute drive with light morning traffic. And I figured I could easily find 10 Peabody Neck when I got there. I was behind the wheel of the Duster at 6:00 a.m. as planned, leaving me an hour to grab coffee and breakfast at the café.

"Good morning, Audrey," I called as I closed the door of the café behind me.

"Good afternoon," the smart aleck called back from the far side of the counter where she wrapped silverware in white paper napkins and stacked them in preparation for the breakfast rush. "Do you think the criminals sleep in, too? I sure hope so, because otherwise I'd feel unprotected for the first two hours of my day."

"Yes," I smiled as I perched on a stool, resting an elbow on the paper place mat. "The local outlaws are notoriously late risers. *All* of them," I teased as Audrey poured a mug of steaming hot coffee and set it in front of me. "Do you have any more of those biscuits?" I asked.

"The day olds? Yeah, but they are now *three* days old. I was going to feed them to the seagulls." My look of obvious horror at the thought of feeding the birds with what I might call breakfast stopped the sassy waitress in her tracks. "Jesus, you're cheap. Okay, you want a stale biscuit? You got it. But I draw the line at mold. If they are green, you'll have to break the bank and spring for the special."

Audrey pushed through swinging doors that led to the kitchen and reappeared before the doors stopped swinging. She held a biscuit in her right hand. Grabbing a small plate from a shelf under the counter, she slid the plate onto my place mat, plopped the biscuit on it, and said, "Bon appétit, girlfriend."

"Thank you. Jelly?"

"Oh, of course! And butter, too, right?" she exclaimed as she presented a small ceramic tray filled with individual pats of butter and assorted jams. I disliked this packaging of condiments, and had voiced this to Audrey many times. They are hard to open if you bite your fingernails, which I do. And I like a lot of butter—so the end result is a large pile of empty plastic things that have been chewed open.

"Thank you," I said as I began the tedious process of picking at the corner of foil sealing a pad of butter. I spun the package around, trying each of the four corners before I managed to lift an edge, giving me access to the butter. Fortunately, the café door opened and a group of four came in, followed by a couple of guys who sat at the counter. As much as I liked Audrey, I didn't need her full attention first thing in the morning. Spreading cold, hard butter on a dry biscuit was at first entertaining, and then frustrating. What initially appeared as a large, lumpy bun had been reduced to rubble on my plate. I chopped the pats of butter into smaller pieces and tried to butter individual crumbs as they flaked from the shrinking biscuit.

The cowbells fixed to the inside of the café door chimed a number of times, to which I paid no attention until I heard Audrey greet my buddy Cal. Cal was one of the first people I had met when I moved to Green Haven. And I knew him as someone I could count on. Cal had retired from commercial fishing, and was always willing and available for hire if I needed a boat ride. We had, in our short relationship, been through a few scrapes and come out basically unscathed. I looked up from my plate of scraps just as Cal took the stool beside me. Cal was not a gabber or a gossip. He was quiet and spoke only when necessary. After a friendly hello, Cal shook out a newspaper and began to read the front page, looking up when Audrey came over to take his breakfast order. "What's it going to be today?" Audrey asked as she refilled my coffee and set a fresh cup for Cal.

"What's that?" Cal asked after checking out the mess on my plate.

"Biscuit," I said.

"I'll have the special, over easy," Cal said with a scowl. "Hold the biscuit."

Audrey giggled and dashed off to place the order. "Hey Cal," I said, "How long would it take for you to get to Great Duck Island?"

"Nice day like this, I guess it would be a bit better than an hour," he said.

"I need a ride out tomorrow to check out a clambake."

"You want to go to a clambake? You can do that right here. Fletcher's puts one on every Sunday—open to the public—only twenty bucks a ticket."

"Well, I have to attend the one on Great Duck tomorrow as part of an active investigation," I said. "Are you free to give me a ride out?"

"Yup. Is this on the insurance company or the sheriff's department?" Cal asked in reference to who would be paying him for the water taxi service that I enjoyed.

"Hancock County," I said.

"What do I need to know?" Cal asked, clearly poking me about a couple of adventures I had gotten him into. Boat ride gone bad is an accurate description of the last time I hired Cal for transportation.

"This is tame. I am tracking down two missing young people who I suspect will surface on Great Duck. I believe the young man and woman are aboard a cruise ship whose passengers and crew are scheduled to be at the clambake at noon tomorrow. No criminals—just kids."

"That's what you said last time. But, yes. I will meet you aboard *Sea Pigeon* at ten thirty."

"That works," I said as I resorted to eating my biscuit with a spoon.

Audrey arrived with a plate of eggs and toast for Cal. Glancing at my breakfast, she said, "That is not good for business."

She pulled a slip from her apron pocket and slapped it on

the counter. I turned it over and said, "You're charging me for the biscuit? I thought you were planning to throw it out!"

"I am charging you for the butter! And for the cleanup I'll have to do when you leave. Looks like Hansel and Gretel have been here, bread crumbs up the wazoo."

I glanced around and was embarrassed to admit that I had made quite a mess. I attempted picking crumbs from my lap, which only crumbled them further. So I brushed them into my hand and dumped them onto the plate as Audrey cleared it. "Well, looks like Wally will have plenty to do when he comes in for his shift," I said with an apologetic smile as I noticed the ring of crumbs circling the base of my stool.

Audrey actually stopped moving, something that is quite rare. She placed her free hand on her hip, rolled her eyes, and said, "Gee thanks. Very thoughtful of you to make work for my employee. You're the best." She shifted back into high gear and flittered around the café, chatting and tossing insults while she single-handedly waited on what had become a full house. Much like the Soup Nazi from *Seinfeld*, Audrey had neither time nor patience for indecision. If a customer dawdled over the menu, she literally snatched it from their hands and ordered breakfast for them—usually the special, which always consisted of eggs, home fried potatoes, and toast. Locals knew to bark out their preferences as Audrey approached their table. And knew that there was a strict "no substitutions" rule. If you ordered a hot dog for lunch with "everything," this did not include ketchup, which in Audrey's words was sacrilegious. There was no complaint department, complaint box, or complaint tolerance. If you ordered eggs and were served pancakes, "Shut up and eat them" was good advice. In spite of (or because of) all of this, the Harbor Café was thriving with Audrey at the helm.

I knew to pay my bill and slip away without saying goodbye, as doing so would invite a snide remark about what I was wearing, or sarcasm about the tip amount. In this case, my tab was $1.50. I felt quite generous leaving two dollars on the counter. That tip was over 30 percent! But, I reminded myself, Audrey worked very hard and was nice to my brother. And I didn't have the time to wait for change.

Phew. A clean getaway, I thought as I left Green Haven in the rearview mirror. Traffic was indeed light. But the condition of the road that led to Northeast Harbor from Route 1 was rough, which forced me to drive below the posted speed limit of forty-five miles an hour. The rough road surface coupled with my unfamiliarity with the twists and turns put me in Northeast Harbor at exactly eight o'clock, which was fine. I continued on the main road through what I assumed was the town of Northeast Harbor, which consisted of a narrow main street section lined with small shops that I had come to recognize as quintessential Down East Maine. You might not find a bank or a grocery store in the middle of most towns. But there was an abundance of antique shops, hair salons, and churches, all of which seemed to be in competition for the worst signage award. Who thought it was funny to name a hair salon "Curl Up and Dye"?

The road widened as I followed it out of the congestion of

Main Street. The absence of parking spots left pavement enough for oncoming traffic to pass without fear of losing side mirrors. I drove slowly to read street signs as I passed them, and quickly found Peabody Neck on my right. The drive was carved out of a thick forest of spruce trees of great girth. All of the green branches were up high, leaving space at eye level to admire the view of the ocean on either side. The land grew broader as driveways appeared sporadically, some gated and some not. A simple wooden sign marked a drive on my right as number ten. A slight incline and a sharp curve opened up to a gorgeous house, barn, and view. This couldn't be right, I thought as I pulled around the circular driveway and stopped directly in front of granite steps that led to a magnificent, heavy mahogany door. I knew that hardworking fishermen made a decent living. But this was not at all what I expected. Too nice, too much, I thought as I flipped open my phone to check the address.

I climbed out of the Duster, deciding to knock on the door and ask for directions to the Thomas house. As I made it to the top of the granite steps, the door opened before I knocked. A handsome young boy of about ten years old stood in bare feet holding the door open. "Hi," I said. "Can you tell me where the Thomases live?"

"We live right here. I'm Bradley," he said.

"Well hello." I tried to hide my surprise. "I'm Jane Bunker from the insurance company Marine Safety Consultants in Ellsworth. Is Liza home?"

"Yep. Mom," he yelled over his shoulder. "The insurance lady is here!" He waited for a reply, and when he didn't receive one, he said, "She is expecting you. Follow me." I did as I was told, following Bradley through a beautiful entryway lined with what appeared to be family photos, black and white and done by a professional. He led me into an ultra-modern kitchen where he offered me a chair. White, crisp, and stark, I thought as I checked out everything I could see from where I sat. The kitchen was fitted with top quality appliances, countertops, and hardware. And the lights and window treatments were in a league of their own. I hated myself for assuming the home of a fisherman would be modest.

I sat and waited and listened to Bradley's bare feet as they padded upstairs over my head. I heard gentle voices, but could not make out words. How sad, I thought. I had always disliked this part of my job. I had never flinched when informing family of death from overdose, drug-deal gunfire, or any self-inflicted crime-related killing. In my profession, victims were *usually* involved in illicit activity of which their loved ones *usually* were aware, and therefore not shocked by news of loss of life. But that was in Miami. That was the vice squad with a heavy focus on narcotics. The death of Ron Thomas was different. I wondered why there were no cars in the yard, and no neighbors or friends here to console Liza the day after her husband died. Maybe it was simply too soon, I reasoned, for anyone to respond to the sudden death.

I heard the bare feet come back down the stairs followed by the clicking of heels. The footsteps slapping the hardwood faded in the distance and the clicking of heels amplified until Liza appeared in the archway. An attractive brunette in a navy-

and-white sleeveless shift, Liza did not fit the fisherman's wife stereotype that I had deeply rooted in my head. With the exception of sniffles and eyes red from crying, Liza was put together in a classy style. She moved with grace as she pulled out a chair and sat across the table from me. Her hair was coiffed in a do too elaborate for any stylist north of Boston, I thought. Tight curls and bangs that grazed dark, thick eyebrows framed a flawless complexion that said natural and unpretentious, allowing me to relax within the stiffness of the sparse furnishings. She extended a lily-white and delicate hand for me to take—not to shake in a masculine way, but to take and hold, which I did.

"Liza, I am Jane Bunker, here on behalf of the insurance company. Mr. Dubois sends his deepest sympathies and wants to assure you that he is working on your behalf. In the meantime, is there anything you need that I can help you with?" This was met with deep, silent sobs that seemed to rack Liza's thin frame. "Oh, I am so sorry," I said quietly. "Please, let me get you a glass of water."

I pulled my hand from under hers, anxious to break free. I was extremely uncomfortable in this role. I found a glass and ran the tap in the main sink, allowing the water to run while I gathered my thoughts. Liza took a breath, smoothed the front of her dress, and began talking. "Thank you for coming. I'm a mess. I have to pull myself together for Bradley. He shouldn't see me like this," she said as I handed her the water and sat back down.

"Your son seems to be handling it better than most young boys would," I remarked.

"Oh, he's stoic. That's the Alfond in him." I couldn't quite believe what I had heard. Suddenly everyone I meet is an Alfond, I thought. That was too weird. My silence was broken by Liza, whose emotions were now unleashed in a verbal landslide. "Yes, I am an Alfond," she confessed. "Or at least I was before I married Ron twelve years ago." I wanted badly to ask how she was related to Pete, but my patience paid off in spades when she admitted that her family had totally disowned her when she became engaged to a fisherman. "Except for my brother Pete. We have remained close, to the chagrin of our parents."

"Sounds like a real Romeo and Juliet story," I said in hopes of learning more.

"Yes, with the exception of me still being alive," she said pitifully. "Oh God, I'm so sorry. That is the type of drama that I detest in others. I really appreciate your coming here. I just can't cope with the fact that my husband is gone. Are you married?"

"No."

"Kids?"

"No." I now felt even more inadequate. I certainly couldn't pretend to relate to what Liza was going through. The fact was, I had been sent as damage control. When people suffer loss, the longer it takes to get the claim processed, the bigger the numbers get for what they think they are due. Attorneys get wind of possibilities, and then it's game on. Lawsuits are filed. And that is why premiums are through the roof, I knew.

"What do you need from me?"

"I don't need anything from you," I said in my most reassuring tone. "I am here to let you know that my boss, Mr. Dubois, is making you his top priority. He will process the claim as quickly as possible. The whole thing should be quite seamless. We don't want to add to the stress you must be feeling, among other emotions."

"Thank you. But you should know that I am not the beneficiary of any insurance payout."

That threw me off. "Well, I am not here to talk specifics. I am not privy to any numbers. I am just here to share our condolences and to see if there is anything I can do for you." This was met with silence, so I continued to fill the awkward void. "Typically the spouse is the beneficiary," I said. "Occasionally the money is put in a trust fund for children of the deceased. Is Bradley the only child?"

"He is our only child. But the beneficiary is Ron's ex-wife. It was her biggest demand, and the only way she would grant the divorce. She won't need any consoling, though. No offense, but small-town Mainers can be so greedy."

"No offense taken," I said. "Small towns don't have a monopoly on that." She needn't know that I had lived the vast majority of my life in big-city Miami. That would put us even further apart, I thought.

"If Ron had picked up with someone of lesser means, things would have been easier. But we fell in love. And we had a wonderful marriage. And Bradley is amazing. I know my family. The Alfonds will now welcome me back into the fold. They aren't cruel, just snobs. I remember the first time I saw Ron . . ."

By the time she needed a refill on her water, I had learned a lot. And while I can't say that I was stunned by anything she shared, I must admit that I had great interest in all she divulged in the name of spilling guts to a total stranger. Liza was being so honest and forthcoming with information, I wanted to share what I knew. I wanted to know what her late husband had told her about the demise of *Elizabeth*, which I now assumed was Liza's full name. I wanted to guide Liza away from the family drama and back to facts and events that led to Ron's fatal heart attack. I needed to steer the conversation to an exit off of Memory Lane.

I interjected. "This may seem a huge coincidence. But I want you to know that I met Ron yesterday." Liza looked perplexed. "I happened to be aboard your brother's boat—on an assignment—when Ron put out his Mayday call. There was no time to waste, so I went on the rescue mission with Pete."

"Wow," Liza said. "Now it makes more sense to me that the insurance company sent you to talk with me." I didn't need to tell her that I hadn't divulged this very pertinent information to Mr. Dubois. "Ron has fished around those ledges all of his life! He couldn't believe he plowed into them. He was so embarrassed and ashamed, he could barely look at me when he told me."

I'll bet, I thought. So Liza knew nothing of the ramming of her husband's boat. I had to push a little, I knew, as I said, "There was another boat that responded to his Mayday. Do you know the boat *Insight*?"

"Oh sure, Larry. He probably responded to be sure he wasn't dreaming. This insurance money will be life changing for them," she said as a matter of fact.

"Them?" I asked.

"Larry Vigue is Ron's ex-wife's husband. Confusing, isn't it?"

Not really, I thought to myself as some of the pieces of the puzzle snapped into place. The ramming had not been part of any territorial war waged by fishermen competing for the same fishing grounds. It was about money. If I had understood Liza correctly, Larry Vigue's wife was the beneficiary to both life and property insurances. Judging from their home, I imagined that the life insurance policy alone was substantial. "I'm sure you can contest the divorce decree and receive at least a percentage of the money," I said. "You do have a home to support and a son to raise."

"I'll be fine. But thank you for your concern. I was disowned in name only. My family paid off Ron's boat and gave us this place. They have an education fund for Bradley."

I waited as Liza shed more tears. She was such a dainty crier, I thought. I wondered if this was a skill taught at finishing school. "I'm sure Ron's death is a loss to the whole community. He is from North East Harbor originally?" I asked, thinking I would need to rally support for Ron and raise questions about Larry Vigue if murder charges were brought.

"Oh, yeah. Ron was fifth generation here. Born and raised. Because of his marriage to me, and my money, Ron faced a lot of jealousy from the fishing community. Some of the guys didn't appreciate that he was catching lobsters when he didn't really need to fish for his living. They saw this as taking food from their tables. But he loved being on the water."

"I can see that," I said. I had experienced similar feelings in law enforcement, and imagined it was human nature to be envious and resent someone who shared your work who didn't need the job. I realized that I had been at Liza's place for longer than I had anticipated. I needed to digest everything Liza had told me. I needed to make some phone calls. I wasn't sure how to bow out gracefully and leave the grieving widow alone.

The phone rang. Liza checked the caller ID and said, "It's my mother. Please excuse me." This may have been my cue to leave. But I now wanted to listen to this end of the conversation, so I remained seated. I nodded and smiled, making it clear that I was fine with her taking the call. "Mom? Oh Mom, I can't believe he's gone." There was a short silence while she listened. "Bradley is taking it better than I am." Another brief silence as Liza wiped tears and nodded in agreement to whatever she was being told. "I wanted to call you and Daddy. The insurance lady is here now, but will be leaving. Please come over. I need you."

There was now no mistaking the fact that I should go. When Liza hung up, I handed her my card and insisted that she call me if there was anything she needed from the insurance company. I considered telling her what I knew about the ramming and what I now knew was a case of murder. But Liza was so emotional now that I thought it would be best to speak with both the sheriff and Mr. Dubois, both of whom might not be happy with me for not telling them everything earlier. Liza surprised me with a hug. I was happy to know that her parents were coming to be with her.

I showed myself to the door and found Bradley sitting on the top granite step. He tossed a baseball into a mitt over and over with great force. "You take care, okay?" I said when he looked up as I stepped by him.

"We'll be fine," he said sadly. "Thank you for coming to see my mother." I believed that they would be fine.

As I drove away, I wondered how learning that his father had been a murder victim might affect Bradley. Liza had mentioned that there was embarrassment and shame in running onto ledges in your familiar grounds. Would there be vindication in knowing that Ron had been intentionally rammed? The sinking was no accident. And the heart attack was just a delayed result that was intended at the hands of Larry Vigue, in my opinion. Or might a murder case make things harder on Bradley and Liza? Maybe word of foul play would make it more difficult to find closure on the loss of husband and father, I thought. An investigation and trial surrounding murder allegations would drive them to seek justice rather than find comfort and peace.

The pending date with Pete tomorrow night just got more interesting, I thought. To be fair, I would let him know what I knew right after hello—assuming the party was still on and that he would be there. I imagined the show would go on, given that the Alfonds, according to Liza, had not approved of Ron, and had in fact been estranged from her for twelve years. And the Alfonds hosting the party were Liza's aunt and uncle, according to what I gathered. And if Liza happened to mention my visit to Pete, I imagined he would want to see me to get the scoop on what I might be thinking. Pete was the only surviving witness to the ramming, other than me, of course.

My law-enforcement soul could not allow Larry Vigue to get away with murder, I thought as I made my way back toward Ellsworth where I had a date with a mountain of paperwork. That mountain had just grown with this morning's visit to Ron Thomas's widow and what she had divulged regarding the beneficiary of the insurance. I now had solid motive in the case against Larry Vigue. He was done, I thought. All I needed to do was get my case in order. Any judge would issue an arrest warrant. And I would happily serve that warrant, cuff him, and toss him in jail to await formal charges, arraignment, and trial. This was a slam dunk, I thought.

My cell phone rang, interrupting my thoughts of bringing a murderer to justice. "Hey Deloris," I answered. "Wow, do I have a lot to tell you."

"Save it, girlfriend," she said quickly and firmly. "I just picked up a call to the Coast Guard on the scanner about a lobster boat. *Insight* was reported to be found going around in circles with nobody aboard."

It took a minute for this statement to become visual and sink in. A boat found going in circles with nobody on board was never a good thing. It nearly always meant that someone was in the water, having fallen, slipped, or been pulled overboard accidently. Yesterday, Pete had told me that Larry always fished alone. But I also knew that there might be people looking to even the score following the death of Ron Thomas. And I assumed that the only people who knew about the ramming were Pete Alfond and myself. Was this tit for tat? Or was this another scheme in the territorial lobster war? Maybe someone had stolen *Insight* and set her off in a circle offshore as a warning to Larry Vigue. I mulled over the possibilities. Again, this might be a situation that had me straddling my two jobs—marine insurance and law enforcement.

"Hey, did you get that?" asked Deloris. "Did I lose you?"

"Yeah, I'm still here," I said. "I was just processing. And pulling off the road. Who made the call to the Coast Guard?"

"I don't know. Sounded like a pleasure boater. Very formal with the radio call. I called the Southwest Harbor Coast Guard station. They responded to the radio call. The dispatcher in Southwest told me that they have sent a boat out to investigate."

"Well, if nobody had been aboard to look around, there's a chance that the captain is there on the deck, or down below," I reasoned. "I have heard of cases when a sailor has been hit in the head with the boom and knocked unconscious, and has not necessarily gone overboard. And there are many cases of cardiac arrest at sea. And there have been times when someone has a mechanical problem that causes them to go below or into the engine compartment," I said, realizing that I was thinking out loud. "I know of two cases where solo mariners were pinned or tangled in the engine compartment, boats were found going around in circles with nobody at the helm, and both times they were rescued and their lives saved."

"Is this the marine insurance gal talking? Or the gal who doesn't want to think about escalating violence and the possibility of a certain potential love interest's involvement?" Deloris was perceptive. And I didn't know the answer to that question, so I sat silently mulling.

I had shared everything with Deloris yesterday. Although she was indeed in the loop regarding events, she was certainly exaggerating things on the emotional side. I sat and pondered my next move. I had nothing other than paperwork planned for the rest of the day. I was free to drive to Bar Harbor, if I could justify doing so. Perhaps I should wait for the Coast Guard to get back to Deloris with their findings, I thought. On the other hand, if someone had retaliated for Ron's death at the hands of Larry Vigue, it was always best to get on scene as quickly as possible. Time is *not* on my side, as opposed to what the Rolling Stones had to say about it.

"Are you still there?" asked Deloris.

"Yes. I want to get to Bar Harbor to ask some questions in the event that Larry Vigue is missing. I can get a jump on the background investigation and hopefully find that it is a waste of time when he turns up at home or aboard his boat."

"In light of everything that happened yesterday, I would call this protocol follow-up on the ramming," Deloris said. "Who else knows about that?"

"I haven't told anyone. But I don't know who Pete Alfond may have confided in," I said. "Hey, let's not get ahead of ourselves. This could be purely coincidental."

"Right." Deloris sounded very skeptical. "Call it karma."

"For now, I will." Before I signed off, I asked Deloris to send me anything she could find in the way of home address, phone numbers, and the like for Larry Vigue. In the interest of getting back on the road, I decided to share all new information I had gleaned from my visit to Liza Thomas with my coworker later. "I'll check in with you when I know more. In the meantime, let me know if you hear back from the Coast Guard."

"Aye, aye," was Deloris's way of letting me know that I was being too bossy. Although in reality, I was her superior officer, Deloris was an equal in every way. Her talents with cyber forensics were invaluable to me. Deloris had great intuition. "And," Deloris blurted a little louder now, "I already know about all of the family intertwinings that you must have just learned of. Another example of what we call the family wreath in Down East Maine."

"Yes, let's compare notes later. It will be noon by the time I get to Bar Harbor. I need to get underway." Her title of dispatcher for the Hancock County Sheriff's Department was a complete undersell, I thought as I laid my phone on the seat beside me and got back on the road. I was quite interested in knowing what else Deloris had been able to dig up on the connections between the Alfonds, in-laws, and outlaws. For now I was compelled to get to the bottom of the status of my homicide suspect, Larry Vigue. I hadn't determined yet whether the appropriate charge was attempted murder or gross negligence manslaughter, so I was very hopeful to find Captain Vigue alive and well and able to be charged.

By now, I thought, Mr. Dubois had learned that my visit to Liza Thomas was out of the false assumption that the widow was beneficiary of the insurance, which is normally the case. I wondered if I would be asked to pay a visit to Ron Thomas's ex-wife. Now that would be twisted, I thought. Especially with the knowledge that the ex is Larry Vigue's present wife. Or could she now be his widow? Maybe I would be meeting Mrs. Vigue soon, I thought as I struggled in stop-and-go traffic that plagued the route to Bar Harbor. I worked to stop the blur of possible scenarios from whizzing in my head as I slowly picked my way to the waterfront.

Luck was with me as I whipped the Duster into a parking spot just vacated. A dense layer of fog smothered the view of the outer islands. But the inner harbor was crystal clear. I hustled through the small park and toward the docks where I recognized *Ragged But Right*. Two uniformed officers stood on the float adjacent to Pete's boat and spoke to him over the rail as he stood at the helm. Pete was dressed in the typical orange bib overalls and rubber boots worn by most commercial fishermen. Pete looked relieved to see me as I walked down the ramp made steep by low tide. "Here's the deputy sheriff now," he said and motioned to me. The men, who I could now see were members of the Maine Marine Patrol, turned and nodded solemn hellos. Pete introduced us and said, "I imagine you heard the news of Ron's death and the abandoned boat, right?"

"Yes, I think I am up to speed. I came down to follow up on *Insight* and her captain. They are both part of an active investigation," I said. "Any sign of him yet?" I asked. "And where is the boat? I'll need to get aboard before anything is disturbed."

"The boat has been towed to the Coast Guard station," Pete replied. "They have not located Larry. I was just in from delivering the pilot to a ship moored in the fog, and getting ready to go haul my traps, when these guys asked me for assistance. The Marine Patrol would normally start by hauling Larry's gear. The theory is that he got wound up when setting out a trawl and went overboard with it. That *does* happen," Pete said skeptically. "But I'm not buying it."

"Well," said one of the uniformed officers, "there are two ways to prove that Larry is not on the bottom with his traps. One is

117

to find him alive. The other is to haul his gear and *not* find his body tangled in it. He isn't home. His wife says that he left before daylight to go fishing. His truck is here in the lot, and his boat was found circling unmanned."

"Has anyone started hauling his traps?" I asked.

"They want me to," Pete said. "But I think it will be a terrible waste of time. Larry Vigue has been fishing his entire life—alone—and he is one tough guy. If anything, he's playing games."

"We'd normally haul the gear ourselves," said the officer. "But our patrol boat is on the hard getting repairs and will not launch again until tomorrow. And Pete has a chart plotter that is compatible to receive the info card from the victim's GPS."

Pete opened his hand and displayed the microchip that had apparently been given to him by the officers. I was somewhat familiar with marine electronics from years of being on- and offshore in Biscayne Bay between summer jobs on fishing boats and later in my career. I did a stint at sea in the distant wake of Nixon's "War on Drugs" that was forever being waged, and found myself appreciating my nautical know-how in many investigations.

"I'm here on behalf of Hancock County," I said. "I'm able to go with you to check Mr. Vigue's gear." This was met with appreciation from the Marine Patrol officers. I wasn't sure whether I had volunteered for the sheriff's department or for personal reasons. It didn't matter. The gear needed to be checked for a body in spite of Pete's opinion that this was a wild-goose chase instigated by Larry Vigue. And, I reminded myself, I needed to follow up on what I thought was my responsibility to find a homicide suspect—dead or alive.

"What the hell," Pete said in a conciliatory tone. "It's a nice day for a boat ride."

The Marine Patrol officers thanked us as I climbed over the rail and onto the deck of *Ragged But Right*. One of the officers handed Pete and me each a business card and instructed us to call with updates of any kind. Pete started untying the boat, and before I could coil and stow the stern line, we were off the float and headed toward the fringe of the heavy blanket of fog.

As we crept along through the no-wake zone that encompassed the inner harbor and mooring field, Pete fiddled with the microchip, flipping it between his thumb and index finger. I couldn't help but notice that the boat's electronics had not yet been fired up. The dash directly in front of the helm was filled with black boxes with glass display fronts. I could tell from the labeling of buttons, knobs, and switches that *Ragged But Right* was equipped with fine marine electronics that included a GPS chart plotter (electronic chart), a radar, a depth sounder, and a VHF radio that was mounted over the captain's chair. "How far to his traps?" I asked, breaking the silence.

"Not far," he replied as he popped open the small drawer-style slot on the side of the black, rectangular piece of electronic equipment that I knew as a chart plotter and slid the SIM card in. As he waited for the information to load, Pete switched his radar from standby to transmit, lighting up the radar's monitor screen with bright green concentric circles in which I knew we were the bull's-eye. The sweep, or radius, went around in a clock-wise rotation like the second hand on a wristwatch—but faster—leaving behind images of boats, landmass, and navigational buoys on the monitor. Now we could "see" through the fog, I thought and relaxed as we approached the wall of murkiness.

As the boat's bow punched a hole in the leading edge of the thick gray vapor, Pete changed the range on the radar with the push of a knob, expanding the captured pings of images out to a full mile. Looking over the bow was senseless. I couldn't see beyond the small wake pushed ahead of us as we ran just over an idle for safety reasons. I watched the radar as land withdrew from the bottom edge of the circular display. In my past life, I had navigated with radar at night. But fog had not been an is-sue in South Florida. Pete was obviously comfortable running in the fog, I thought as he pushed up the throttle a bit.

Pete manipulated the chart plotter while I watched in amaze-ment at the technological advancements made to marine electron-ics in recent years. The chart plotter consisted of a large screen that displayed the navigational chart and our position on it. We appeared as a boat icon, the bow facing in the direction we were traveling. Dotted lines I knew as "bread crumbs" marked the his-tory of the boat's travels. In this case, as the GPS was reading the card from *Insight*, we were looking at our present course and speed on the chart, and seeing where Larry had been. Pete scanned through the menu and found how to show only the recorded information from today's date, including marks Larry had put on the plotter to record where his lobster traps were placed. "This makes it easy," I said.

"Yes, I assume that this was his course line leaving Bar Harbor this morning," he said as he pointed at the dotted line we were now following. "We'll just stay on this line until we find where the boat went in circles. Then we can haul whatever gear he has marked in the vicinity." Pete changed the range on the plotter to include a larger area. He placed a finger on the screen. "Looks like he started hauling at Bay Ledge, and used these symbols for the traps he fished today," he suggested of the string of red triangles that were scattered along the bread crumbs marking his travels. "I apologize for my pessimism," Pete said. "I have known Larry all of my life, and staging his own death is not a stretch. I don't know whether I want to find him or not. And I am thankful to have you aboard."

"As a witness?" I asked, hoping to glean some feeling or emotion from Pete, who I suspected might have a theory on the demise or non-demise of Larry Vigue.

"That, and I didn't know I would be seeing you before party. This is a bonus."

I was flattered. But then I realized that Pete might think I had been fishing for that compliment. So rather than say something stupid, I clammed up and stared at the radar, which showed a number of green blips of light that signified boats within a one-mile radius from us. As the boat icon approached the first red triangle on the chart plotter, Pete said, "Larry's buoys are fluorescent orange."

I stepped around Pete and out of the pilothouse where I could see better without straining my eyes through the windshield that had misted up from the fog. Pete instructed me to sing out when I saw the first orange buoy, which he explained marked a pair of Larry's traps. Just as he pulled the throttle back to an idle, a bright orange buoy appeared off our starboard bow, bobbing slightly. "One o'clock," I said loudly as Pete threw the engine out of gear and joined me at the helm station at the starboard side of the open work deck. "Should we haul it?" I asked.

"There's no point in doing that. The track on the plotter shows that he hauled and reset this pair, and moved southeast to the next one. I'll just follow his track until I see something abnormal," he said. "Then we'll haul. Until then, we can keep our eyes peeled."

I wasn't quite sure what I was looking for. But I looked hard. I scanned and searched 360 degrees as we steamed from red triangle to red triangle, spotting orange buoys before moving on to the next. I wondered if Pete secretly thought a dead body was possibly floating, and was therefore really glad I was here. I put that thought out of my head and kept hunting. The fog was wet and cold, and clung to tendrils of my hair that were now sticking to my temples and forehead. Droplets hung in my eyelashes and cascaded down my cheeks when I blinked.

"This is strange," he said after about an hour. "The track line indicates that Larry steamed offshore here, let's see, for close to seven miles. Looks like he stopped and drifted close to Schoodic Ridges, then steamed back and started hauling traps again."

"Maybe he went offshore to ram someone," I suggested sarcastically as I tried to recall why I knew the name Schoodic Ridges.

"Hey, there was a lot of bad blood between Ron and Larry.

The ramming was a fit of rage, I think. The fishing has been slow this season. That always fuels the fire. Larry must have just lost control of his temper."

Was Pete really defending his sister's husband's ex-wife's husband? I understood that fishing was the livelihood, and that poor times might tend to make one irritable. But did Pete expect me to buy the theory that this could escalate to attempted murder? He was playing it cool, I thought. He may have been in denial. Pete must still believe it would be best to let this all go, and he certainly wasn't letting on that there might be a financial motive involved. I wanted badly to believe that Pete was protecting me from whatever he imagined might happen to a deputy sheriff who might ruffle some feathers. I decided that I should divulge that I knew more than he thought I did about what may have driven the incident. "Yes, I understand the bad blood," I said. "I met your sister this morning." I hoped that sharing this would allow Pete to open up with any information that might be helpful in sorting out what I assumed would be difficult to unravel. Wouldn't Liza Thomas want to press charges if she knew Larry Vigue had been responsible for her husband's death? We were searching for a trace of the man who had caused Pete's brother-in-law to suffer a fatal heart attack!

"Poor Liza. She is so dear. How is she? I should be with her now, and not out here poking around in the fog." I didn't bother answering as I knew Pete had agreed to assist the Marine Patrol, and by doing so was actually assisting me. I needed to learn the status of Larry Vigue. And this seemed like the best possibility, even if just to eliminate it. "Well, here's the last red triangle.

The track is definitely going in circles here," Pete said as he stepped aside, allowing me to see the full screen of the chart plotter. "It looks as if he only hauled and set back one pair of traps after his trip to The Ridges. There is nothing whimsical about Larry. Every move is deliberate and calculated. So I assume he made efforts to throw off anyone who might be looking for him."

I studied the chart plotter and understood what Pete was saying. I saw the red triangles leading to the straight, unmarked track offshore. The dots displaying the offshore steam and return tracks were spaced farther apart, indicating a faster speed of travel, Pete explained. I saw the area labeled Schoodic Ridges. And I saw where the track thickened with dots nearly on top of one another and zigzagged slightly, indicting a slow drift. "Do you know of anyone other than us who would be searching for him?"

"I can't think of anyone who would care. Well, other than his wife."

"Let's go back and start hauling the gear he appears to have handled today before the steam offshore. Then we can compare apples to apples," I suggested.

Pete agreed and pushed the boat into gear and headed to the string of icons on the plotter just west of where Larry took a break from fishing to ride south. Five red triangles bunched up in a tight group represented what Pete defined as a single string of gear—or five pairs of traps, two per buoy; or ten traps total. "We'll haul this whole string. Normally, when a fisherman dies, we would have been asked to bring gear ashore for the widow to sell. But that would be premature."

Pete pulled on a pair of white cotton work gloves and grabbed the gaff from the starboard rail where he now stood, driving the boat with his left hand. The first orange buoy popped out of the fog just off our bow. Pete swung the boat so that the buoy came along the starboard side within reach of the short gaff. He knocked the engine into neutral while he gaffed the line under the buoy and pulled it aboard. He placed the buoy on the wash rail forward of the davit and hydraulic trap hauler, placed the line leading toward the traps sitting on the ocean floor below us between the plates of the hauler, and twisted a handle on the dash. The plates of the hauler, mounted vertically on the forward bulkhead and at waist level, turned counterclockwise, pinching the line between them and pulling it in aboard where it coiled neatly on the deck at Pete's feet.

Pete and I stared into the water where the rope exited, looking and not expecting anything other than lobster traps. As the first sign of color appeared beneath the surface, I stiffened and took a deep breath. Pete slowed the hauler until a yellow trap broke the surface. I almost said "Phew." Pete grabbed the trap with his right hand, pulled it onto the wash rail, and started the hauler turning again. More color below instantly became the second trap on this line. Pete broke the trap over the rail and landed it just ahead of the first one. "Both traps have fresh bait in them," he said. I could see that. "Freshly salted herring. It's what we all use this time of year. The bags are full—no sign of anything. This pair was hauled earlier today, as we know."

"Let's check the next pair," I said. With this, Pete swung the boat around in a hard starboard circle, pushed the trap closest to him back overboard, and allowed the line connecting the two traps to become taut, which automatically dragged the second trap over where it splashed and quickly disappeared. The coil of line on the deck straightened out and followed the traps into the water until the buoy flew off the rail and smacked the surface.

I watched the buoy fade into fog in our wake, and turned toward the bow to see the next buoy grow from faint to bright as we closed in on it. Pete stabbed with the gaff, slid the line between the plates, twisted the valve control, and watched with nervous anticipation. Two traps were boarded and set back into the water. We silently went through the motions for the remaining three pairs of lobster traps that produced nothing more than a handful of small lobsters and a mixed variety of crabs. All ten traps in this string had been hauled and freshly baited, just as Pete had expected from the evidence on the chart plotter. "This would be more fun if we waited a few days," Pete said as he steered *Ragged But Right* toward the solitary red triangle remaining in this area. "Then we might be catching a few bugs! What a waste of time. I should be hauling my own gear, not this idiot's."

"Well, I appreciate your help here. It is necessary to eliminate the possibility that Larry met with an accidental death while fishing. So, let's keep going," I said. The fog was starting to burn off a bit; dense, dark patches eased to light, misty clouds that shifted across the water's surface. The sun dissolved a hole that grew in circumference until blue sky hung like a distant awning overhead.

"How did you come to meet my sister?" Pete asked as he neared the orange buoy.

"My other job is with Marine Safety Consultants with whom Ron carried insurance for *Elizabeth*," I answered, consciously avoiding the topic of the life insurance policy. "When my boss learned of Ron's death, he sent me to visit Liza to offer support and instill confidence that we are on her side and will work as efficiently as possible on her behalf. And when I left your sister's place I heard from the sheriff's dispatcher that *Insight* had been found circling with nobody aboard. So I switched into my deputy sheriff's hat, and here we are."

This explanation seemed to satisfy Pete. It was truthful in itself, even if it left out a few details. "How is Bradley?" Pete asked as he grabbed the gaff and plunged the hook toward the line that dangled beneath the buoy.

"He is better than I would have expected in light of the fact that he lost his father. Maybe he's in shock," I offered. "Liza is distraught, of course. They'll both be fine," I said, hoping Pete would share an opinion. He did not.

We stood staring at the hole the line pierced in the flat surface of the water. A yellow blur became a trap that scraped the wash rail as Pete slid it to make room for the second trap that we now anticipated would break the surface. Suddenly Pete stopped the hauler. I peered down deep as far as the sunlight allowed. A dark, amorphous shadow hung just at the edge of my vision. I placed my hands on the wash rail and leaned over the gunwale to get closer in hopes of distinguishing what lay below. I turned to look at Pete. His face was ashen and he had broken out in a sweat. "Can you haul it in a little more? I can't quite make it out." I said.

Pete's left hand grasped the valve handle, cracked it open slightly, which turned the plates ever so slowly and gently. The shadow took shape as it neared the surface. "Is that him?" I asked.

"Yup."

SEVEN

Pete gulped his lungs full of salt air and swallowed audibly. He seemed to be trying to compose himself, which was understandable. Most people do not have experience with corpses. And Pete had made it abundantly clear that he did not believe that Larry would be found tangled in his own gear. The limp, dead body, tethered to the boat by trapline, swayed the slightest bit in the tide, making the scene even more eerie. "Let's get him aboard," I said, taking command of a situation that was most definitely within my comfort zone.

Pete shook off what I assumed was a sick feeling. His complexion regained its deep tan as quickly as it had drained to paste. "Okay," he said. "I'll haul him up to the surface hydraulically. Then we'll have to manhandle him over the rail." This was a statement to himself, I knew, so I did not respond in any way other than to position myself with my thighs pressed against the gunwale perpendicular to the body that drooped lifelessly and bobbed facedown below. Pete twisted the hydraulic valve to spin the plates of the hauler slowly. One booted foot rose to the surface, trapline tightly wound around the ankle.

Pete reached down with his gaff and snagged the back of Larry's T-shirt, bringing his upper body to the top of the water. He passed the end of the gaff to me to hold, which I did. Pete then bent over at the waist, laying with his belly on the wash rail, and grabbed Larry under his left armpit. "Okay, I've got him. Drop the gaff and grab his other arm," he barked, taking charge. I did as he instructed. "Now on three. One, two, three . . ." We pulled together with a unified grunt. The corpse landed on the deck at our feet with a thud that I was certain would reverberate in Pete's head for some time.

Pete sat on the rail and stared at the body while I snapped pictures with my cell phone. Medium height and build, I thought as I started at the top and worked my way down. Larry's head was pure white and hairless from the temples up; his hat, now missing, was apparently a permanent fixture that covered total baldness. From the hat-line down, Larry was a hairy guy. A bushy salt-and-pepper horseshoe fringed his head, and a gray, wild beard joined wiry chest hair that escaped the neck of Larry's T-shirt like the frayed root system of weeds from under a rock. His exposed arms and hands appeared to be unharmed. Thick callouses common on working hands sheathed both palms and had turned to white prunes from water saturation. Black dungarees and black leather belt, black boots . . . "I wonder why Larry wasn't wearing bib overalls like yours," I said. "Don't most fishermen live in those?"

"Yeah. Some don't, though. Especially if it's really hot out," Pete answered. "I never saw him without a hat. Never knew he was a cue ball. I guess you can't be too careful," he added. "If Larry Vigue got wrapped up and pulled overboard, it could happen to any of us. That's what happens when guys get too comfortable. They get careless."

I nodded, understanding that carelessness was often a fatal mistake in my business as well. I concentrated on Larry's right boot. The line was so tight around his boot's ankle that the boot had been pinched to half of the diameter of the left. The trapline had been cinched to form a perfect clove hitch; one end of the line led to the trap that was still on the rail. The bitter end of the line that normally would have been tied to the second trap in this pair appeared to have been severed. I noted that Larry wore no sheath in which a knife may have been kept. "I wonder what happened to the other trap." I held up the bitter end of the line that trailed after the hitch around Larry's ankle.

"Looks like it was cut. Or it may have gone into the propeller of his boat while he was setting out," Pete offered. "But *that* trap"—Pete motioned to the single trap on the rail—"hasn't been baited. So this had to have happened while he was hauling the traps. Maybe someone waked him so hard that the traps slid overboard before he had baited them, and got wound up in his prop. Then he stepped into the coil, got caught, and pulled over."

I knew that Pete's theory of "waking" meant that someone had driven their boat by Larry at full throttle and close proximity so as to throw a huge wake toward him, aimed to roll his boat uncomfortably. Pete was either trying to be helpful or just making nervous chatter. I appreciated the observations and discernment from him as a commercial lobster fisherman. His knowledge of the fishery and of Larry Vigue would be extremely helpful, I thought.

He continued. "I realize that *waking* someone is pretty tame compared to *ramming*. But it's fairly common practice around here."

"Let's get him ashore," I said. "I'll call the sheriff and request that he send the county coroner. You call the Marine Patrol and advise them that the body has been found and was indeed fouled in his own gear as suspected."

Pete quickly got the boat headed toward land. He called the Marine Patrol as I called the sheriff. "We'll be at the commercial dock in Bar Harbor in about forty-five minutes," I said, repeating what I'd heard Pete relay as our ETA.

We steamed in silence until we entered the inner harbor and Pete pulled the throttle back to an idle. Small rivulets of salt water trickled from the corpse to the scuppers in the stern of the boat. Larry's T-shirt and jeans had dried in blotches. The sun was still high in the sky at nearly 4:00 p.m. This day had certainly been a whirlwind, I thought as I grabbed the stern line. "I'll want to get aboard *Insight*," I said. "Where is the Coast Guard base?"

"Southwest Harbor," Pete said. "It's faster to go by boat than by car this time of year. I'd offer to take you, but I'll need to get over to my sister's when we finish here. And by the looks of the crowd that has gathered, that might be a while."

I placed my right hand in a salute to shield the sun from my eyes and observed a rather large and growing mass of people on the dock above the commercial floats. "Looks like a lot of people want to see Larry Vigue dead," I said, knowing that this could be taken in different ways, and hoping for a telling response. Pete didn't take the bait.

Pete swung the wheel hard to port and reversed the engine, kicking the stern toward the float. *Ragged But Right* lightly caressed the chafe gear that protected the edge of the floats and came to a complete stop. I handed the stern line to a man in a fireman's uniform while Pete wrapped the bowline around a cleat. The only men on the float were in uniform—fire, police, and EMTs. Civilians were here purely out of curiosity, it appeared, and were politely standing off above where they could see and not be in the way. Getting a peek at a dead body was something that would fill cocktail conversations tonight, I thought. A lot of people are intrigued with death and corpses as long as they keep them at arm's length. I wondered how many onlookers were visiting tourists, and how many were locals. Landing a dead body would surely not be acceptable to the local chamber of commerce, I thought. If I had been asked to postpone all drug busts in the name of bolstering tourism, this would be frowned on for the same reason. Accidental death by drowning is a risk inherent in Larry Vigue's chosen occupation. I had some doubts about the accidental part, but I'd keep those to myself for now.

A man in a suit and tie scrambled down the ramp. As he approached, I wondered who he was, and assumed possibly the coroner. When he addressed the small group on the float, I understood that he was indeed *not* the coroner. "Really? You had to bring him *here*?"

"Sorry, Joe," Pete said. "But where else would I land? I live *here*. I fish out of *here*. I keep my boat *here*. My truck is *here*. And I want this body *out* of here so *I* can get out of here." The man quickly apologized and offered his condolences to Pete for the loss of his brother-in-law, Ron Thomas. "This is Hancock County's deputy sheriff, Jane Bunker," Pete introduced me.

Joe introduced himself as Bar Harbor's city manager, which explained his concerns surrounding unloading a corpse in the heart of the town's tourist district. "Welcome to Bar Harbor, Ms. Bunker," he said. "I do hope you've had occasion to visit our paradise while not on duty!"

"Well, actually I have not," I answered honestly. "I was here yesterday looking for a young woman who has been reported missing. And this morning I was in Northeast Harbor on other business when I got the call about the boat circling. And now I should get to the Coast Guard station in Southwest Harbor and get aboard the victim's boat to close the loop on this," I said. Joe probably did not want my report, considering it was all bad and had all transpired in or around locations within his jurisdiction. He politely excused himself.

Pete pulled gently at my sleeve and motioned toward the wheelhouse, suggesting that we have a little privacy. I happily followed. "So far our time together has been . . . well, strange," he said. "But I am really looking forward to seeing you tomorrow night. We're still on, right?"

"Umm, sure," I stammered slightly. I had been wondering

whether the Alfond family would go through with the party. My hesitation was not that my initial feelings about Pete had changed. I was deeply interested. Maybe some weird fate had thrown us together, I thought.

"You probably think it terrible that my aunt and uncle would not cancel the Solstice Soiree." Pete must have sensed what I was thinking. "But the family never approved of Ron. He wasn't what the older generation had in mind for Liza. Even Ron's death will not be acknowledged," he said just above a whisper. "The ultimate snubbing."

Pete had mistakenly assumed that I came from a family that would shut down to mourn a similar situation, I thought. He couldn't be further from the truth. I didn't even know my blood relations, forget about various in-laws. I resisted the temptation to ask Pete about his feelings.

As usual, I had no idea how to appropriately respond. So I just said, "Take care, and I'll see you tomorrow." Inwardly excited about the rendezvous plan, I climbed off the boat and onto the float just as the EMTs zipped up the body bag and muscled it onto a stretcher.

That I could mention a date and a body bag in the same sentence is telling in regard to my relationship history . . .

Back in the Duster, I removed my phone from my pocket and laid it on the seat beside me. Just as I did, a text message dinged. It was from Anika, the missing Romanian's roomie. *Are you still looking for Bianca? Worried here.*

I texted back: *Yes. Am following up on a lead. Believe she is fine. Let me know if you hear from her.*

Will do. Thank you very much.

I appreciated text messages for their pointedness, I thought as I poked my way out of Bar Harbor in stop-and-go traffic. Deadpan texts were much easier for me to deal with on the job. Texts did not relay a sense of urgency, pain, sorrow, or anxiety. They were simply detached in a way that live phone calls were not. I got the reminder. I answered. And I had a record of it—yet another plus on the side of electronic, written communication.

Signs indicating the way to Southwest Harbor were abundant and conveniently placed before every necessary turn. Once in Southwest, the Coast Guard station was equally well-marked. My stomach growled as I passed Beal's Lobster Pier. I hadn't eaten since breakfast, I realized as I considered stopping for a quick bite. The line of people waiting for tables at Beal's was a testament to the quality of food served there, but also acted as a deterrent as I intended to be aboard *Insight* while I had daylight on my side. I sighed and drove on by the restaurant. I would wait and eat dinner with the Vickersons and Wally, I thought. That would save me the cost of a lobster roll.

A guard shack with an electric gate formed a conspicuous entrance to the Coast Guard station. I stopped and was greeted by the officer on duty. "I'm looking for *Insight*," I said.

The young Coastie smiled and replied, "I have wisdom beyond my years. Insight on what?"

"Oh yeah," I said with a grin. "The boat that was towed here. A lobster boat named *Insight*?" I opened my wallet and flashed my deputy badge.

"Slip number four, ma'am. You can park in one of the visitor spots straight ahead. And I'll call for an escort to the vessel. Please wait at your vehicle." Interesting, I thought, how the badge brought out formality in most instances.

I did as instructed, and was greeted by the escort as soon as I stood beside my car. Polite and proper, the young coast guardsman serving as my escort had little to say, which suited me fine. He guided me quietly to slip number four where *Insight* was tied with bow, stern, and two spring lines. I noted the scrape of green paint on the stem and starboard bow: remnants of foul play that I knew had led to the death of Ron Thomas. And perhaps the same was true of Larry Vigue's demise. At least, I thought as I excused the young officer, Larry's death could be considered self-inflicted. Was his fatal misstep an act of karma? My belief in unexplained quid pro quo for bad deeds had developed in my maturity. A young Jane Bunker would have said "bullshit" to any theory that included kismet. And now, as I was indeed an eyewitness to the ramming that I had considered attempted murder, I liked to think of Larry's subsequent death as providential payback.

I snapped pictures of the green paint that I knew came from contact with Ron's boat. The fact that *Elizabeth* sat on the bottom of the ocean meant that there would never be a sample available to match. I wondered if it even mattered now. The only two people who knew *most* of the true story were me and Pete. And it was clear that Pete preferred tight lips regarding sinking ships. I hadn't been assigned the duty of investigating Larry's death. But I knew that my investigative duties required by Marine Safety Consultants would include exactly what I was doing now, which was climbing aboard *Insight* for a quick inspection and a few pictures.

Insight was a crudely built, plainly finished utilitarian vessel. She was, I noted when I read the hull ID number on her transom, a forty-one footer built in 2007. She was configured nearly identically to *Ragged But Right*, with a split wheelhouse allowing two helm stations, one inside the house and one outside. She had a short house and a long cockpit; a configuration allowing more work space on deck. She had the typical hydraulic trap hauler, davit, and block. She had a welded plastic holding tank for lobster, fitted with twelve-volt pumps to circulate raw water to keep the lobsters alive. There was nothing out of the ordinary.

My first overall impression was that *Insight* was much cleaner than I had anticipated. No mud on the wash rail. No seaweed, bait, or crabs on the deck. There were no lobsters aboard. And there was very little bait aboard. If Larry had gone overboard with his traps, I thought the scene would have been different. After hauling a few traps with Pete, I knew that Larry's gear was fairly fouled up with growth and slime that spattered all over the place. I doubted the Coast Guard would have touched anything. And they certainly would not have cleaned the boat. Would they have tossed bait overboard? No way, I thought as I continued to snap pictures and grew more skeptical.

The electronics were similar to Pete's setup. There was a chart plotter, VHF radio, radar, and depth sounder. I knew the Marine Patrol had grabbed the SIM card from the GPS, as they had given it to Pete to find Larry's gear. There was an additional black box mounted on the port dash that I was not familiar with. The box was labeled "Furuno—FA-150." My cell phone indicated full service. I googled the machine's label out of curiosity and learned that it was an AIS, or automatic identification system, used on boats and ships. My reading was interrupted by a man's voice from the top of the wharf. "Hello there!"

I stepped onto the deck and said hi to the young coast guardsman who had escorted me to the boat.

"My team leader sent me back to assist you. Do you need any help?"

I wondered if the kid had been reprimanded for not staying with me. I certainly didn't need or want him here while I poked around. "No thank you. I'm all set here. Just taking a few pictures—protocol for completing accidental death reports." I hoped he hadn't been given an order to babysit me.

"Well, dinner is at five. And it's almost five. Do you need an escort back to your vehicle? If you're going to be a while, I can check back after dinner."

"I'll be gone by then," I said, relieved to know that he was hungry and didn't care what I was doing or why. "But thank you for the offer." He left quickly, as if he thought I might change my mind. My stomach growled, reminding me again that I was starving. Just a few more minutes, I thought, and I'll be out of here. I continued my inspection of the boat.

An aluminum beverage can wrapped in a bright red insulated cozy sat on the dash just ahead of the helm. The cozy, purposed to keep drinks cold, was also a good way to keep them upright in rough seas, I thought as I snapped a picture. I spun the cozy around and read the advertisement: *"Princess of the Seas*—Bimini." How interesting, I thought, that Larry Vigue would have a souvenir from the very cruise ship that was featured in my active investigation of missing girls and boys. I fought the urge to tie the two cases together, as I knew that in small-town Maine everyone and everything were connected or separated by far fewer than the six degrees.

There was no beer cooler aboard. No lunch pail. The usual orange rubber bib overalls that old timers call "oil skins" hung on a hook. A framed picture of a very much alive Larry Vigue and an attractive woman who I assumed must be his wife (formerly Mrs. Ron Thomas) was secured between two side windows. I searched through all cubbyholes and drawers and found nothing unexpected. Bands for lobster claws, various plastic replacement parts for traps, a tool used to splice line that I knew as a fid, cotton work gloves, a tube of grease and a tube of sunblock, spare hoses, gaskets, fittings, duct tape, et cetera. I found a ship's log that was flipped open to today's date. Blue ink scribbling indicated that Larry had fueled the boat this morning, noting that he had pumped aboard eighty-six gallons of diesel and recorded 9,550 total engine hours. There were two sets of numbers that I didn't recognize scrunched up in the upper-right-hand corner of the page—42030 and 13275. I snapped a picture of the page and flipped through the entire log, finding numbers of traps hauled and pounds sold. Prices were recorded every day that Larry had sold lobsters. I took special note of yesterday's page, hoping to see something different to prove that the ramming and sinking of *Elizabeth* was premeditated. I don't know what I expected to find. But there was evidence of nothing.

I left the wheelhouse and walked around the perimeter of the cockpit or work deck. There were knives secured under the transom at both corners. I realized that these had been placed there for emergency use. There were also knives secured at the davit and under the wash rail at the hauling station. All knife blades were held by strips of leather that had been screwed into bulwarks at strategic places, places where a man could easily grab one and cut himself free if tangled in gear and being pulled overboard at the stern or starboard rail. It appeared that Larry could not reach a knife or didn't have time, as all knives were in their holders. There were no empty strips of leather. I slid one knife out and thumbed the edge of the blade. It was razor sharp. So it appeared that Larry had taken the usual precautions to save himself should he ever get wound up. I reasoned that these were things that only men who choose to fish alone do.

The only remaining thing I could think of to do was to get a look at the propeller. The bitter end of the line that was hitched around Larry's ankle appeared to have been severed by a propeller, as it was frayed in a jagged way, like it had been chewed. A knife would have made a cleaner cut, I thought. So if the line had been fouled in Larry's prop, there should be line remaining there now and wrapped around the shaft and possibly the rudder as well. There may even be a lobster trap hanging from the boat's running gear, I thought. The second trap of the pair was missing. I had no way of getting a diver right now. And I had no idea when or if the boat would be hauled out of the water for inspection. That, I thought, would depend on the widow's wishes and intentions for the boat. I wanted badly to be thorough and avoid another trip to Southwest Harbor if possible.

Call me MacGyver. I found a used Ziploc bag in the trash can in the wheelhouse. I grabbed the duct tape from a drawer. I placed my phone in the video mode, sealed it in the bag, and taped it to the end of a gaff pole. I plunged the rig under the surface of the water at the stern of the boat, and moved it back and forth, slowly rotating the pole in hopes of capturing what I needed to see. I prayed that the bag wouldn't leak, as I had purchased the most inexpensive phone on the market, which was not waterproof, or even moisture resistant. After thirty seconds, I retrieved my underwater camera and was happy to see that it was dry.

I had done a good job of filming. The prop, shaft, and rudder were all clean. No pot warp. No trap. So, I reasoned, it was unlikely that Larry's gear had been caught in his own propeller. I was mildly satisfied to at least eliminate that as a possibility. But, I knew, there were many other scenarios that could explain the evidence at hand. I felt good about having been thorough, even though I didn't know whether I was on the insurance company's or Hancock County's clock. I had covered the bases, and realized that my jobs had a lot of overlap.

I put everything back as I had found it, and climbed out of the cockpit and onto the wharf. Walking briskly in the direction of the visitor parking, I inhaled a breath of bait-filled air. It wasn't unpleasant. But it was distinct and salty. Beal's Lobster

Dock hummed with activity next door to the Coast Guard base. I stopped and watched as working boats unloaded their catch into plastic totes that were slid onto a set of scales and then splashed into wet storage. Most boats had two people on board, and a couple of larger vessels had three. It was a bit unusual for serious fishermen to go solo, but not unheard of, as Pete had explained. Totes of freshly salted herring were hefted onto decks and stowed for the next day's fishing. Boats zipped quickly from the dock to moorings where they replaced dinghies and skiffs that acted as placeholders while boats were offshore. It was almost time for this working section of the harbor to go to bed, I thought as the day dimmed slightly.

As I started back toward the Duster, suddenly a siren blared. It was so loud, I covered my ears with my hands and scrunched my neck down into my shoulders. The siren silenced and a whistle sounded seven short blasts followed by one prolonged blast. I recognized this sequence as a general alarm meant to alert crew of an emergency on board ship. I wondered briefly whether this was a practice drill for the coast guardsmen. A door was flung open at the front of the building closest to me. The sign pointing that way indicated that it was the mess hall.

I counted eight Coasties as they sprinted from the open door in single file fashion. I followed them with my eyes as they literally jumped into two hard-bottom inflatable boats, four men in each boat. Helmets and life vests were donned. Outboard motors purred, lines were cast, and rooster tails of water were thrown from behind the boats as they quickly disappeared to seaward. Small wakes dissipated into shoreline on either side of Southwest Harbor and everything was still. The man I knew as my escort hustled down to the float from which the boats had disembarked and coiled all dock lines neatly from where they had been tossed haphazardly.

As he made his way back toward the mess hall, I intercepted him. "Thanks again for your help," I said. "What's the commotion? Drills?"

"No ma'am," he answered. "We received a call of a person in the water. Search and rescue teams have been deployed in hopes of reaching the scene before dark."

"Wow. Well, I am impressed with the speed of getting underway. There's a lot more excitement here than I expected. Never a dull moment, right?" I said, hoping to get details of the emergency, mostly out of curiosity.

"Yes, we are kept busy in the summer, for sure. Too many pleasure boaters who have no training or experience. We play a lot of cards in the winter months."

"Was this call a pan-pan, or a Mayday?" I asked, not testing the young man's knowledge of the difference, but rather in hopes of gaining credibility with him. (PAN—Possible Assistance Needed. And Mayday—signifying grave and imminent danger.)

"Our radio operator heard the call as a pan-pan first. It was a man overboard in which the vessel putting out the call was maneuvering to recover the victim. But I guess the captain must have decided he needed help because—well, you heard the alarms. Our search and rescue squads are responding to the Mayday." I maintained eye contact, relaying that he held my interest. I nodded, hoping for more information. Even though I knew this was none of my business, any time there is an emergency of any nature, I am compelled to assist. In this case, I was trying to figure out if I was needed in any way, but trying not to interfere with the Coast Guard. "We have responded to eight calls already this week. And it's only Thursday! The weekend warriors will keep us hopping starting tomorrow night," he exclaimed. "All eight calls were responded to successfully, thankfully. Five boats needing a tow, two taking on water, and one fire."

"You guys are good," I complimented him with total honesty and admiration that I had gained through many years of experience working hand-in-hand with the USCG stations in Fort Lauderdale, Key West, and the Air Station base in Opa Locka, Florida. "I'm sure whoever is treading water right now will appreciate the quick and efficient response."

"Yes, ma'am, probably teenagers hacking around and got in trouble. Or maybe an elderly sailboater. It's tough for some people to get back aboard a boat after they go over. Especially if there's no ladder." The young Coastie conveyed a fairly light attitude about the gravity of this situation. And he was probably right. Most often with a Mayday call to the Coast Guard, it involves novices to boating. They tend to overreact, which was sure better than the alternative, I thought. "Well, I guess I can go finish my dinner. Maybe I can scoff an extra dessert now that the guys are out on a mission."

Food! Wow, was I hungry. I was not needed here, I knew. "Okay, thanks again. I'll be leaving now," I said as I gave him a half wave and started toward the parking lot. Many people

145

might question my thoughts and growing focus on dinner. In light of today's activities revisited from behind the Duster's steering wheel, perhaps my stomach should not have entered the picture. But it did. Yes, I had visited a widow who had lost the love of her life to what she believed was cardiac arrest facilitated by his boat sinking. Yes, I was one of only two witnesses to the malicious attempted murder that I believed brought on the death of her husband, Ron Thomas. Yes, I had helped pull a corpse from the ocean and transport it ashore. Yes, the corpse was my homicide suspect. Yes, my suspect was the husband of the ramming victim's ex-wife. Yes, my single and long awaited romantic interest was involved and very much connected to my investigations, both insurance- and deputy-wise. The fact that my tally of today's activities did not include lunch was now the most prominent item on the list. Gnawing doesn't even come close to this degree of hunger, I thought as I pulled into the Vickersons' yard. This hunger was tearing big bites, like a shark.

I would be remiss, I thought as I climbed the stairs to my apartment, to not mentally note my schedule, which included following up on missing people. Bianca Chiriac and Franklin Avery had been pushed to a back burner. I defended my conscience by reminding myself that their whereabouts were actually known. They were aboard *The Princess of the Seas.* They were both adults, and seemingly not wanting to be found. I had hired Cal to take me to the clambake tomorrow, where they should be making a last memory of a three-day tryst that would end on Saturday morning when Franklin would disembark from his internship with the cruise liner company and from his secret fling. I had a lot of things to sort out, I thought as I dropped my jacket and bag into a chair and bolted back down over the stairs.

"Hello," I called out as I entered the Vickersons' home. "What's for dinner? I'm starving."

"Janey! Come right in!" Mrs. V was always very enthusiastic with her welcome greeting, which made me feel good about becoming such a fixture at her dinner table. "Henry is pouring our second round, so you have some catching up to do."

"The usual?" Mr. V asked as I plunked myself down into "my" chair in the living room.

"Yes, please." I almost laughed with the realization that I had become so predictable. At the café it was the least expensive item, and here it was Scotch on the rocks. "Where's Wally?"

"Walter has a date this evening—dinner and a show," Mr. V said in a casual manner in which one might think that this was not actually noteworthy. I knew he was looking for an audience response. And I gave him what he was looking for.

"A date? With whom?"

"I don't think he said," replied Mr. V, knowing this would really get my hackles up. "Why? Are you nervous?" He was teasing me, and I knew it. But I just *had* to know where my brother was and with whom.

"Call me curious."

"Curiosity killed the cat." He smiled. It was clear that Mr. V was really enjoying this.

"And you're smiling like a Cheshire cat," I replied, knowing that I was falling into my landlord's word game that used to drive me nuts.

"That's because you're like a cat on a hot tin roof!"

I paused, unable to snap back with anything appropriate. Mrs. V entered with a plate of smoked mussels and rescued my end of the game with, "Walter is the cat's pajamas, isn't he?" Then she winked at me and added, "There's more than one way to skin a cat. I score two for that," she said proudly.

"Well, I'm not ready to let the cat out of the bag," defended her doting husband. Then he looked at me and asked, "What's the matter? Cat got your tongue?" With that he raised two fingers in the air and mouthed, "Two."

"Look at him," Mrs. V insisted. "He's smiling like the Cheshire cat."

"Copycat! That has already been played, dear. Game over. I win," Mr. V said satisfiedly as he held his drink up in a cheers to himself. "Ooooh, what's the dipping sauce?" he asked of the small bowl nestled among the mussels on the platter that his wife now held for him to sample.

"Whole grain mustard, sour cream, maple syrup, lemon juice, and fresh tarragon," she recited as she passed the platter to me. "How was your day, Jane?"

"Hectic, as usual," I said as I plucked a mussel between my thumb and index finger, dredged it through the dipping sauce, and popped it in my mouth. Mrs. V always waited patiently and expectantly for a review of whatever morsel she had offered. I chewed and savored the delicate smoke flavor that melded so well with the zesty lemon and mustard.

"Too much maple?" she asked.

"Not at all," I said. "Perfectly delicious." I grabbed two more mussels before Mrs. V set the platter on the table between her husband and me. The Scotch and the smoked mussels tamed my growling stomach. I relaxed into the easy chair. "I think it's wonderful that Wally has a social life. And it's totally appropriate that he keeps it private. I certainly would never share relationship and dating details with anyone." Now I was the one smiling with delight, as I knew that my landlords were insanely nosy when it came to my life.

"Foul! That's just unfair," whined Mrs. V. "Just because Henry's a grinch, doesn't mean you should keep things from *me*." She turned and gave her husband a look. "I wouldn't exactly call Walter's evening a date. And dinner and a show is a stretch. Come clean, dear," she advised her husband.

"Oh, okay, spoilsport. Walter is at the church potluck with the Old Maids."

"Marlena and Marilyn have taken a real liking to your brother," said Mrs. V. "As has the entire town. He is indeed the darling of Green Haven." We all could agree on that, I thought as I sipped my drink quietly. We enjoyed a little chitchat until Mrs. V declared it time for dinner and asked us to move our conversation to the table. Although I am not a multitasker, I was able to hold up my end of the dinner conversation with work in the back of my mind.

Dinner was nothing short of spectacular. Tonight's mussel entrée had an Asian flair. The coconut milk base infused with ginger, lemon grass, fresh lime, and a dab of red curry paste was simply delicious. The mainstay ingredient, mussels in their shells sprinkled with chopped scallions, was served over plain white rice. I polished off a healthy portion and excused myself from the table before I yawned. Although Wally hadn't come home, I knew he was in good hands with Marlena and Marilyn. "Thanks for dinner," I said as I stood to leave. "And give Wally a hug good night for me."

"Yes, you get a good night's sleep," Mrs. V advised. "You have a date tomorrow night!"

"Yeah, God knows I need all the beauty sleep I can get," I answered with a wry smile as I closed the door behind me and scrambled through the Lobster Trappe, ducking my head to avoid bumping the gift shop's hanging inventory.

Before diving into bed, I gave my phone the obligatory check, noting that I had missed two calls while dining. I listened to the first message, which was from Anika, the roommate of the missing Romanian girl. "Hi, Deputy Bunker. There is still no word from Bianca. Are you still looking for her? I am really scared. You said to call. Here I am. Please call me back." Rather than call, I chose to text Anika.

Hi Anika. I am following up on a solid lead tomorrow, and will let you know. I am not worried about Bianca. There is evidence that she is fine.

A text came back faster than I could imagine. *Is there anything I can do in the meantime? I can't stand just waiting.*

If you have access to a copy machine, you can put up posters around town. That might be premature, but it never hurts to get the word out. I thought this might indeed be unnecessary. But, I reasoned, it would serve as a lesson to Bianca when she returned to Bar Harbor to find how she caused such worry.

Okay, thank you.

The second message was from the sheriff asking me to please call him ASAP. There was no way I could put him off with a text, I thought. So I called him. "Hi, Jane. Thanks for getting back to me. I got a disturbing update from Earl Smith at the Academy. The cruise line company that owns *Princess of the Seas* is now reporting that Franklin Avery is missing from the ship."

EIGHT

I woke up completely disoriented. I lay on my back and gazed at the ceiling over my bed as it swirled and slowly came into focus. I'm not sure what this says about me psychologically, but if this were a Rorschach test, the knots, rings, and grains in the pine boards looked like knots, rings, and grains to me. No matter how hard I tried, I could not make out a bunny or a clown anywhere. I yawned and stretched and thought that perhaps I hadn't needed that second Scotch last night. Mr. V was notorious for his generous pour.

As I gained clarity, I thought about the conversation with the sheriff that I'd had just before bed. It seemed that the missing persons cases (yes, two of them) were reemerging when I had hoped to focus on the hows and whys of double deaths—Ron Thomas and Larry Vigue—which I found more challenging and mysterious. I shook myself to a higher level of alertness and hopped out of bed and into the shower where I recounted the scant details of last night's conversation with the sheriff.

"That is all I know," the sheriff had insisted when I questioned the reported disappearance of Franklin Avery.

"Who reported him missing?" I asked.

"Someone from the cruise line company office called the Academy hoping he had shown up there," he said. "Earl Smith called me last night hoping that you would reopen the investigation."

"Well, I have made arrangements to attend a clambake tomorrow that is part of *The Princess of the Seas'* itinerary. I had hoped to find both Franklin and Bianca there rather than waiting for the ship to land in Rockland on Saturday morning," I recalled assuring the sheriff last night.

The sheriff had seemed satisfied that I was following up on this vague information. In light of our working theory that had not been discredited, there was no sense of urgency. Everyone still believed that Franklin and Bianca were shacking up: she as a stowaway, and he as an officer-in-training who had been led astray. I imagined that now even Franklin's shipmates had grown weary of the situation. Enough is enough, right?

I checked my cell phone to confirm that the texts that I had sent to Deloris last night had gone through. They had. I had sent her two pictures: one of the AIS unit on *Insight* with a note asking her to research and to let me know the unit's capabilities and typical use aboard commercial fishing vessels, and the other of the series of numbers Larry had recorded in his logbook yesterday with a note asking Deloris to decipher what significance they had to lobster fishing. Deloris had responded with her usual, "Aye aye." So I knew she had received them and was on it. I would catch up with Deloris at the station this morning, I thought as I mentally scheduled my day.

The empty refrigerator placed breakfast at the café first on the list of things to do. I would run to the sheriff's station and organize my long-neglected paperwork, and then meet Cal at 10:30 a.m. as planned for a ride to Great Duck Island where I would check out my very first clambake in the name of business. In the back of my mind was the fact that I still needed to find something to wear to the Alfonds' Summer Solstice Soiree. I had a date tonight—again, in the name of business. The sheriff had insisted that I go on behalf of Hancock County's finest. Otherwise I had not intended to attend, I lied to myself.

I was dressed and out the door in time to witness first light as it crept over the eastern horizon. The air was crisp and warmed slightly as the colors of sunrise glowed and transformed dawn to day. I marveled at my present living situation. What had I done to deserve this? The natural beauty was inspiring. My landlords had become family. I loved the work I was doing. My brother was thriving. All that was missing, I thought as I tore myself away from the truly awesome view over the bay, was a life partner. But, I reminded myself as I drove to the café, I had gained hope recently in the form of Pete Alfond. I sort of hated myself for allowing this thought. And I would never express it out loud. For God's sake, I scolded myself, I barely knew the man.

Nothing like a little romantic intrigue to brighten up one's disposition, I thought as I suppressed the bounce in my step from the Duster to the café. I would put on my game face before entering, as I knew that Audrey would notice and call me out for being "giddy." True to form, Audrey did not disappoint. "Good morning, girlfriend!" she called as I grabbed my usual stool at the counter. "You are absolutely glowing! Must be the rush of excitement about your big night. Did you buy a dress?"

"Nope. How about some scrambled eggs?" I asked, knowing that the out-of-character splurge would distract Audrey from grilling me on my wardrobe. I knew that I would face the same questions and disgust at my answers from Deloris this morning, so was somewhat braced and prepared to be mildly insulted.

"Oh, then you must be borrowing something from your landlord, right? Vintage is in style. She must still have her prom dress from 1910. And I know that the smell of mothballs drives men crazy." I almost laughed, but didn't want to encourage more of this. "You are friggin' kidding me. You have a much-needed date tonight and you are thinking about eggs? Get real!"

"I don't *need* a date," I defended.

"Oh, believe me. You do. Ask anyone."

I lifted both shoulders and raised my hands with palms up in my most exaggerated shrug and looked around the café. "If you had any customers this morning I would."

"Yes, and if you had a man in your bed, you would not be the first customer *every* morning. Look, Janey." Audrey was now pleading. "You have been in Green Haven for over a year, and you're still playing the happily single role. You need to put yourself out there, and . . ." The lecture that I had heard many times before was suddenly interrupted by the clanging of the cowbells that hung on the door.

"Ah, saved by the bell!" I said and smiled as I turned to see who had done me the favor. It was Clyde Leeman.

"You did say dumbbell, didn't you?" Audrey rolled her eyes and exhaled audibly in what I knew was borderline revulsion for Clyde Leeman, Green Haven's very own village idiot.

I was genuinely happy to see Clyde this morning and knew his presence was an opportunity to get the young, sassy Audrey off my back. When Clyde was in the mix, he took all the heat. I had come to know that whatever hat Clyde was wearing on any particular day dictated who he was. This morning, he would be a cowboy. "Good morning, Clydie," I said as I patted the stool next to me, inviting him to join me at the counter. "Saddle up, amigo." I could, I reasoned, put up with Clyde's nonsense for a few minutes if it meant not discussing my love life.

Audrey, who is always on her game and usually miles ahead of everyone, saw what I was attempting and turned it around, hitting me where it hurt most. "Deputy Bunker is fixin' to buy your breakfast! What'll you have, pardner? Sky's the limit, right, Janey?"

My stomach turned with the thought of shelling out some large sum of cash. Clyde was stunned (and so was I!). When it finally sunk in that he had actually been welcomed by me, and was in fact being treated by me, he tipped his Stetson politely and said, "Much obliged, ma'am."

I was now forced to go along with the gag, and preferred breakfast with cowboy Clyde to being berated by Audrey for my lack of style and total void of life outside of work. In short, I understood that Audrey found me marginally boring. But she did like me, and her intentions were good. We were friends, I reminded myself as Clyde stepped up his charade. "I've got a hankerin' for cackleberries. Fetch me a plate plumb full of 'em, lassie. And grab me a mug of that belly wash."

Audrey plunked a steaming cup of black coffee in front of Clydie and disappeared to the kitchen where I could hear her snickering while placing our orders of the most expensive combo on the menu. "Two times four, over easy. Drag the spuds through the garden. Loaded cakes. Double meat and rye." This was going to cost me a fortune! I felt sweat beading up on my forehead as I tried to remember how much cash was in my wallet.

The only thing more painful than wasting money on breakfast was listening to Clyde. By the time our platters arrived (with a flourish, I might add), I had exhausted every bit of cowboy lingo in my repertoire. However, the same could not be said of my breakfast companion and waitress. By the time Clydie had polished off his mountain of food, I had heard all the high-falutins, lookie yonders, reckons, ifins, and fixins I could stand. "Them was mighty fine vittles," Clyde said, smiling. "I'm full as a tick."

I could not recall a single time that Clyde had not been ordered to leave the café before even ordering breakfast, never mind eating it. Audrey usually had no patience with him, but was clearly delighted to put me through this. Audrey's end of the western jargon had devolved to things like, "You're jawin' me to death," and "Your brain cavity wouldn't make a drinkin' cup for a canary," and my favorite, "You couldn't teach a hen to cluck." The beautiful thing about Clyde Leeman, in my opinion, is that he does not know when he is being insulted. When she couldn't take anymore, she pointed at the door and said, "Vamoose." When Clyde appeared to be forming some argument for staying, she got stern and said, "Get along, little doggie."

Clyde reluctantly stood and placed his Stetson back on his head. As he had been banished from the café many times, he must have realized that he was pushing his luck with Audrey. But he would never go without a parting shot. "You're as ornery as a mama bear with a sore teat."

Understanding that he had now crossed a line, Clyde thanked me for breakfast. He hitched up his pants by his wide leather belt, and sidled toward the door with his legs bowed in his best cowboy walk after advising me, "Keep your powder dry."

Audrey stood with her hands on her hips and did her usual eye roll of disgust. "And *that*, girlfriend, is why you should be taking your date with Pete Alfond very seriously. Clyde is the only bachelor I'm aware of in Green Haven."

"He's harmless," I said, defending Clyde, sort of.

"Harmless? He kills me," Audrey said. "I was actually relieved that he didn't show up in his buccaneer hat today. Customers question all the arrs." I joined Audrey in a much-needed giggle. Then she made the rounds through the now filling-up restaurant. When she passed by me she slid the check onto my place mat with a wink. Although I had really enjoyed the huge breakfast, I was extremely nervous about paying for it. Sure, I could afford it. But it was like a psychosis with me. Audrey had dubbed my apparent underspending disorder, "Pennypinchingitis."

I took a deep breath and flipped the check over. Audrey had charged me only for my usual biscuit and coffee. She had also written, "You are an amazing woman. Have fun tonight!" This gesture was so kind and unexpected, I didn't know how to react. I wanted to thank her. But I was a little embarrassed. Return kindness with kindness, I thought. I swallowed hard and I left Audrey a 25 percent tip. To be truthful, I again didn't have correct change and wanted to get away without further discussion about my romantic future. I literally dashed out the door while Audrey was making coffee with her back to me.

It was almost 7:00 a.m. when I hit the road for Ellsworth. I figured that I could spend approximately two and a half hours catching up on paperwork and anything Deloris had for me before I had to head back to meet Cal for the boat ride out to Great Duck Island. I would call Earl Smith at Dirigo Academy in hopes of getting a few details on the renewed missing status of his cadet, Franklin Avery. It was shaping up to be a glorious day. I was looking forward to a few things; namely, a boat ride with my pal Cal, checking out an authentic Maine clambake, and seeing Pete Alfond this evening. As I drove, I mentally went through my closet looking for something special to wear this evening for my date. By the time I shuffled through the hangers from end to end, I was wishing I had heeded the advice of Audrey and Deloris to buy something. But that seemed so wasteful when I have perfectly good clothes literally hanging around waiting to be worn. Well, I acquiesced, it's too late now to go shopping. I'll make do.

As I entered Hancock County Sheriff's Department, I was greeted by Deloris. She sat at the main desk and peered over her glasses at me. Before she could speak, I said, "Yes, I have a great outfit for tonight."

"Not that I'm questioning your fashion sense, but can you describe it to me?" I took a breath and tried to imagine what I might wear. Before I could come up with anything, Deloris spoke up again. "Just as I suspected. You don't have a clue, do you?"

"The only clues I need are those that might line up with missing people and dead people," I said, impressed with my quick comeback. "What were you able to find?"

"Okay, but don't blame me when you join Marilyn and Marlena as the third old maid." Deloris pushed her glasses higher onto her nose and focused on one of her laptops. "Let's start with your most recent requests—the AIS unit aboard *Insight*, and the series of numbers scrawled in the captain's log. The FA-150 is a transponder that is basically a piece of safety equipment. It transmits and receives data in real time, including position and speed and course over ground. The data is specific to the boat and includes the ship's name and hailing port."

"In light of the ramming incident, I didn't think Larry Vigue was that safety conscious. I guess that won't tell us much," I said.

"Not so fast, girlfriend," Deloris advised. "I was able to *find* the history of what Larry Vigue's AIS had recorded the last two days that he was aboard his boat. It appears that he rendez-voused with none other than *The Princess of the Seas* yesterday just prior to his boat going in circles."

"Okay, now I'm interested. Just two ships passing coincidentally, or is there more?" I asked.

"The series of numbers that you photographed and texted me are loran bearings. The local fishermen use loran bearings instead of latitude and longitude in navigating and setting gear."

"And?"

"And, the bearings that Larry Vigue recorded in his log are the exact position where the AIS shows *Insight* visiting *The Princess*. The recorded data from the cruise ship's AIS confirms that the two vessels shared that position for about fifteen minutes."

"Okay. When Pete and I were looking for Larry, we were following the track left on his chart plotter. It appeared that he steamed away from his traps, then returned to haul again, which is when he went overboard," I said as I tried to put pieces together. "I wonder why he got together with *The Princess*."

"That's your department," Deloris answered, although I was merely thinking out loud.

"Well, I will get to the bottom of that today at the clambake. I'll question the captain and see what he has to say. I hadn't thought there was a connection between the missing kids and the ramming and subsequent death and homicide cases. But maybe there is something there." I rubbed the corners of my jaw with both hands as I fought the urge to clench and grind my teeth. I was suddenly getting nerved up about what Bianca and the now missing Franklin might know about Ron Thomas and Larry Vigue. "Probably a stretch," I conceded as Deloris continued to work on two laptops at the same time.

"Yes, that would be too easy," Deloris said. "I've been digging through the marriage and divorce records and all insurances held in the Vigue and Thomas names. It seems that Liza divulged to you the complete and honest story. Larry Vigue's widow is indeed Ron Thomas's ex-wife. And she is the sole beneficiary to all property and life insurance payouts."

"That makes her the prime suspect," I said. "But I'm not sure what I suspect her of. That's a problem that may start to unravel when I join the festivities at the clambake. I really need to find Bianca and Franklin—now more than ever." As love, revenge, and money are the three most prominent motives for all crimes, I knew that I would be seeking out Ron Thomas's ex and Larry Vigue's widow soon after the funeral service. It made it easy that they were one and the same, I thought as I excused myself to start writing up the long-neglected reports.

As I shut my office door, I heard the phone at the main desk ringing. Unfortunate, I thought, with all of the skill and talent possessed by Deloris in the way of cyber forensics and research, that the bulk of her duties here at the station involved answering the phone and dispatching. I realized that until I started as deputy here, Deloris must have been grossly underutilized. The sheriff was aware of her talents, but never really pursued cases that required more than writing a summons or doing some smooth negotiating over the phone. The sheriff, I knew, was a tad lazy. He was liked and respected by all of the county. Especially the criminals! He kept the peace. And I suppose that was generally what the position required until I upset the balance by actually fighting crime. This thought brought me back to silently bemoaning the fact that I had been asked to put my drug-busting self on vacation until the end of tourist season. The fact that the county sheriff was an elected position spoke to his likability. And also forecast that I would never get that promotion.

I realized that all of this going through my head was a way of procrastinating. I sighed audibly and got busy, starting with my trip to Bar Harbor to follow up on the call about the missing girl—Bianca Chiriac. I had barely typed the date into the electronic form on my monitor when Deloris rapped on the door, opened it enough to stick her head in, and said, "I received a call on the Find Bianca tip line."

"The what?" I asked, confused.

"It's news to me, too. The caller claims to have seen a picture of Bianca on a poster in Bar Harbor and says this number was listed to call with any sightings or information. Some guy they call The Wharf Rat claims to have some information that might be related." I had forgotten about the brief encounter with The Rat. "He doesn't have a cell, and called from the only pay phone in the area. He said that you would know how to find him." Deloris paused for a few seconds, then asked, "When did we start putting up missing-person posters?"

"We didn't. Bianca's friend wanted to do something to help. I thought she was just bugging me for information. I didn't think she would actually do anything, so I told her to beat the bushes."

"The Wharf Rat sounded like he knew something. But how credible is someone with that name?" Deloris asked, skeptically.

"I was led to believe he's a bum, and my first impression was not a good one. Maybe he needs a little attention. I'll find him next time I go to Bar Harbor if I don't find Bianca today at the clambake."

This seemed to satisfy Deloris, who excused herself to return to her post, leaving me to the much-dreaded reports. Time escaped before I got caught up. I quickly and happily shut down the office and bolted for the Duster, yelling a goodbye to Deloris as I hustled by. "Have a wonderful time tonight," she reminded me. "Don't do anything I wouldn't do." I wondered briefly what Deloris would not do. More importantly, what *would* I do? Would there be opportunity to *do* or not *do*? I forced images from my mind as I drove just over the speed limit. There was no point in allowing myself to indulge in a daydream, I thought. Time would tell what might transpire between Pete Alfond and me. I secretly hoped, but did not dare to admit that I wanted to get to know Pete. My gut told me he was, at the very least, a viable option. Or were those butterflies driven by work-related anxiety?

I had just enough time to get to the dock in Green Haven by 10:30, which was the time I had agreed to meet Cal for my ride out to Great Duck Island. When I pulled into a vacant parking spot above the dock, I could see exhaust coming from the stack of *Sea Pigeon*. As I locked up the Duster I could hear the low rumble of the boat's diesel engine as it idled, waiting patiently for me to climb aboard and cast off the lines. I slung my messenger-style seabag over my head and pushed my right arm through the strap, allowing the bag to rest on my right side. I scampered down the ramp and was greeted by Cal, who was starting up the boat's electronics. "We'd best plan to leave Great Duck by three o'clock. I've been warned that you'll need some time to get dolled up for your date."

"Let me guess. Audrey?"

"Among others." Cal smiled and nodded to me to cast off the stern line as he unleashed the *Sea Pigeon*'s bowline from a piling. Cal wound the boat's wheel hard to starboard and pushed the gearshift into forward, sending the stern to port and away from the float. He shoved the gearshift into reverse and gave three short blasts of the boat's electric horn, indicating that he was using stern propulsion. Backing away from the dock, Cal spun the steering wheel hard to port, put the engine in forward, and watched as the boat's starboard port quarter just cleared the float.

As Cal maneuvered between moorings, I stepped out of the cockpit and into the wheelhouse. I placed my bag on the bench-style seat against the aft house enclosure and joined him at the helm. Cal drifted up to a dinghy tethered to a mooring, gaffed the pennant, untied the dinghy's painter, and secured it to a ring on the *Sea Pigeon*'s transom. Taking the dinghy in tow, he said, "We'll need to get ashore. No dock on Great Duck." I nodded in understanding. Although it was flat calm, I held the forward dash with both hands, mostly out of habit, and gazed over the bow as Green Haven Harbor's east and west sides faded and disappeared from the periphery. I knew Cal to enjoy silence, so I did the same.

The course to Great Duck Island was dotted with islands as green and wild as they come, I thought. I noticed a couple of crude dwellings and a makeshift dock on one island. I watched as it passed by the portside windows and wondered how difficult construction must have been on these islands protected by a forbidding, ragged coastline. Protected or imprisoned, I wondered. I imagined either could be accurate, depending on the circumstances of one's residing there. My own mother, for instance, felt she had been held hostage by Acadia Island, a victim of island-ness, not islanders. On the other hand, I thought, I had come to know people indigenous to islands from Florida to Maine whose entire identities were defined by and embodied in their island homes. To them, "islander" was the most coveted descriptor of any that could be attributed. As if reading my mind, Cal broke the lull. "My wife is from Swan's. Been in Green Haven since 1967, and it's still not her home." This required no comment, so I remained silent.

Thirty minutes into the ride, Cal pointed at a long, low landmass over the bow. A large white ship lay in the foreground. It was *The Princess*. Ten minutes later the mass had gained clarity. And we could see that the cruise ship was anchored off the island at a safe distance. Maneuvering by the ship, Cal swung the *Sea Pigeon* into an opening in treacherous ledges that reminded me of jagged teeth. Granite gave way to a peaceful, bowl-shaped cove spattered with moorings. Several small boats and a few bigger ones bobbed ever so slightly, tethered by their bows to moorings marked with orange poly balls. Cal threw the engine into neutral and picked a mooring pennant off the surface of the water and ran it up to the bow where he placed it firmly onto a rugged bit. Back at the helm, he turned off the electronics and shut down the engine. "You buying lunch?" Cal asked.

"Of course," I replied. "I can expense it." Thank God, I thought as I imagined how costly a meal might be here in this remote setting where there were no options for food other than what a ticket for the clambake provided. I hadn't planned to eat. I had planned to ask some questions and possibly get aboard *The Princess*. But who am I to deny Cal lunch? And this was my first real clambake. I should have the full experience, I thought. I'd enjoy fresh lobster, clams, and all the fixings on Hancock County's tab. And it would be good to mix with the crowd that I could see all along the shore of the cove. Sticking out as a law enforcement officer is not always the most productive tactic for investigative work.

Cal climbed into the dinghy and motioned for me to take the seat in the stern, allowing him to row from the middle seat. As Cal rowed, his back to the scene on the shore, I couldn't help thinking about lunch. What I knew about clambakes wasn't all that appetizing. I recalled my single acting experience. I was a reluctant chorus member in my high school's rendition of *Carousel*, in which the lyrics of some number regaled the eating of lobster at the clambake . . . *We slit 'em down the back and peppered 'em good, and doused 'em in melted butter. Then we tore away the claws and cracked 'em with our teeth 'cause we weren't in the mood to putter.* Proof that Rodgers and Hammerstein were indeed carnivores. (Hey, my participation in that performance fulfilled my entire arts requirement!)

I enjoyed being rowed ashore. There is simply nothing as primitive and peaceful in the world as rowing a boat in calm water. Cal dipped, pulled, and returned the oars in perfect cadence to propel the dinghy silently except for the squeak of wooden oars in locks. I could see several dinghies high and dry—having been dragged onto a short patch of gravel beach. Cal steered toward the same beach, peeking over his right shoulder every few strokes. People were strewn throughout the cove, some in pairs and others in clusters. They sat on grass above the high-water mark, or on flat ledges and overturned dinghies. "Wow," I said. "There are more people here than I expected." Cal nodded. Soon the bow of the dinghy grazed the beach and came to a stop. Cal boated the oars, and climbed over the bow and onto dry ground without getting his feet wet. He motioned for me to do the same. I helped him pull the dinghy out of the water as he noted that the tide was low so he would keep an eye on things while I did my job.

Before I left the beach, a woman approached and welcomed us to Great Duck Island's famous clambake. She asked if we would be eating, and sold me two tickets for fifty bucks. I handed one ticket to Cal, and told him I would meet him back at the dinghy where I would join him for the seafood feast. "First, I'll make rounds and ask questions," I said. "I would like to find crew members of *The Princess*. Someone will spill the beans about the missing kids. I would prefer to not go to Rockland tomorrow if possible."

I started by walking around the cove and checking everything out. I figured that eventually I would be greeted by some friendly and talkative guy or gal who would strike up a conversation, as the gift of gab was not mine. All I hoped to achieve was getting confirmation that Bianca and Frankie were indeed being young and irresponsible. And once the lost were found, I could concentrate on the deaths of Ron Thomas and Larry Vigue, I thought as I wandered upon the cooking area where several galvanized washtubs sat on hot coals.

A man in a white uniform approached me. I immediately recognized him as the ship's steward whom I had met the other day when Pete delivered the pilot to *The Princess*. "Hello, Deputy," he called out as he stopped and stood with his hands crossed at his chest. "We meet again. You here for a lobster and clams?"

"No, this isn't a social event for me," I started. "I am still looking for the Romanian girl. And since I saw you last, another missing person has been reported—Franklin Avery. He is finishing up a cadet shipping stint aboard *The Princess*. I have reason to believe that both of them are aboard the ship and would like permission to get aboard to search."

"I think I explained that a search is not possible. Legally, you are not welcome. I can't believe you are wasting so much time and money looking for those who may not want to be found."

"Recent reports indicate the possibility of foul play. I just want to wrap this up. Have you seen Frank or Bianca?"

"No. And you'll have to come with a search warrant next time if the lovers don't come up for air in Rockland tomorrow."

I made a mental note of getting a search warrant before heading to Rockland tomorrow, but assumed this would be unnecessary if I could find someone in the crowd to assure me that they had seen either Frank or Bianca aboard. "Okay, well what can you tell me about a rendezvous the ship had with a local lobster boat yesterday? *Insight*?" I asked, trying to get something from the tight-lipped steward that might impact the case I really wanted to be working on.

"We purchased lobsters from Larry yesterday for this event. He always delivers to the ship the day before." Of course, that made perfect sense, I thought, almost disappointed to have that piece of the puzzle fit so tightly and unsuspiciously. I thanked the steward with a degree of sarcasm. I understood that he was just doing his job. But I didn't like him. I continued my surveillance and was hopeful of finding a talker.

I watched as men and women tended the fires and tubs. Empty tubs were taken to the edge of the water where they were filled from the cove with a few gallons of salt water. The tubs were then placed on fires, filled with lobsters, clams, and ears of freshly shucked corn, and covered with seaweed. I assumed the seaweed acted as a cover to keep the heat from escaping and helping to boil the water quicker. Small pans with pounds of butter topped the seaweed—perfect for melting, I thought. Some tub tenders declared theirs done, and picked tubs from fires using steel rods with hooks on either end with which to grab hot tub handles. Straddling steaming tubs, two men would walk the full tubs over to the dumping area where the piping hot food was gently deposited onto metal cooling racks held off the ground by beach rocks. Two women used long tongs to separate lobsters and corn from the clams and plated all three on stiff paper platters. A third woman poured melted butter into small plastic cups and placed one each on the full platters. Hungry guests exchanged tickets for platters and dispersed to various picnic spots to enjoy.

I was number ten in line for food when another tub was brought over and dumped to cool. A woman behind me said, "Now this is the way to eat lobster!"

"Yes," I said as I turned to chat with her. "This is my very first Maine clambake. Are you a guest from the cruise ship?"

"Yes. My husband and I are celebrating our twenty-fifth anniversary. We are from Texas!" she exclaimed with a smile. "Are you on the ship? I haven't met you, have I?" she asked almost apologetically.

Now I was faced with a challenge. Do I lie, or tell the truth? I realized that I had nothing to lie about—this was not a criminal investigation. I was looking for kids! "No, I am here on duty. I am a deputy sheriff, and have been assigned to follow up on two missing persons reports. A young Romanian woman named Bianca and a cadet from the maritime academy named Frank Avery."

The woman's sunburned face went to ash. "There was a girl, too?" she asked. "We were told only about the boy. How tragic. And we are supposed to go on without a care and enjoy the rest of the cruise . . ."

"What exactly were you told? And by whom?"

"Well, we assumed that it was a drunken incident—the

booze flows quite freely aboard ship. And all we have heard is rumor. Nothing confirmed. But that's why you're here, to confirm, right?"

I gently pulled the woman from the food line and walked her away from the crowd for some privacy. I flashed my badge briefly and tucked it back into my pocket. "You need to tell me everything. I have to locate two people, and whatever you can tell me will be helpful. Even if you believe it's just rumor."

"Of course," she said, then cleared her throat as if she might be talking to a tape recorder. "At breakfast this morning, I heard that a female passenger *thinks* that she witnessed something last night. She was up wandering the upper deck, late—seasickness, I guess. She swears that she saw something fly by her from above and splash into the water. She looked and saw what she described as a body in a khaki uniform disappear in the wake. It was dark. She may have been drunk."

"Can you tell me the name of the woman who thinks she saw this? Or help me find her? I need to speak with her, obviously," I said.

"I never heard her name. But she'll be easy to find. Just look for a purple hat. She has been surrounded by curious passengers all morning. We came ashore here in the same launch, and all the focus was on her and her story. Even the launch captain was glued to the drama."

I thanked the woman and allowed her to rejoin the food line that was moving quickly again. I made my way around the perimeter of the cove, looking for a purple hat. At the far side, between the beach and trees, were a few picnic tables where some of the elderly people sat and enjoyed the sun and the lobster dinners. The purple hat stuck out from the green backdrop of spruce trees. The woman faced me as I approached. She was sitting with a broad-shouldered man who had his back to me as he sat across the table from my subject. As I neared, I saw that the man held her hands in his. When she noticed me, her eyes caught mine, causing her companion to turn and see who was interrupting their privacy.

"You're stalking me, right?" said Pete Alfond.

NINE

I attempted to mask my nervous confusion by laughing. When I realized that I was laughing alone, I stopped abruptly and stared, awkwardly waiting for Prince Charming to save me from sheer embarrassment. It was clear from the looks on their faces that I had thrown whatever train the two had going off track. Although I was sure there was a logical explanation for Pete's presence here, and in fact everywhere I had been lately, I was now forced to question this degree of coincidence. I counted my heartbeats until Pete stood. He introduced us and shared the name of the woman he appeared to be "with."

"Deputy Jane Bunker is with the local sheriff's department," he said to his companion, whom I now perceived to be annoyed by me. There was a noticeable absence of *and my date for tonight* in his introduction, I thought. When I didn't excuse myself and disappear, Pete finally stood and begged the woman's pardon and promised, "I'll be back in a minute."

Pete gently took my arm and led me away from the picnic table, I supposed so that the woman couldn't hear his fumbling apology and lies. Or maybe that was my imagination. Just because I had a date with him tonight didn't mean anything. We were not in a committed relationship, I reminded myself. We weren't in *any* relationship. But I couldn't help but be disappointed to see him occupied, and perhaps not as eligible as I had assumed. But if the woman wearing the purple hat was a passenger on the ship, how could she and Pete have connected so quickly? He sure works fast, I thought as he spun me around, forcing our eyes to meet. "Business or pleasure?" he asked gruffly.

"Purely business," I answered. "I am here following up on the same missing kids that I was looking for when I first met you. And the purple hat is part of my investigation," I said, consciously avoiding the use of her name, which I had already forgotten. "It's been reported that she may have seen something or someone fall from the ship last night. So I need to speak with her."

"Well then, you should know that the purple hat is in crisis. She is an alcoholic and has been severely intoxicated the entire cruise. Her companions have suggested intervention, which is why I am here. I am a substance abuse counselor and am here at the request of the cruise line to evaluate and advise."

I almost let out an audible "phew" when it registered that Pete was actually innocent of whatever I assumed he might have been guilty of. "I didn't know that about you. Cool. I still need to speak with her, though."

Pete acquiesced, and warned me that the woman was fragile

and not in her right mind. "She is borderline in withdrawal, and may even be delusional."

We walked back to the picnic table where I sat across from the purple hat and next to Pete. He explained that I had questions for her related to what she reported to have seen. "Well, it's about time," she said disgustedly. "Hey, hon," she said to Pete. "Can you find me a drink? I'm parched." Her voice was dry and shaky. Her accent was pure New Jersey.

"I can grab some water. Be right back," he said as he left us alone.

"I'm sure you've repeated this several times already, but I need to hear about what you reported," I said. I noticed sweat on her face and trembling in her hands, classic symptoms of withdrawal from alcohol. I peered under the wide brim of the straw hat that shielded the sun and hid signs of age and abuse that had no doubt taken years to achieve. Her clothes were rumpled.

"I guess I partied a little too hard," she started. "But it is a cruise."

"Okay, but you reported seeing something. And I am here to follow up. Can you tell me what you saw?" I was very careful to not put words in her mouth or assist her soggy memory or imagination. She took a deep breath and looked around, I assumed for Pete.

"At this point all I can do is tell you what I have been told by others. I think I must have blacked out at some point."

Oh great, I thought. Now she has amnesia. "Why don't you start by telling me what you had for dinner last night," I suggested in an attempt to get her talking. It worked.

"I had the same thing that I had for lunch and breakfast," she confided. "Liquid diet." She swallowed hard and continued. "Late last night, I was feeling lousy. I don't know if I was seasick or just needing another drink. The bartender at the all-night club cut me off, so I went out on the main deck for some air."

"What time was that? And were you alone?"

"I think it must have been one or two. I was alone. My friends deserted me when I got flirtatious with a stranger. But it is a cruise." She defended whatever she regarded as reason for her companions to abandon her. She looked around again for Pete. "Where is he with my drink?"

"He'll be back," I assured her. "So continue. Where were you and what were you doing?"

"I was trying to sober up enough to get another drink," she said honestly. "I sat in a deck chair and wondered why there were no stars or moon. And that's when I saw a body fly by. I got up and looked overboard and watched it disappear behind the ship."

"It was dark, right?"

"Yes, it was dark! But the ship is lit up like a football stadium at night. That's why I couldn't see any stars. And that's how I got such a good look at the body. I have explained this to *everyone*," she said with growing impatience and thirst.

"All right. What did you do? Who did you tell, and how much time elapsed between what you saw and your report?" I asked, knowing that she was less than credible. I noted that she was more concerned about her next drink than she was about what she claimed to have witnessed.

"That's when things get blurry," she said. "I was told that I was heard screaming at the top of my lungs. I am not sure who responded, or what I might have told them." Wouldn't anyone in their right mind be distraught about seeing a body go overboard? And wouldn't that event act to sober a person up? I was getting antsy, and wanted to wrap this up and get out to the ship to ask around about Bianca and Franklin. She walked me in stages, with plenty of prodding, back through what she recalled. By the time Pete showed back up with a tray that held three full lobster dinners, I knew that my time would be wasted by continued questioning of the purple hat.

Pete placed the tray in the middle of the table and said, "Help yourselves."

"I think I'm going to puke. Excuse me." And the woman in the purple hat staggered away and toward a group of young people who were enjoying the clambake with a cooler of beer.

"More for us," Pete said. "Did you get what you came for?"

"Not yet," I answered as I pulled a platter from the tray. A bright red lobster and a perfect ear of corn were nestled in a pile of steamed softshell clams. "Did you? I mean, are you here to intervene, or advise?"

"I spoke with her friends just now. They tell me she is notorious for making up stories for attention when she's drunk, and then recanting when sober." Pete pulled both claws from his lobster and separated the tail from the carapace. I watched and mirrored his actions. "They are getting off the ship tomorrow in Rockland and taking her home. So my work here is done." He pushed succulent-looking meat from the tail, pulled a strip from the back, dunked it in drawn butter, and slurped it up. "Is this your first lobster?" he asked with a smile.

"No. Second. My first clambake." I pushed a piece of lobster into my mouth. Butter dripped down my chin. It was perhaps the most delicious thing I had ever eaten. "Wow. Thank you so much. You didn't have to buy my lunch."

"No, I didn't *have* to. I *wanted* to," he said. "I think it's something I would like to make a habit of."

Did he really just say that? I was stunned. Yes, it was something I wanted to hear. But I didn't know how to respond. So I kept eating, following his lead. I devoured the lobster and started on the clams, pinching off the outer skin from the necks, then using the neck as a handle for dipping into butter. We were both too full to eat the corn, so Pete placed both ears on the untouched platter he had provided for the now partying purple hat, and asked me to take it with me. "Lobster and clams to go?" I asked. "Sure, I'll give it to my ride if you're going to throw it away."

"Your ride?" Pete asked. "Who might that be? Should I be jealous?"

Now he was really flirting, I thought. And I loved it. But the mention of Cal reminded me that I was here on business, and needed to act accordingly. "I need to get back to work. I'm hoping to avoid a trip to Rockland tomorrow, so I need to locate the missing kids. I'm sure the ship's crew will talk."

"Okay. See you tonight. Are you sure I can't pick you up? Now that we have our first date out of the way?"

"No." I blushed. "Let's stick to the plan. I'll see you at your aunt and uncle's. Six o'clock?"

"I am truly looking forward to it. And all I have left today is to take the pilot back ashore. Then I can get to work making myself beautiful for tonight. Can't wait!" he said with a twinkle in his eyes. I wished that I had been the one to exclaim excitement for our anticipated date.

We got up from the table and walked together—me with a lobster dinner plus extra corn—to the edge of the water. Pete pushed a small rowboat from the beach into the incoming tide, stepping into it over the bow. I forced myself to stop watching him row and went to find Cal.

Cal was close to where I had left him. He had perched on a rock where he could watch both the dinghy and *Sea Pigeon*. I handed him the platter of now-cold food. "I already et mine," he said. "But I'll take it home to Betty," he said, meaning his wife. "We ready to go?"

"Not yet—I have to question some of the ship's crew," I said. "All I need is confirmation that someone has seen the people I'm looking for. That, or I'll have to get aboard *The Princess* tomorrow to do my questioning."

By now the crowd had thinned a bit. Two launches from the ship shuttled passengers from the shore back aboard in groups of ten or twelve. People who had come in private boats began disappearing too. I had wasted a lot of time with the purple hat, I thought as I scrambled to meet a launch before any passengers could get into it. "Hi, I'm Deputy Sheriff Bunker from Hancock County. I'm investigating two missing persons reports. I'd like to ask you a few questions."

"Fire away," said the skinny young man driving the launch.

"Do you know Franklin Avery or Bianca Chiriac? Franklin is a cadet doing an internship aboard, and Bianca is a nineteen-year-old Romanian who we believe may be stowing away aboard *The Princess*." I opened my phone to Bianca's Facebook profile picture and held it for the launch driver to inspect.

"Wow! She's hot," remarked the young man. "Nope. I have never seen her. And I'm pretty tight with the ladies onboard."

I found the picture of Franklin in full uniform and showed it. "Not to sound like an idiot," he said. "But they all look alike." When I scowled in disapproval, he continued. "All of the officers think their shit don't stink. Except for the steward, they don't even ride in the same launch with the passengers! Do you see any uniforms here at the clambake? No, you know why? Because they are too good for us common folk."

The launch captain was not going to be much help, I thought. Setting aside his attitude, which displayed the same derisiveness between the classes aboard a ship that everyone who had ever seen *Titanic* is aware of, I believed he had been honest in not recognizing either Franklin or Bianca. "I can take you out to the ship if you want to interrogate some of the brass," he said snidely.

"Thanks, but they won't let me aboard without a search warrant—already tried." I believed that telling him that I had been forbidden access might win him over—make him feel like we had that in common, being perceived by the ship's officers to be of a lower rank and class, and therefore unfit to even ask questions of them. "Unless the lost is found, I'll see you in Rockland tomorrow."

"Yup. I imagine that the presence of local law enforcement

181

aboard ship isn't good for business," he added as he lent a hand to the first passenger to board for a ride back to *The Princess*. "And we wouldn't want to rock the boat, would we?"

It seemed that I had been hearing a lot of that rhetoric lately. Don't bust any druggies. It might upset tourism. Don't make a scene about looking for two missing people. It might be bad for business. I smiled and nodded as the launch quickly filled with happy passengers, many of whom chatted about the lovely time they had had at the clambake. The launch shoved off, leaving me on the beach with nothing more than I had come with. Unless you count the short yet meaningful repartee I had enjoyed with Pete. That was something I would take home that would buoy my spirits until seeing him again tonight.

I glanced at my watch and realized that I was ahead of schedule. There was nothing else I could do here, I thought. As the trip to Rockland tomorrow was now unavoidable, I knew that it would eat up most of my workday. I still needed to follow up with The Wharf Rat on his call to the tip line that nobody knew we had, I thought as Cal rowed efficiently and methodically from the shore to *Sea Pigeon*. "Hey, Cal?" I asked. "How long would it take to steam to Bar Harbor from here?"

"If I push the throttle up, maybe forty-five minutes. You're paying for the fuel." Cal glanced over his right shoulder and pulled hard with the left oar as he boated the right one. The dinghy glided perfectly against the side of the boat. "Hop out."

I stood, holding the gunwale with both hands, and swung my right leg over and into the cockpit of Cal's boat. Once I was fully aboard, Cal tossed the bitter end of the dinghy's painter onto the deck and climbed aboard himself. Cal tied the painter into the ring bolt on the transom, and then walked the starboard wash rail to the bow where he cast off the mooring pennant and quickly returned to the helm. "Bar Harbor?" he asked.

"Please." And off we went—a lot faster than I was accustomed to going aboard Cal's boat. "Where have you been hiding this power?" I asked teasingly.

"Good to have, ain't it? I like to be home and at the dinner table by four thirty. And I haven't forgotten about your date." Cal took a good look at me, shook his head and said, "If she had another hundred, I'd use it." I knew he was referring to RPMs, and making a not-too-subtle comment about my appearance and the necessity to travel quickly to allow maximum time for some magical transformation from uptight, straitlaced Deputy Bunker to sexy, eligible, and desirable.

"I guess it would take more than just another hundred," I chuckled. And I knew that by not denying my date or the need to look as good as I could for it, I was confessing my anticipation to see Pete tonight. I was fine with this unspoken admission to Cal as I knew he would never divulge a confidence and was not inclined to gossip. In fact, Cal would likely never mention my date again. He would not question me, or even wonder how it went, unlike Audrey, Deloris, and my landlords. The remainder of the ride was spent in silent reverie sporadically interrupted by the reality of my job.

I took note of the absence of *Ragged But Right* in the harbor, or on a mooring. Pete must have gotten delayed, I thought. I certainly wanted to get out of here before running into him yet again. We had left on such a sweet note. No sense risking dampening that with another chance encounter before our big date. I spotted The Wharf Rat before we landed at the commercial float. He sat on the pier and tossed a mackerel jig out lazily, jigged it a few times, then slowly reeled it back in. He repeated this several times as we secured *Sea Pigeon* to the float. He was keenly aware of our presence, I knew. But he never glanced our way. Instead, he remained focused on fishing. I asked Cal to wait for me, and made my way up the ramp and onto the pier.

"I guess you got my message," the man, in need of a shave, said.

"Yes, I did. And you must know something that you thought relevant to the missing Romanian girl," I said.

"Is there a reward?" he asked.

"How about doing the right thing?"

He shrugged and sighed. "Maybe I didn't see anything after all."

"How about I buy you a meal?"

"How about a rack of beer and a pack of butts?"

"How about a cheeseburger?"

"Fuck the cheeseburger."

"Just as I suspected," I said disgustedly. "That's the problem with a tip line. Every idiot in Bar Harbor is calling with useless information," I lied. "And everyone wants something in return. Well, you're out of luck, pal. And sadly, so is Bianca Chiriac. Why don't you go crawl back into your hole, Rat." I turned on my heel and headed back toward the ramp.

"Wait," he called after me. "I'm not just any idiot. I'm the Rat. I see everything. Fuck you and your cheeseburger."

Now I was mad. Nothing makes me crazier than waste, be it time or money. And I had just squandered both by hiring Cal to bring me here to listen to this kook. I walked back to the man and put my finger on his chest. "You're a bum. You hang around the dock trying to look tough. But you're not tough. You're a punk looking for attention. I am searching for a good girl—a hardworking girl who is going to make something of herself—with no help from anyone. She's here all alone, from another country. Now that's what I call tough."

"The bitch didn't look too tough the other night when she was so wasted they carried her aboard the pilot boat."

"Who's 'they'?"

"I don't know. I'm just a punk lookin' for attention," he said, mocking me.

"Why didn't you tell me this when I met you Wednesday?"

"Because you didn't ask. You were amused by me—like I'm some kind of freak or something. Oh, look at the poor white trash hanging around the dock. He's filthy. He's ignorant. He couldn't possible help *me* in any way."

"I did not ask, you're right. But I never had those thoughts about you," I said truthfully. If he knew the facts surrounding my upbringing, he'd realize that we were kindred spirits. "If you really saw something, you need to tell me right now. And all you get for your trouble is a bit of self-respect and integrity."

"Well, whoop-de-fuckin'-do. Okay, just to show that I am an

185

honorable man," he said indignantly, "I saw the girl on the posters. She was wasted—real bad. I didn't think too much of it, 'cause it happens all the time with cruisers. They can't hold their liquor. Normally they get poured into a launch and taken back to the ship. But the last launch had already run, so I guess the pilot boat was the only option." Now I was somewhat stunned, but not certain whether or not I could believe him. I knew from years of experience with tip lines that the vast majority of calls are hoaxes, often well-meaning citizens who want in on the action. "Why don't you ask your boyfriend?" he asked flippantly. The Rat's black eyes pierced mine like lasers.

"Oh, I will. And when I find out that you're a liar, I'll be back to arrest you for making a false statement and obstruction of justice." The Rat had just tipped his hand in my mind by making it personal with the *boyfriend* comment. If he had real information, he would be more forthcoming and would keep it factual.

"I expect you'll be back to buy me a fuckin' cheeseburger."

I shook my head and left The Rat casting and reeling his jig back and forth. He had enjoyed toying with me. People like him would go out of their way to mislead law enforcement or any person of authority, I knew. And he had no idea, I was sure, how he had struck a nerve by bringing Pete into his fabricated "tip." Or maybe he did, and that was the point. I would certainly let Pete know that he does not have a friend in The Rat. Now, if he had placed someone else at the helm of the boat delivering a drunk girl, I would be taking his statement with some degree of seriousness. Someone like Larry Vigue. The thought of Larry Vigue set the normal string of dominoes in motion, tumbling into Ron Thomas and freshening my annoyance at the valuable time I was passing looking for missing people when I really wanted to resolve a homicide case.

"False alarm," I said to Cal as I stepped back aboard *Sea Pigeon*.

"Wild-goose chase?" he suggested while loosening a line that held the boat to the float, shoving off with a gaff and pulling away.

"Wild Rat chase," I said, and knew that Cal neither needed nor wanted any explanation. "Home, James. And don't spare the horses!" I said, quoting some old movie cliché in an attempt to lighten my own mood, which was teetering on anger and fully immersed in frustration. Happily, we managed to get out of Bar Harbor without running into Pete. And at least this trip could serve as fodder for conversation tonight, I thought. Most men like to hear about police work, I knew from experience. And often boyfriends got very involved in my cases—to the point of getting angry when I held back information. And Pete had been on the fringe, if not near the core, of everything I had going on with both my insurance and deputy assignments. So we would likely have plenty to talk about.

At four o'clock, I was slinging my bag over my shoulder and climbing off the *Sea Pigeon* back in Green Haven. Cal quickly secured his boat and followed me up the ramp with the full lobster dinner for his wife. I thanked him for his assistance, told him I would see him in the morning at the café to settle up, and wished him a good night.

I may have driven a little above the speed limit on my way

home from the dock. But I was excited about the first, actual date that I would have since I could remember. Pete was such a catch! I badly wanted to give this my best shot. And, I told myself, if it didn't work out romantically, I had lost nothing and perhaps gained some perspective. As much as I was looking forward to tonight, I had to understand that this was something I did indeed need. Although I would never admit it to Audrey, Deloris, or Mr. and Mrs. V. I would, as urged by those who care about me, put myself out there. I glanced at my own reflection in the Duster's rearview mirror and gasped. I had a lot of work to do.

To say that I am not a clotheshorse is an understatement of grand proportion. As I charged up the stairs to my apartment, I was dreading the closet search and praying for a miracle. My prayers were answered by Mrs. V, my personal, earthbound God. Hung on the outside of my closet door was the most classic black cocktail dress I could ever imagine wearing. And on the floor below it was a pair of simple yet elegant flats. I found the note on my bed. "Found this little number in my wardrobe. Never worn. I'm too old! Have a wonderful night, and we'll expect a full report tomorrow." It was signed by all three: Mrs. V, Mr. V, and Walter.

The dress fairy had saved me, I thought as I showered and shampooed. I stood in front of the bathroom mirror and wondered about makeup. To use or not to use—that was the question. I owned eye shadow, mascara, and lipstick. But I never used them, so was a little nervous about doing it correctly. Go natural, or go all out and face the possibility of looking like a clown? I blew my hair out poker straight and liked the refined appearance it gave me. My cheeks had great color from my day at the clambake, I thought. I summoned the courage to brush on a bit of mascara. Then I opted for a lightly tinted lip gloss, forgoing the deep red that I had purchased on a whim and had not been brave enough to experiment with. I tried out a couple of smiles in the mirror, and preferred the shy, non-teeth-baring to the confident, toothy beam. I wanted sultry, not spicy.

I could have spent more time practicing looks in the mirror, but knew that I needed to hustle. Suddenly the summer solstice—the longest day of the year—had grown short. I took a deep breath and pulled the dress over my head and stepped into the flats. Pure magic. I stood admiring my full-length reflection in the picture window. The dress did more than extenuate, it created and exaggerated what was not there in the way of contours as the jersey-spandex blend hugged and clung. The square neckline needed no necklace. Thin straps crisscrossed over the open back. The pencil skirt's hem fell at the knee and was slit thigh high on one side. My appearance bolstered my flagging confidence that this date was a good idea. Oh, those last-minute second thoughts! I exhaled and braced myself to leave the apartment. For such a successful gal, I sure was wavering now. I grabbed the sleek, black clutch that Mrs. V had thoughtfully left to complete my ensemble, packed it with my phone and wallet, and scurried in the most unladylike way to the Duster.

I felt the three noses pressed against the window, watching as I drove out. I had to admire the restraint they exercised by not whistling, snapping pictures, or cheering. Probably in shock, I laughed as I got on the road.

Although I had never entered the Alfonds' gated driveway, I knew exactly where it was. I guessed that everyone did, because it was frequently used as a landmark when giving directions. Everywhere of note in Green Haven was some number of rights or lefts after the sign for Bold Sound, which marked the entrance to the Alfond estate. I forced my right foot to ease up on the accelerator. I was anxious but needed to relax. Fashionably late was not in my repertoire. In fact I had always been a chronic early bird, to the point of absolute panic when faced with the possibility of being tardy. I saw the gate. It was 5:45. I needed to arrive at 6:00. I passed by the Bold Sound sign and turned around in someone's driveway. I passed the gate again. I wanted to be greeted by Pete, and not seem overly anxious. Being the first to arrive might spell desperation, I thought. I found a wide shoulder to pull off onto. I needed to kill about ten minutes.

I parked and fumbled for my phone. I saw that I had missed a text message from Deloris asking me to call her ASAP. I knew she would never miss an opportunity to coach me on this date and provide a pep talk. I could not deny her the pleasure, I thought. And besides, I needed to kill a few more minutes. "Hi Deloris. You'll be proud of me," I said. "I am literally around the corner from the soiree, and I am even wearing makeup."

"Hi Jane. I don't want to be a wet blanket. And there's nothing you can do about this tonight, so enjoy your date. But the sheriff thought you should know that Franklin Avery is no longer missing. He was found clinging to a lobster trap buoy. He's dead."

TEN

H ello? You still there, Jane?"

"Yes, I'm here. Just . . . wow, I don't know . . . um, geez." I felt a lump forming in my throat and gulped hard in an attempt to swallow what might otherwise result in tears. Although words had stalled, my mind was racing. The lady in the purple hat had seen something after all. Had Franklin fallen, jumped, or been pushed? "Cause of death?" I asked.

"Initial report looks to have been exposure. The parents have requested an autopsy."

The human anatomy cannot withstand overnight submersion in water—especially with temperatures in the sixties as in the Gulf of Maine and surrounding bays. "When was he discovered and by whom?" I asked.

"A lobsterman out of Bass Harbor spotted him on his way in from the fishing grounds late this afternoon. The report I have states that it appeared that the victim had tied himself to a lobster trap buoy. So he must have been alive when he went overboard," Deloris reasoned. "And get this," she emphasized, ensuring that she had my full attention. "First responders in Bass Harbor who transported the corpse to the morgue have suggested suicide. They found a business card in the victim's pocket for substance abuse and grief counseling—Peter Alfond."

"Oh my God," I whispered. I didn't know what this meant, but would find out. Had Pete met with Franklin? Or had he left cards aboard when transporting the pilot? Or had someone else given Franklin the card out of concern for him? There must be a logical explanation, I thought. If I hadn't just learned that Pete was a counselor today at the clambake, I would likely have responded to this bombshell in a manner more in line with what Deloris may have anticipated.

"Should make for an interesting date," Deloris again prodded. "The sheriff just wanted you to be aware, and knows that you are going to meet the ship when it arrives in Rockland tomorrow morning. Now you have yet another reason to get aboard."

"I'll need a search warrant."

"Done. It's on your desk and ready for you to pick up when you come by in the morning. Now you had better get to the party. I'm on standby if you need anything—just call."

There was a noted lack of "Have fun" from Deloris as she knew that I would now be consumed with work—even at the risk of fumbling this opportunity with the greatest guy I had met since moving to Maine. I disconnected from Deloris and pulled onto the road, heading the short distance to the soiree. Although I had not met Franklin Avery, I felt a real sadness for his passing, more than the usual job-related stuff. By all accounts, Franklin was a good boy with a promising future. I couldn't help feeling an intensified concern for Bianca now. How would she be implicated in Franklin's death? And would she be forthcoming and helpful in the event that he had taken his own life? And had the Averys and Franklin's fiancée been informed of his secret relationship with the Romanian girl? This could get ugly, fast, I thought as I turned into the gate to Bold Sound.

I barely noticed what would normally have taken my breath away in scenery. As I parked, I wondered how I would fill Pete in on the sad news about Franklin. I climbed out of the Duster at exactly 6:00 p.m., leaving my cell behind to ensure that I would not be distracted by incoming texts from nosy friends. My mood was now somber with the news of Franklin Avery, and I yearned for someone to talk to. I needed to lay out all that had happened in the past three days, and kick some theories around—a sounding board. Pete would be perfect as he already understood a lot of the background information, I thought as I tried to concentrate on the surroundings. I smoothed my dress, ran a hand through my hair, and took a breath of fresh confidence to bolster my entrance into what I assumed was a world with which I was somewhat unfamiliar. I was happy to not be wearing heels when I navigated the slate walkway to the granite steps that led to the front door, which was wide open and attended by a male servant in a white uniform.

"Good evening . . . Ms.?" I was greeted by the very formal yet friendly man.

"Hi. Jane Bunker," I responded with a smile.

"Welcome to Bold Sound, Ms. Bunker," he said as he quickly scanned the list of invited guests he held on a clipboard. "The Alfonds are so happy that you could join them in their thirty-fourth annual celebration of the summer solstice."

"Thank you. I'm happy to be here. I'm meeting someone—Pete Alfond. Is it all right if I wait here in the foyer for him?" I asked politely.

"Of course," he smiled and motioned for me to come over the threshold, inside and out of the way of the next arriving guests whom he greeted by name. I stood in a vantage point to see who was coming up the walkway. And I planned to have my back to the door when Pete arrived, feigning admiration for the maritime art that filled all available wall space. I certainly didn't want to appear to be waiting with the hired help, I thought. I wanted to come off as cool, yet enthusiastic, and wasn't sure how to strike that balance. I shifted my weight from foot to foot and changed my pose slightly every few seconds, trying to achieve my most attractive profile. Guests passed and disappeared through swinging doors, and laughter and conversation levels rose as the crowd grew.

Guests continued to arrive, mostly coupled up, as I waited anxiously and nervously for my date. I wanted to check the time, but thought that would project impatience. When the flow of arriving guests slowed to a trickle, I had a sudden panic that Pete had arrived before me and was waiting inside. I fell in behind two couples who appeared to be traveling together, and followed them from the foyer through the full-length mahogany swinging doors that revealed a grand ballroom.

The right side of the large room was lined with a long and fully stocked bar that had six tending stations. No waiting for drinks, I thought. I bellied up to the bar and ordered a glass of pinot noir. It was served in a huge glass with a very long and lean stem—real crystal. I noted the extensive menu of single malt Scotches, and thought I'd wait to sample one of those with Pete. I strolled, sipping my wine. The opposite end of the room was wide open to a remarkable patio and view of the ocean. Most of the ballroom was filled with tables that seated groups of eight. Food was scattered throughout. There was a carving station with rare roast beef and pork tenderloin and turkey. My mouth watered. But I would wait for Pete before digging in. There was a pasta station, an enormous smoked seafood platter, and a table with every vegetable known to man, all brilliantly displayed. There was an ice sculpture of a boat that served as an elaborate raw bar where a man in a pristine white apron shucked oysters. I made the rounds, inspecting and admiring every person and morsel of food. I had never seen anything like this. And I didn't see my date anywhere. My mind tiptoed around thoughts of Franklin Avery.

Pete must have been running late, I thought as I ambled around the perimeter of the outside deck, admiring both the air and the view. People were friendly, always saying "Hello," but not engaging me beyond "Nice night" or "Great party." I didn't recognize anyone, which did not surprise me as I did not mingle or socialize outside of my small and comfortable circles within the café and home. I began feeling a bit awkward when I realized that I had not seen anyone in attendance who appeared to be alone.

I found a quiet corner from where I could watch the partying crowd. I was overcome with sadness when I found myself wondering about Franklin Avery's death. Wrapping up what had seemed to be a benign case had certainly taken an unexpected and dramatic turn. All along I had assumed that I would simply embarrass Franklin and Bianca by letting them know that they had not been good at keeping their relationship under the radar. Franklin could have stuck to his "extended work duties" excuse to soothe his parents and girlfriend, I thought. And there's always the excuse of the dead cell phone with no charger that I was certain Bianca would rely on to cover her irresponsibility. But now that scenario was impossible. What was assumed to have begun as an innocent love affair had become tragic and sad, which should have put my dismal, present situation into perspective.

I spotted a couple whom I assumed must be the hosts—Mr. and Mrs. Arnold Alfond. They were working the crowd, making their way to personally greet every guest. As they approached, I stuck out my hand and introduced myself. "Of course! Deputy Bunker, we are so pleased to meet you!" exclaimed Mrs. Alfond. I was hoping for her to mention that her nephew had told her all about me. But it was clear that Pete had not mentioned me. I understood that doing so would have been a bit premature. Men are typically slower than women in sharing news of potential relationships, I reasoned.

"And we are delighted to know of your brilliant work on behalf of the sheriff's department. Our guests can relax—we are joined by Hancock County's finest, I'm sure," said Mr. Alfond with a chuckle that put me off slightly. He quickly released my hand and was on to the next greeting before I could even thank them for including me. I would have much preferred making their acquaintance on the arm of their nephew, I thought as I watched and listened to people as they milled and made small talk. I wondered if I should have been insulted by Mr. Alfond's somewhat snide tone. No, I resolved. He probably meant it sincerely. No need to have a thin skin. That, coupled with my ineptitude for socializing with the elite, would only add to my discomfort.

Where was Pete? I was getting tired of posing to make the best impression upon his first sight of me. And my anxiety was growing in need of hashing through the events that had resulted in what I assumed must be one of the deadliest three days in Hancock County's history. This was exhausting, I thought as I decided to check the foyer again. What if the greeter hadn't told Pete that I was here and inside? He might be waiting and thinking that I was late. But he was not. And the greeter was now wishing the first departing guests a good night. "Excuse me," I said, getting the attention of the greeter. "Have you seen Pete Alfond?"

"No, I am sorry, I have not. His is one of only three names on the list that I did not check off."

"With whom would I check to ask if he has called and left a message?"

"That would be me. And I am sorry. He has not."

"I guess I shouldn't be worried. He's a grown man, right?" I tried to hide my disappointment. "I'll grab a bite to eat and wait a little longer before giving up on him. Maybe he had car trouble."

"Perhaps," said the greeter, skeptically.

I felt myself shrink—literally. All of the anticipation for a fun and possibly romantic date had decanted from my puffed-up psyche, leaving me flat. I hardly tasted the food. The platters were now looking sparse and the ice sculpture was quickly receding. I plucked a shrimp cocktail from a pool of melted cargo space. There was no sense prolonging this any more than I already had. I placed my empty glass on the bar and hit the swinging doors.

"You look lovely tonight, Ms. Bunker," said the greeter. "I am sorry that you have been stood up. His loss."

Although this was meant to comfort me, his kind words humiliated me. Was it that obvious that I had been stood up? I felt that I had been made a fool of. Waiting and primping and posing and posturing and practicing smiles and looks. And imagining the sweet nothings to be whispered. I had been denied the shoulder I needed to lean on and the non-judgmental ear I needed to talk to as I worked through my present caseload. I was crushed. I was an idiot for allowing myself the indulgence in this fantasy. How had I managed to build Pete, whom I admittedly knew nothing about, into Mr. Right? And how would I answer the questions from Audrey, Deloris, and my "family" when they asked about my date? I climbed into the Duster and slammed the door hard enough to create a cloud of road dust that billowed in the headlights of the last cars to leave. I opened my phone to check the time, knowing that this would only verify what a dolt I had been to wait all night for a no-show.

I had a text message from a number that I did not recognize.

I opened it and read, *Work late. Later. P.* This incensed me. I didn't even rate a full sentence.

Two possibilities crossed my mind. One: Pete had succumbed to second thoughts about a date with me. And Two: Pete had learned of the death of Franklin Avery and was actually performing emergency counseling to whoever was in need. His absence may have been a combination of both, I realized as I remained parked on Alfond property, unwilling to go home and face the interrogation that awaited me. Maybe Pete wanted to back out, and given the opportunity to use work as an excuse, realized that I of all people would understand. But, I thought, Pete knew that Franklin Avery was the subject of one on my missing persons investigations. What about *my* work? Didn't Pete at least think enough of me professionally to inform me of Franklin's tragic turning up? I checked the time of the text. It had been sent, or at least received, at 6:07.

It was just past eight o'clock, and the light of day was beginning to dwindle to dusk. I couldn't sit in the Duster all night, and I couldn't bring myself to go home. The Vickersons were night owls, and Wally would be up with them until they retired, which wouldn't be until after the eleven o'clock news. The only emotion I was experiencing now that was stronger than rejection was self-loathing. I had put my work aside for a man. I had somehow neglected to pursue reports of missing people in the dogged fashion in which I had always prided myself. If I had forced my way aboard *The Princess of the Seas* when I'd had opportunity (twice!), I might have been able to talk sense to Franklin and Bianca. Certainly whatever had gotten to Franklin, whether it was his own conscience, a fatal misstep, or a shipboard enemy, could possibly have been averted. I would never know, and I would always feel a tad responsible. No, this was not the first, or even second time that I'd assumed an inkling of personal responsibility for the loss of a subject during an active investigation. And although I knew this went with the territory, it did nothing to soothe my growing angst. I clasped my hands in my lap and closed my eyes in a brief prayer. I begged my God for the emotional and professional wherewithal to simply do my job. And with that, I twisted the Duster's ignition key and resolved to get to work. I had some catching up to do.

I needed to start back at the beginning, I thought as I drove. I would retrace my steps tonight, staying up all night if needed. And I would be in Rockland by daylight to greet *The Princess* when she arrived in port. My first stop would be the Bar Harbor Inn and Resort. I would find Bianca's roommate, Anika, who had made the initial call to report Bianca missing and who had since plastered the town with posters pleading for help. Everyone had believed that Franklin and Bianca were involved in an innocent love affair. What if everyone had been mistaken? If I hadn't been blinded by my own prospects of love, I might have found them prior to Franklin's death. I vowed to banish all thoughts of Peter Alfond and anything remotely personal from my head, returning to all business after the short sabbatical.

As luck would have it, this was the right time of night to be driving to Bar Harbor. Traffic was light, and I made the trip in thirty minutes. I pulled into the Bar Harbor Inn and Resort, and was greeted by the same valet I had met on Wednesday. I knew the drill, so handed him my keys without question. "Leave them on the tire?" he asked. I nodded and walked directly to the basement-level entrance used by employees only.

The door was kept ajar with a plastic jug of water. I noted that the door would otherwise automatically lock from the inside. There was a motion-detecting spotlight, but no sign of any security camera. A large tin can filled with cigarette butts indicated this was the employee smoking area. I let myself in and found the laundry room bustling with activity. As soon as I was spotted, work and chatter slowed to a pace that allowed the employees to appear busy, but to also watch and listen to what this intrusion might mean. Anika emerged from behind an ironing board and said, "Detective Bunker?"

"Yes, hi Anika. I am here following up with you on Bianca. I assume you have still not heard from her," I started. "But have you thought of anything else that you may have not told me that might help?"

"No, nothing. I put up the posters like you said."

"Yes, we did receive one tip that did not pan out. But I am going over that again tonight," I said.

"You are working undercover on this?" Anika questioned as she checked out my dress and shoes. She scowled and added, "Or did you just stop in for dinner and remember that we are missing our friend." She sounded fairly frustrated, which I understood. The longer Bianca was missing, the less likely it was that she would ever surface. This was a cold statistic of which I assumed Anika was aware.

"I am doing everything I can to locate your friend."

"Oh, like going to clambakes and parties? Did you think you would find Bianca hanging out with rich people?"

There was no use defending myself, I knew from past experience. When citizens on the fringe of an investigation are frustrated, law enforcement seemingly does nothing right. Everyone who watches police dramas on television is an armchair detective. I asked permission to search her living quarters. Anika agreed, giving me the unit number and confirming that the door was unlocked in case Bianca came back without her key. "If anything at all comes to mind, let me know," I said as I turned to make my exit. "You never know what might help. Nothing is too small or insignificant."

I knew from what Deloris had told me that the vast majority of service employees in tourist destinations in Maine are working on J-1 visas. As J-1 visas were limited in numbers issued, I also knew that there were many job openings that locals would not lower themselves to fill, preferring to be unemployed. That must make for some tension, I thought as I found the path to the employee barracks I recalled were referred to as the UN. I would speak to some local Bar Harbor residents to learn about possible bad attitudes and resentments that may have been acted on. Most areas that enjoyed tourist trade also had seasonal residents. There was usually friction between the wealthy summer folks and the year-rounders. But the immigrant workforce was yet another faction that was an angle worth exploring, I thought. I imagined that in some cases, immigrant workers might be the darlings of local business owners and wealthy summer residents looking to be pampered and served, which may be another sore spot chafing on locals prone to being disgruntled about life in general. With all of this in mind, I was still leaning toward an innocent, albeit sad, resolution to this case.

I let myself in at the housing unit shared by Anika and Bianca. It looked exactly like what I would have expected to see in a room shared by young women. There were two beds, two nightstands, two dressers with three drawers each, and two mirrors. Both beds were made neatly, and things were basically organized. Drawers of both dressers were stuffed with clothes. Nightstand drawers held personal mail, handwritten in a language foreign to me. The single bathroom was the exception to doubles on everything else. The vanity was full of beauty and maintenance products typical of nineteen- and twenty-year-old women. Makeup, hair, nails, hygiene, acne; they had it covered. I found no prescription drugs. I checked under the beds and between the mattresses and box springs. I found no sign of anything even remotely illicit.

On the top of the dresser I assumed was Anika's by the family picture in which she appeared, there was a yellow legal pad with notes printed in blue ink. It looked like Anika was keeping a timeline of events since Bianca's disappearance. The list was short, but well documented with dates and times. I ran my finger down the numbered list and stalled on the last line—"207-347-6645—Counselor." I hoped I was wrong when I opened my phone and checked the last text message. My stomach knotted when I saw that the number belonged to Pete Alfond. I snapped a picture of the list and let myself out, leaving the door unlocked as instructed by Anika.

I walked quickly back to my car, found the key over the driver's-side back tire, and started toward the waterfront. I finally allowed the ugly thought to surface. Pete Alfond was just too involved at every step of every move I had made since the initial trip here on Wednesday. I couldn't ignore it any longer. I couldn't justify his Johnny-on-the-spot presence any more. I could not rationalize that it was normal in small towns to have a single person emerge at every part of a multi-faceted case. I could no longer explain or excuse or make alibis for Pete Alfond. I recalled that his name had been handwritten on the police report of the missing woman last year—nearly a year to the date of Bianca's disappearance. Pete had taken me to witness the ramming and sinking of *Elizabeth*, never mentioning that the victim, now dead, was his brother-in-law. He had taken me to haul the suspect's traps, finding his corpse mysteriously tied to the line with a perfect clove hitch. He had been at the clambake. The Wharf Rat had implicated the pilot boat in delivering an intoxicated Bianca to *The Princess*. His business card had been found in the deceased Franklin Avery's pocket. And now his name was on Anika's list. Pete knew that I would be out of circulation tonight, as I was at a party. Too many coincidences to be considered anything but prime suspect. Pete was involved in, if not directly responsible for, a lot of things that had "happened," I surmised as I entered the center of Bar Harbor.

I parked and walked toward the waterfront, hoping to find The Rat. The restaurants that lined Main Street served late diners as shops swept up and flipped signs from "OPEN" to

"CLOSED." It was now dark, and the park was deserted. I sensed being watched, and brushed it off as paranoia. Headlights lit up the wharf area as a vehicle circled into the lot between me and the dock. The vehicle stopped and I saw a flash of a lighter followed by the red glow of a cigarette. I approached and found it was the cabbie I had met. I recalled that his name was Dudley and that he and his wife, Dolly, owned and operated Tag Team Taxi. His presence here was fortuitous, I thought.

"Good evening," I called through the open window of the Subaru wagon.

"Hello there!" the cabbie said pleasantly. "Looking for a ride? I can accommodate you after I pick up a fare due here in five minutes. Where are you headed?"

"I'm Deputy Bunker. We met on Wednesday. Remember me? I am following up on the missing Romanian woman," I reminded him as I realized that he met a lot of people.

"Oh, of course! I almost didn't recognize you—all dolled up like that. You working undercover?" he asked, but not sarcastically as Anika had.

"No, just happened to be on my way from an event, and thought I'd swing back through here to see if I had missed something. You're working late tonight," I said, secretly relieved to have company as this area was a little creepy after dark. Too many shadows and hiding places, I thought.

"You too! Usually the only one here at night is a kid they call The Wharf Rat. He's a sneaky guy. I don't trust him and always tell Dolly to keep her distance." He quickly snuffed out the cigarette against the outside of his car door and said, "Jesus, don't tell Dolly I'm smoking! She'll have a fit."

"Who are you waiting for?" I asked, more out of conversation than for an investigative motive.

"The ship's pilot. A new cruise ship came in a while ago, I guess. I just made my last trip back and forth to the airport for the night. Last flight out to Boston just left. I'll be late home and dinner will be cold. But it's part of the job," he said with a smile and patted his big belly.

I supposed this was confirmation that Pete had indeed been working late. But I couldn't believe he didn't have a firm schedule of duties with the ship's pilot, or couldn't find a replacement for tonight's transport if it had come up unexpectedly. There was no way I wanted to see Pete, or be seen by him. "Well, I'll see if I can find The Rat. Have a nice night," I said and waved a quick goodbye.

"Yeah, The Rat sure lurks around. He must see and hear a lot of things that don't need hearing or seeing. You might find him at the service entrance of one of the restaurants. The cooks feed him in exchange for *deliveries*. I just don't trust the kid. Makes me nervous. You be careful."

I heeded the advice, and shared a distrust of The Rat with the cabbie. But I wasn't ready to go searching back alleys for the guy who may well be receiving handouts; not yet. Instead, I found a dark park bench from which I could see and not be seen from the dock. Street- and floodlights were blocked by the roof of a gazebo strategically shielding me in blackness. I waited patiently as the summer air cooled and left its mark in goosebumps on my exposed calves and upper arms. When I heard the faint humming of an outboard motor, I strained to see through the dark. As the motor grew louder, running lights came into view and approached the commercial fishing section of floats. Two figures stepped from the boat to the float. I could not see faces in the distance—they could have been any two average-size men. The only thing I knew was that the boat was not Pete's. It appeared to be one of the launches. It left the float and disappeared into the ink-black night as the two figures made their way up the ramp and into the idling taxi.

I watched the cab until its taillights faded out of sight. I walked, trying to stay in the shadows cast by surrounding trees, down toward the ramp that fed the working floats where many skiffs and dinghies were tied, resting like horses at a hitching post. I stopped and hid behind a Dumpster to ensure that I was alone before proceeding. The launch's stern light had dissipated into the murky backdrop of the inner harbor. I listened as the gurgling of the outboard motor grew faint in the distance and finally stopped as it reached whatever cruise ship had arrived tonight. It was a breathless night, totally silent and motionless save the slight lapping of the incoming tide. I checked the entrance to the parking lot above me for any sign of activity, and was certain that the lot was completely empty. I couldn't shake the eerie feeling of being watched. But I couldn't stay behind the Dumpster until daylight, either.

My plan, which was being reformulated continuously, was to commandeer a dinghy and row out to see if *Ragged But Right* was on a mooring. While I am sure that some might see this as a scorned woman thing, I was dead set on Pete Alfond as a suspect now. I hoped to get aboard his boat and have a look around. I would check his chart plotter for travel outside of what I knew about already, and see what could be connected to the recorded courses and positions of *The Princess* and *Insight*. I made a mental note to ask Deloris to look into any AIS information, and expected that I would learn that I had been played by Pete.

But Pete was good, I thought as I walked quickly and quietly down the ramp to the dinghy float. He had sucked me in with his charm. And now that I had been chewed and spit out, I was wise to him. Pete had been conveniently at every scene to intervene under the guise of assistance. He had orchestrated my whereabouts this evening by ensuring that I would be at his family's Summer Solstice Soiree. I wondered what evil activity he had been engaged in tonight that required that I would be off duty. He had gone out of his way to discredit The Wharf Rat, and now I understood why. The Rat was a witness. And as soon as I inspected and got what I needed aboard *Ragged But Right*, I would track down The Rat. I would gladly ply him with the requested rack of beer and pack of butts to nail Pete Alfond.

I stood and scrutinized the many skiffs and small rowing boats that hung like a cluster of grapes from the designated finger float. A floodlight from the dock shone down, lighting up my options. The stench of rotten bait permeated the area. The small boats belonged to fishermen who were less than meticulous about their appearance or fragrance, I thought. Although outboards were numerous, I would be stealthier in a rowboat. I picked one that appeared to be cleaner and a bit more stable than some of the other tea-cup alternatives. I chased the painter hand over hand to where the end was tethered to a wooden tie-down, unlashed the line, and carefully stepped into the dinghy. I sat on the middle seat facing aft, flipped oarlocks into position, and slid the oars into them as I drifted out and away from the float where the spot I had left was quickly filled by the remaining dinghies, a bit less jammed now.

Although the oars were not a matched set, I pulled and quickly found a comfortable rhythm. I thought about what an odd sight I was, rowing this stinky misfit of a boat while wearing a cocktail dress. I pushed the image from my mind, and vowed to get home for a wardrobe change before heading to Rockland. As soon as I escaped the floodlight, my eyes adjusted and I was able to see boats all around me on moorings. The chill in the air was warmed by the exercise. I circled the mooring field, looking for Pete's boat, stopping occasionally to just drift quietly. There was no sign of *Ragged But Right*. I wondered where else Pete might tie up, or whether he had returned from the clambake. I would ask The Rat, I thought as I continued to pull and glide. The Rat had the waterfront under constant surveillance, I knew. Maybe that explained why I felt that I had eyes on me tonight, I reasoned. I rowed by an empty mooring and saw the lettering on the poly ball—"P. ALFOND." That answered part of my question, I thought. The boat was not here, and so, I reasoned, neither was her captain.

As I returned to the dinghy float, I thought about asking Deloris to track Pete's cell phone. Ping triangulation from various cell towers was not extremely accurate, I knew. But it would be helpful. I would also request that Deloris get records of Pete's recent banking activity. Deloris could easily hack into email and other social media accounts for evidence that would perhaps connect Pete to three deaths, I thought as I nosed the bow of the dinghy between the sterns of two skiffs. It was too late to call her now, I knew. But I would have time behind the Duster's windshield tomorrow morning to place that call. I scrambled over the bow of the rowboat back onto the dinghy float and secured the painter. I figured that I would look around for The Rat on my way out of town, and get home for a nap and a shower before hitting the road and the case again in the morning.

Halfway up the ramp connecting float to dock, something caught the corner of my eye. I stopped and peered down below the ramp. My breath caught in my chest. In the seaweed, just at the edge of the water, was a body lying facedown. I could clearly make out the back of a head and a bright red T-shirt. I looked around and saw that the only way to get to the body other than jumping from the ramp was to go ashore and make my way down to it. I sprang into action, running to the top of the ramp at full speed. I sprinted the length of the dock and hurdled a guardrail, landing on grass adjacent to the ramp. I scrambled down a steep embankment and onto the beach where I slipped and fell on seaweed-covered rocks. I twisted an ankle and skinned a shin on barnacles. I lost a shoe in the mud before making it to the body.

I grabbed the victim by his armpits and dragged him out of the water. I turned him over and started CPR before even feeling for a pulse. When I put my fingers on his carotid artery, I focused on his face. It was The Wharf Rat. And he had no pulse. I assumed there was nobody within earshot, but started yelling as loudly as I could for help while I continued to work hard on the limp body—trying desperately to pump some life back into it. My cry for help was answered in the form of feet pounding pavement and then slopping and sloshing through the weed and muck toward me from behind. I kept working and yelled, "Call nine-one-one."

A shadow hulked over me. I heard a grunt and a swish. Then everything went black.

ELEVEN

The tide had come in around me when I came to. Like waking from a very sound, drug-induced sleep, I was disoriented to a degree that bewildered me. The side of my head throbbed. I slowly rolled onto my stomach and crawled higher on the shore to get out of the water. I sat and felt my right temple. I was not surprised to feel a huge contusion over my ear. My hand became sticky with what I assumed must be blood. I looked around, trying to decipher what I can only describe as a dull kaleidoscope that swirled lackadaisically until the scene gradually stabilized. The confusion of one bare foot and one black flat slowly cleared, and everything came back to me. I had been trying to revive The Rat when someone whacked me from behind, leaving me for dead and for the tide to claim.

I stood unsteadily and looked around for The Rat, whom I presumed was already dead when I had started CPR. I shivered and shook from cold and trauma, but forced myself to stumble along the beach at the high-water mark, searching for the body of the Wharf Rat. I gave up, knowing that it was too late for him but wishing that I had the corpse, mainly to substantiate what would certainly sound like a crazy story. I combed the surrounding area for whatever had been used as the weapon to clout me. But darkness made that impossible. I would have to come back in daylight. And with help. I would search at low tide. I would have Deloris contact the State Police to send a diver to explore the ocean floor as far out as someone might be able to throw an object heavy enough to kill a person. Or, I reminded myself, to nearly kill a person. Or, I thought, to kill a person of normal skull thickness.

I hobbled up the steep embankment and through the park to my car. The Duster was one thing I could count on, I thought as I climbed behind the wheel, locking all four doors. From the safety of my trusted vehicle, I gathered my thoughts. I started the engine and cranked the heat. Then I checked my phone for the time and learned that it was 1:30 a.m. I figured that I must have been unconscious for over an hour, which made sense with the distance the tide had come in from where I had dragged The Rat prior to being knocked out. Whoever wanted The Rat dead was willing to kill me, too. I suspected that I was onto something big—much bigger than missing kids and territorial wars waged amid and among local lobster fishermen. Although I knew that money was always a motive for murder, I couldn't tie Bianca and Franklin into a motive of insurance fraud, benefitting from the death of Ron Thomas or Larry Vigue. No, this was something much bigger.

The Duster's fan began to blow warm air. My head ached severely. I switched on the interior light and tilted the rearview mirror to inspect the damage above my temple. I parted my hair, which was sticky and clumped together from blood, with both hands. A deep gash and large hematoma had trickled and left a trail of dried blood at the corner of my eye and along my jawbone. The laceration had crusted over now, so there was no need for stitches, I convinced myself. There was a possibility of a linear fracture of my skull, and the likelihood of a concussion. I had always been good at self-diagnoses. No need to waste time and money on a hospital visit, I thought as I got my wits about me. I was now thinking clearly. I was safe to drive home.

I recalled the feeling of being watched when I had arrived in Bar Harbor earlier, and pondered the possibility that whoever had tried to kill me might still have an eye on me. If so, they might try to do me in again. I had to call Deloris, just in case something more happened before I got out of town. I dialed and got her voice mail. I hung up without leaving a message, believing that leaving an accurate one was not a good idea, and would be difficult to do in the short time before getting automatically disconnected. Where would I start? Better yet, where would I end? I ran through a rehearsal in my head, knowing that Deloris would call me when she realized she had missed my call. "Hi. I was stood up by my date, then knocked on the head and left for dead in Bar Harbor where The Wharf Rat was killed and whose body disappeared while I was unconscious. Oh, and I lost a shoe."

That eerie feeling of being in someone's crosshairs stayed

with me like a haunting refrain from a song of which the lyrics remain just below the surface of memory—teasingly frustrating. I drove Main Street slowly enough to consider the trip a tour, peering into every black storefront and examining each access to the alleys between shops from within the safety of the Duster. I glanced into the rearview mirror periodically, but saw nothing. Once I turned onto Route 1 I relaxed my grip on the steering wheel and thought about a plan of action.

I obviously needed to report the death of The Wharf Rat. God, I didn't even know his real name! And I needed to go back to Bar Harbor to interrogate Peter Alfond. First I would have Deloris pull every trick from her overstuffed bag to find every single morsel of Pete's past. I needed connections and correspondence with Ron Thomas, Larry Vigue, the harbor pilot, and the administration of the cruise line company that owned *Princess of the Seas*. I needed every electronic device, every bank record, and receipts for every transaction on Pete's record since before the girl was reported missing last year. I needed to know about any possible connection or counseling Pete may have done with Franklin Avery and Bianca Chiriac. I needed information about The Rat. Who was he? And where was he? I knew that making murder cases usually required a body. I needed the preliminary autopsy findings for Larry Vigue. The chance of his death being accidental was now nil, I knew. And what about Franklin Avery? I needed that autopsy, too.

By the time I entered Green Haven, my list of things to do and to ask Deloris to do was enormous. And time was short. I would not waste time and energy scolding myself for being sucked in by the charming Pete Alfond. I would not rehash every bad relationship in my past. I would not relive the times when my personal and professional lives had become intertwined, to the degradation of both. There will be plenty of time for introspection and self-loathing when Pete is behind bars, I thought. Only then would I consider myself vindicated for this silly, half-baked dalliance with my now prime suspect. Sadly, this would not be the first time that my feelings had been misplaced. And this would not be the first prospective significant other to land on the wrong side of the cell door. The most critical thing, right now, was for me to locate Bianca Chiriac. If she was still alive, she would be key to putting the puzzle together. And in light of the number of deaths involved in the two cases of which I was now convinced were one, her minutes were numbered. Whether Bianca was involved in whatever scheme I was ferociously tackling or just more collateral damage, it was crucial that I find her.

I couldn't help but think about the growing possibility that drugs were at the root of all that had transpired since Wednesday. It may have been a result of the bump on my head, but I actually laughed out loud when I realized that I might be on the brink of busting open a large international drug-running ring while I was supposed to be hands-off until the end of tourist season. This little missing person case had sure escalated, I thought as I switched off the headlights before pulling into the Vickersons' yard. No need chancing waking them or Wally, I thought. My appearance would frighten them, and I didn't have time to explain.

As I climbed out of the car, my cell phone rang. Seeing that it was Deloris, I answered it before the second ring. "Hey, thanks for getting back to me," I said.

"I figured that you must have had one hell of a date to be calling me at one thirty! What's the matter?"

I cut her off with some chilling facts that included The Rat's death, his missing body, and my close call. I somehow avoided mentioning the humiliation of having been jilted by my date, but assumed that Deloris deduced that from the subject of the research project I gave her, titled Peter Alfond. "I have to stop by the office to grab the search warrant for *The Princess of the Seas*," I said. "What are the chances that you'll have anything for me by six?"

"I'll have everything worth having. I'll be at my desk in ten minutes. See you at six."

"And I'll need a warrant for the arrest of Pete Alfond."

"No chance of that by six," Deloris said. "But I may be able to give it to you verbally later in the morning. Do you have evidence?"

"Purely circumstantial. I'm betting on that to change in Rockland." I let Deloris go, as I knew she would need every available minute between now and six o'clock to adeptly scour every resource.

I crept into and through the gift shop below my apartment, using the light of my cell phone to avoid upsetting any of the many displays that crowded the Lobster Trappe. I needed to grab some ice from the Vickersons' freezer for my head, I thought as I tiptoed through their door and into the kitchen. I opened the freezer and found a bag of peas—perfect for the swelling, I thought. And better late than never, I knew. I closed the freezer and turned to leave when I met my brother, Wally, face to face. "What are you doing up?" I whispered, deflecting what was surely coming in the way of questions about what *I* was doing up, and relieved that it was dark enough to hide my injury.

"I am having milk and cookies. Are you hungry?" Wally said in his usual quiet voice.

"No, I'm just tired."

"Why are you eating peas?"

"Oh, I'm not eating them. I have a headache and thought these might help," I muttered somewhat truthfully. I consciously turned so that Wally was seeing only my left side.

"How was your date with the rich man?" he asked, parroting what I knew he had been told by the landlords or Audrey.

"Interesting. How was your date with Marilyn and Marlena?"

"It was fun. But we didn't have dessert because the lady who made the cupcakes is always sick. Even red velvet isn't worth whatever germs she is spreading." I could hear Marlena's tone and attitude in Wally' voice.

I fought off a giggle and said, "Okay. I'm heading to bed. Good night."

As I moved closer, Wally bowed his head in expectation of the usual kiss on his forehead. "Where is your other shoe?"

"I think I lost it."

"Like Cinderella?"

"Yes," I said, thinking how far off that comparison was, yet impressed that Wally had made it. As I opened the door to leave I heard Wally's faint protest about the missing shoe being one of Mrs. V's favorites.

I wanted to collapse on the couch when I got into my apartment. But I knew better. I needed to shower, clean and disinfect my head wound, and then get a catnap. I peeled off the still-damp cocktail dress, kicked off the single shoe, and hobbled, sore, into the shower. I could see fresh scrapes and bruises on my thighs and shins. But they were superficial. I could endure stinging and searing, I thought. But the pounding in my head would be impossible to ignore. I watched the drain between my feet as red tinted water gradually grew clear. I toweled off, carefully slipped a nightdress over my head, gulped down three aspirins with a glass of water, and went to bed with the frozen peas on my lump. I didn't set an alarm, as I knew that my internal clock would wake me up at precisely 5:30.

One hour and forty-five minutes later, I was awake. I hadn't slept long or soundly enough to be out of it. I was fully alert and ready to go. I flipped my pillow over to hide the bloodstained case. I tossed the thawed peas into my freezer, hoping to get a chill back into them before I left the house. I knew that the more I iced my head, the less swelling and discoloration I would have. I took a deep breath and entered the bathroom to inspect myself in the small mirror over the vanity. The beginnings of the inevitable black eye would be easily concealed with sunglasses, I thought. And my hair was fairly lumpy from sleeping with it wet, so the hematoma over my temple would play well in my bad hair day. The bump was extremely tender to the touch. But the aspirin had taken care of the headache. I popped three more for maintenance, and tucked the bottle into my bag along with a number of other items I might need in Rockland today, not the least of which was my loaded Glock.

Twenty minutes in my freezer hadn't firmed up the peas. But they were cold enough to help a bit, I thought as I held the bag on my injury with one hand while I shut off lights and closed the apartment door behind me. I realized how hungry I was when I left the driveway. The café had always been part of my daily routine. I needed to make a quick decision. Do I face Audrey with her questions and smart-ass commentary, and get much-needed food? Or do I avoid the whole scene and go hungry until I find an open restaurant where nobody knows me? My stomach growled, tipping the balance to the café for a quick bite and a short barrage from the sassy waitress.

I tossed the peas into my bag and slipped through the café door, being extra careful to not jingle the cowbells. I was relieved to be the only customer. I took my usual stool at the counter and waited for Audrey to appear from within the kitchen where I could hear her kibitzing with the cook. She quickly excused herself saying that she had a customer. I had never been able to sneak in undetected and could not figure out how Audrey always knew I was there. She called it her seventh sense, the sixth sense being her ability to read minds—her words, not mine.

Audrey made an entrance. She hit the swinging doors in her usual self-assured way that I suspected was her style even when nobody was around. Her special, personal panache set her apart from the crowd in her mundane world of the café. She took one look at me, placed her hands on her hips, and said, "Okay, you can lose the sunglasses. Too much to drink last night? I'll whip up my never-fail hangover remedy." She grabbed a glass from under the counter and pulled tomato juice from the fridge. "You can talk while I mix," she said as she gathered various ingredients for her concoction. "Start with what you wore. And end with who took what off."

While her back was to me, I removed the sunglasses and placed them on the counter. She turned and served me the glass of juiced up juice and said, "What the hell? Did he hit you? Oh my God. Put the glasses back on."

I put the shades back on and forced a smile. I chugged down the juice and ordered two muffins to go. Audrey stood her ground, not making any move toward obliging my request for breakfast to go. She cocked her head to one side and scowled in disapproval, I supposed from my lack of disclosure about my date. I glanced at the clock, and knew that I should hustle. I sighed and said, "Coffee?" Audrey snapped two mugs onto the counter and splashed them full of hot, black coffee, indicating that she was joining me. She remained silent, waiting for me to speak. And I finally did. I figured the fastest way out of the café was to play to Audrey's feminine side, getting sympathy for my humiliation at the soiree. "He never showed up. I waited until guests were leaving. And he didn't show up." I tried to sound pathetic. I expected a hug of reassurance or something in the way of what a jerk Pete was. But Audrey remained silent. So

I continued. "I have never been so embarrassed. I even wore makeup. I thought he was special." I grabbed a napkin and faked wiping a tear from under my shades.

"So what's with the black eye? Failed suicide attempt? Get a grip, for Christ's sake." Audrey was disgusted with me. "Since when are you such a . . . a . . . girl?"

"The black eye was in the line of duty. Late night. Muffins?"

"Well since you are thinking about your stomach, I'll assume that your psyche is fine. But you'll have to do better with some details," Audrey said as she placed a couple of what appeared to be blueberry muffins in a paper bag and handed them to me. "So, Pete is not Prince Charming. Big deal. What are you working on that resulted in the gash on your head? This story *has* to be juicier than your stunted sex life."

I felt the bump and realized that it was bleeding. Audrey wetted a clean cloth and handed it to me. "Thanks. You know I can't discuss a case in progress," I advised, giving my usual reply when asked about work. "No, not even with you," I added, knowing that Audrey was about to start pleading. She would normally bring up the fact that she had helped me solve a case one time.

"Yup. I get it. But when should I worry about you? That cut is serious. Shouldn't you see a doctor?"

"Head wounds bleed. I'm fine, and I have to go. I promise you'll be the first to know what's up as soon as I can talk about it." I plunked some cash on the counter, grabbed the bag of muffins, and left holding the wet dish towel on my head.

"Good. Get out of here before my customers show up. Git. Scram. Shoo. Scat." She didn't say "Loser," but it was there.

"And be careful!" This seemed heartfelt, I thought as I closed the door behind me. Audrey had no idea how much I wanted to confide in her. I had relied on and benefitted from her insight and local knowledge on many occasions. But giving her the scoop at this point would be unprofessional, unwise, and unfair. I could live with unwise, but not the other two-thirds of the equation that added up to my reticence. Besides, I didn't have much to share even if I *could* talk with Audrey about the case. Or cases.

I pressed the wet cloth on my head until the bleeding stopped again. I devoured both muffins, gnawing at them like a mouse, since opening my mouth for a true bite sent pain through my temple. The drive to the Hancock County Sheriff's Department was uneventful, which was appreciated as I am sure that my driving was slightly distracted. I found Deloris at her desk in the main lobby. The printer was cranking out pages, and the fax machine beeped repeatedly while Deloris furiously tapped keyboards, working on two laptops simultaneously. "It's only a quarter of," Deloris said without looking up from her work. "I have fifteen more minutes to produce another miracle." I loved the fact that Deloris was so confident in her abilities. And deservedly so. She was good.

"Do you need all fifteen?" I asked as I pulled a chair from the opposite wall and sat across the desk from her.

"Nope. I'm—" Deloris hesitated when she looked up from a monitor. "Okay, how bad is it? Take off the sunglasses and let me have a look." I pulled the aviator-style glasses off gingerly, avoiding contact with my right cheekbone and temple. "Whoa."

Deloris grabbed her stomach and grimaced. "Oh, Jane. That makes me sick. You should go to the ER." Deloris literally squinted her eyes up as if doing so would lessen the horror of my face, distorted from swelling and discolored from bruising. "Keep the glasses on."

"I'll be fine. Good thing I have a thick skull," I said in an attempt to lighten the conversation. "What do you have for me?"

"Well, I hope I'm not overreaching here," Deloris said, raising both eyebrows. "But are you thinking serial killer?"

"I am thinking drugs, which I know from experience can leave a trail of dead bodies. I hadn't thought about a serial killer because there is no consistent MO and the victims are too dissimilar. Serial killers generally have a type and a signature. And serial killers typically have an inactive period between strikes," I quoted from memory what I had learned in a textbook. Truth was, serial killers were not my expertise. I had spent the bulk of my highly decorated career as a detective in Dade County, Florida, fighting drugs. "What did you find that suggests I am looking for a psycho?" I asked, thinking that I had no reason to believe any of the four deaths had been premeditated. They all appeared to have been straightforward homicides that I had intuitively thought were to cover up whatever the killer was up to. And in the case of Ron Thomas, he had actually died from a heart attack—yes, directly related to the ramming and near drowning. And his blood was on the hands of Larry Vigue, who was the next victim. "No, there's no serial killer."

"Well, something is up. *The Princess of the Seas* started coming to Maine ports five years ago. And every time that cruise ship has entered Bar Harbor, Camden, and Rockland, there have been missing persons reported—all young girls—all of whom have been in Maine from foreign countries, working on J-1 visas. And because the ship is flagged in the Bahamas, local law enforcement can't get aboard to investigate."

"How many girls are we talking about?" I asked.

"Including Bianca Chiriac, fourteen."

"And none of them have ever been found?"

"Well, they haven't been looked for very thoroughly. Like Bianca, everyone assumes the girls are simply AWOL and will resurface. But there's never been any follow-through from what I have found. I think the psycho is a crewmember of the ship. And I think he has gotten away with thirteen murders. Who knows what he's doing with them before he kills them. And he probably dumps the bodies in the middle of the ocean."

"Well, you might be onto something. But how do The Rat, Larry Vigue, and Ron Thomas fit in?" I asked, humoring Deloris. She had clearly dug something up that needed to be looked into, I knew. But other than the Bianca connection, her theory didn't do much to solve the majority of my problems.

"Witnesses?"

"Maybe," I said. "What did you find on Pete Alfond?"

"Nothing. He's like a ghost. Clean slate, to the point of weird. Not even a traffic violation. Would have been a very boring date, in my opinion. And, so you know, he wasn't in Maine when the first three young women went missing."

"So, he's not a serial killer?"

"Hey, you asked me to dig. I dug. And now I have voiced my

opinion, which I know was neither requested nor appreciated. What else can I do for you, boss?"

I had clearly hurt Deloris's feelings, which was not my intention. I just needed her to stick to her part of what worked well for us as a team. I would not apologize for expecting her to simply do her job. "What about The Rat? Real name? Rap sheet?"

"I'll need more than fifteen minutes for that." Deloris took a breath, clearly deciding to let me slide on what she perceived as my insensitivity to or lack of appreciation for her. "Without a name, I can't do much. And until a body is found and ID'd, I won't have a name. The State Police should be on scene now, with the diver."

"Okay, good work," I said as I stood to leave. "Keep me posted. I'm on my way to Rockland to investigate the death of Franklin Avery."

"Awww, it was nothin'," Deloris said sarcastically. I knew Deloris was ultra-sensitive to what she considered being talked down to. But I didn't have time to treat her with kid gloves, or to figure out an alternative way of expressing that she had done a good job that would not insult her. Deloris wanted badly to get out from behind the desk and join me in the field. But the one time that I had allowed her an assignment, she ended up with two broken heels. Since then, she hadn't been overly pushy about another chance. But I sensed that her next suggestion was coming. "I should go with you."

"I need you here. Too many loose ends hanging for us to team up. We'll cover more ground on separate paths this morning," I said honestly.

"I know, I know," Deloris complained. "I'm a spoke on the wheel, right?"

I smiled. "Not just any spoke. I rely on your wizardry! You are good at the things where I am lacking, as you know. I *need* you here."

"By the looks of your face, you *need* someone to watch your back. Be careful," Deloris called as I ducked into my office and grabbed the search warrant she had obtained for me.

Rockland was a forty-five minute drive south, making the Green Haven and Ellsworth area the middle ground sandwiched between it and Bar Harbor. It was a beautiful morning to be on the road. Route 1 bustled in spurts with local morning commuters as I drove through a number of main street villages comprised of small shops. As I crested a hill at the Rockland town line, I drove into a thick wall of fog. I knew the harbor was ahead and to the left, but I couldn't see a thing. I slowed the Duster to below the speed limit as I was unfamiliar with the road. The fog collected in droplets on the windshield.

I followed signs to the waterfront and found a parking spot adjacent to the public dock. I could see the edge of the water, but the fog concealed anything beyond the immediate shore. As ridiculous as the sunglasses were in these conditions, I kept them on to avoid questions or assumptions. I stood with the car door open and prepared. I tucked my loaded Glock into the holster and strung it onto my belt at my left side with the butt of the grip forward, then untucked my shirttail to cover it. I pushed my head and right arm through the strap of my messenger-style bag, allowing it to rest on my right hip. I checked the status of my cell phone, and was happy to see full service and charge. I silenced the ringer and pushed the phone into my hip pocket. I shut the car door and took a deep breath.

It was time to pull out all of the stops, I thought as I walked purposefully toward the docks. Unfortunately, it had taken getting clocked on the head and left for dead to realize that I had penetrated something more serious than I had originally assumed. I felt that Deloris had missed the mark with her theory of a serial killer. But there was a killer involved—no doubt about that now, in light of The Rat's situation. Sure, even The Rat's death could have appeared to have been accidental, I reasoned, if I hadn't been whacked while trying to revive him.

I had been investigating and busting drug lords for more years than I liked to admit, and therefore recognized their work. Sometimes cops follow the money trail to the kingpin. In this case, I was following dead bodies. The only difference I saw now was in the non-brutal killings, if there is such a thing. Normally, drug-related murder was overkill and gory beyond explanation. Maybe the druggies of Down East Maine had not graduated to that height of torturous savagery of which I had admittedly too much knowledge from my work in Miami. The culprits had made efforts to disguise their work as accidental deaths. The drug-cartel hit men that I had dealt with would never have wasted time and energy on that, preferring to leave their mark and escalate fear. Whatever the reason for the relatively tame killings, I needed to get ahead of the drug ring's next move before another "accident" was committed.

And the missing girls? Well, I had never met a drug baron who didn't have a taste for young, innocent women. It made perfect sense for the underlings to provide their boss with foreign students on visas, I thought. Especially when the deals were conducted aboard the foreign-flagged cruise ship. It was clear that law enforcement hadn't or couldn't investigate. And with local law enforcement's hands being tied until the end of tourist season, the outlaws had free rein. Well, that was about to change.

I didn't have to guess where passengers of *The Princess* boarded the launch for transport back and forth to the ship. There was large sign on a post above a double-wide ramp that announced "Boarding for *The Princess of the Seas*" in bold red lettering. A young man sat in the only launch tied to the float, looking at his cell phone. I ascended the ramp quickly and asked, "Can you take me to the ship?"

"I could if they were receiving guests. But they are preparing to weigh anchor. Takes them about an hour to get disconnected," he said as he politely slipped his phone into a pocket.

I pulled out my wallet and flashed my badge. Stepping aboard the launch I said, "Hancock County Sheriff. I have a warrant to search *The Princess of the Seas*."

The launch captain's face grew red. He started stammering about something that made no sense to me. "I knew it. I knew it. Am I in trouble, too? Here, take the twenty bucks." He was so nervous his hand shook uncontrollably as he withdrew a crisp twenty-dollar bill from a shirt pocket and handed it to me.

"Save it for the judge," I said as I pointed to the boat's outboard motor and said, "Start it up."

"I'll make a deal. I'll talk if it saves my job. Will my name be in the paper? This will kill my mother. I'm still in high school." He started the outboard with a single pull on the cord. He allowed it to idle as he cast off a line. "I knew it."

"Are you sure the ship is weighing anchor? Didn't they just arrive this morning?"

"No, they got in last night. My boss called and asked me to work late. Too foggy offshore for the whale watching trip. And I don't know why they're leaving already, but they are."

"Why don't you tell me everything on the way to the ship? It will be better for you if you cooperate," I said, still not knowing what exactly he had been paid to do. I suspected that it was simply to keep his mouth shut. Little did he know that he would likely have been found facedown before nightfall had he not been confessing something to me. "Start at the beginning," I said as I wiped a seat with the sleeve of my shirt and sat down facing the man.

"Well, the ship's steward asked me where he could buy some cheap lobsters. So I called my uncle. He fishes, and needs some extra cash. All I did was deliver the crate of lobster to the ship. I never even looked in the crate."

"When did you deliver it?" I asked.

"Ten minutes before you showed up." The young man pushed the launch away from the float with his foot, and put the motor in gear. "Then I gave the cash to my uncle, and he went back to his traps. All but the twenty bucks that I got."

"What do you think was in the crate? And how much cash did you deliver to your uncle?" I asked, and wondered if this was part of the drug ring. It was clear that the launch captain knew that something illegal was going on, and that he had participated.

"Shorts and V-notched, I guess. My uncle would never keep an egger!" he said, defending his uncle.

"Shorts? Undersized lobsters, you mean?"

"Yup. You can't legally sell shorts and V-notched lobsters, so they are worth less on the black market. A hundred bucks a crate, which is about one hundred pounds. The ship buys legal lobsters that are delivered by the pilot boat—those are served to passengers. The crew gets the shorts."

A granite breakwater emerged from the fog. The launch driver followed the massive stone wall purposed to protect the harbor from storm surges to the end where a sparkplug-style lighthouse sounded a horn every ten seconds. Just as the lighthouse faded into fog, the bow of the ship appeared. The fog was so thick it hid the stern section of the ship until we were almost touching the hull side. I could hear the grinding of the anchor chain as the giant windless turned on the bow. The boarding door above us was wide open, but the ramp and float had been retracted. The ship's steward appeared in the doorway and yelled, "Now what?"

"Deputy Sheriff Jane Bunker. I have a search warrant. I'm coming aboard," I yelled.

"Too late, Deputy," he called back. "We will be underway in less than five minutes. And three miles offshore, your warrant is meaningless."

231

"I am coming aboard. Now deploy the boarding ramp. I want to speak with your captain."

"No. You can catch up with the captain when we land in Portland this evening. Oh, that is out of your jurisdiction, isn't it? Bye bye," he said as the door slid closed.

Oh yeah, I thought angrily. By this evening, there may be a couple more bodies bobbing around. And whatever illegal drugs are aboard may be handed off at sea before *The Princess* makes Portland Harbor. "Now what?" asked the launch driver.

"Take me around the ship. Maybe I can flag the captain's attention before he gets up a full head of steam."

"In this fog? You're kidding, right?"

"Your cooperation will make things easier on you," I reminded him. "Come on now. Take me around to the port side. Go around her stern. Might be dangerous to go by the bow while the anchor is coming up," I said with a real sense of urgency. I knew that if the anchor broke the surface before I was onboard, I would be out of luck.

The young man did as I instructed, running the launch faster now. As we swung under the transom, I was close enough to touch the lettering, reminding me of the issues that could arise with foreign-flagged vessels. Bimini, I thought, must be a major link in the chain of drugs. And if I didn't break this case wide open between Rockland and Portland, the murder investigations of Ron Thomas, Larry Vigue, Franklin Avery, and The Rat would go cold. And the possibility of learning anything about Bianca and the other girls who had been reported as missing would be nil.

Just as the launch turned to starboard to run along the ship's port side, I saw an opening in the hull. I pointed to it and said, "Take me over there." As we neared, I saw that the opening was a cargo loading door that was often referred to as "the grub hole" for its intended purpose of loading food and other supplies onto a ship out of the sight of passengers. Fortunately, the grub hole had not yet been secured.

The launch driver pressed the bow of the launch against the ship's hull just below the door after some muttering about how stupid this was. But he was clearly afraid of what he would face if he did not oblige me. "Call the Hancock County Sheriff's Department and tell Deloris where I am," I said. I stood and grabbed either side of the door casing firmly, hopped, and pulled myself through the opening. I turned and waved the launch driver away. He disappeared into the fog in an instant.

I knew that someone would be coming to secure the cargo door. I had to assume there were no friendly crewmembers, as doing otherwise might be dangerous to me and the investigation. Maybe I could find my way to the main salon and mingle with passengers. That would be the safest place, I thought as I looked around the storage area. I saw work boots coming down a gangway, and quickly ducked behind a pallet of cardboard boxes. I waited, and listened to the door being closed and the suction of the watertight seal. I had to remain unseen until I could get into a crowded area. Then I would insist on seeing the captain and hope that he would cooperate with, and possibly assist with, a search and some questioning.

Within minutes, I heard the main engines increase RPMs

and felt the ship lurch forward slightly. We must be underway, I thought as I peeked out from my hiding spot. I was alone. I quickly scurried over to the gangway, seeing no other exit. I climbed the steel stairs and slowly opened a door to a long corridor. I turned to the right, hoping to find signs that would lead me to an area of the ship where I could find safety in numbers. A door ahead suddenly opened out into the corridor and toward me, concealing whoever was behind it from me, and me from them. I grabbed the knob of the closest door, and was relieved that it opened. I entered another corridor, closing the door quickly behind me.

A door at the end of the corridor opened to another set of stairs, these going back down. I was certain that I needed to get up a couple of decks to find passengers, and up to the bridge to find the captain. But I would have to get up by first going down, as this was my only option. At the bottom of the stairs, I heard voices. When a door slammed, I jumped and pulled my gun out of its holster. There was no way out other than this door, I thought. My best chance was to fling the door open quickly and lead with my Glock. I took a deep breath and kicked the door open.

Again, I was alone. But I knew it would not be for long. The room was part of the engineering department. Walls were filled with gauges and panels, all electronically controlled with computer monitors that were secured to bulkheads at eye level. The door on the opposite side of the room had a sign that read "Hard Hats and Safety Glasses." The door was made of heavy steel, made to dampen sound. I opened it slowly with my Glock in hand, poised to be taking someone by surprise.

I entered a room filled with pipes and valves. I slowly closed the soundproof door behind me. I turned away from the door and found myself looking directly down the barrel of a gun. Instinctively, I drew my gun up to waist level, pointing it into the guts of none other than Pete Alfond, who had his gun pointed at my face. "Drop it," we said in unison.

TWELVE

Slowly, I slid my thumb to release the safety on the trigger. There was no doubt in my mind that Pete intended to shoot to kill. I took a step backward and raised my Glock to eye level, squaring off to meet my nemesis face to face. If my index finger so much as twitched, Pete would drop with a slug in his head. And I suspected that I would have already been dead if Pete didn't need information from me. I had been down this road before. I was not nervous. My training and instincts took over. "Drop it, Pete. There's no way out of this for you. My team is aware that I am here to bring you in. If you kill me, you'll lose your alibi for the murders that have already been committed," I said, meeting his steely stare with one of my own. It was difficult to breathe in this steam-filled room. Without looking around to confirm, I knew we were in the ship's boiler room.

"Okay, okay," Pete said as a bead of sweat rolled down and

dripped from the end of his nose. It was extremely and dangerously hot in this area of the ship, I thought. Steam pipes perspired and valves hissed as Pete deliberately and smoothly removed his finger from the trigger of his gun, squatted down and laid it on the floor, then stood back up and raised his hands in surrender. "Easy now, Jane," he said nervously.

"Back away," I commanded as I thought about how Pete must have been living a nightmare, and actually been ready to be caught. No, this was too easy. I would have to be careful now, I knew. Obviously an expert manipulator, Pete would not go down without a fight, I thought. Pete may have partners waiting to ambush me as soon as they were made aware that I was on board. Pete would wait for an opening and try to overpower me. He must realize that I needed to have him alive to confess and explain. Pete slowly backed away from his gun. I stepped in and slid it aside with my foot, the sights of my Glock never leaving his forehead. Now out of his kicking range, I stooped and grabbed his gun, a .38-caliber revolver. Old school, I thought as I pushed in the safety and tucked the piece into the back of my waistband that was already soaked and sticking to my sweaty skin. "All right, now we are going to make our way to the bridge and have the captain put the brakes on. This ship isn't going anywhere."

"It's too late for that," Pete said. "We are already underway. And we can't trust the captain. Some of the officers are in on it."

"We?" I asked mockingly. "There's no *we* here. Now get your ass in gear, and keep your hands over your head." I assumed that Pete knew his way around the ship and might lead me into a trap. But I knew we couldn't stay in this steam bath and wait for his accomplices to find us.

"Jane." Pete collected himself with a deep breath. "I am FBI Special Agent Peter Alfond. I have been working this case for two years undercover." He stopped and waited for my response. I remained silent. "Now I am going to show you my badge which I wear under my clothes and protective gear." He slowly lowered his hands to unbutton his perspiration-stained, oxford-cloth shirt, exposing a bulletproof vest. He reached inside the vest, never breaking eye contact with me as I stood poised for him to pull a second weapon and attempt to gun me down. He gently removed his hand from his vest and flipped open a credentials wallet for me to see.

"Toss it over here," I said, unwilling to allow him to hand it to me, a rookie mistake that had killed many young officers. Pete pitched the wallet underhand to my feet, then raised both hands again over his head. I grabbed the wallet and opened it to find what appeared to be official credentials. The bifold black leather case displayed both the FBI ID card, which indeed indicated that I had "Special Agent Peter Alfond" at gunpoint. The badge displayed the scales of justice and the thirteen golden stars that encircled the FBI shield and laurels. Below was a scroll that read "Fidelity, Bravery, Integrity." I had no desire to apologize. And I assumed that we had no time to spend talking. We needed to escape the extreme heat that had intensified as the ship's engines increased throttle. I holstered my Glock and handed Pete his wallet.

"I'll explain. But let's get out of here first," Pete said as he held his hand out for his gun. I reluctantly withdrew my revolver from my waistband and handed it back to him. He flipped the safety back off and led us away from the wet heat with the barrel ready to blast away. I followed Pete through a steel door, my Glock drawn and ready to back him up if needed. On the opposite side of the door it was relatively cool. We both breathed deeply, enjoying the relief. This room was filled with generators, air compressors, feed pumps, and fuel pumps. We were alone except for the security cameras that we both noticed and acknowledged. "The engineers will be monitoring this room," Pete said. "Let's keep moving."

We crept around like mice, in and out of various compartments—manned and unmanned—until we found ourselves in a utility closet with cleaning supplies. The closet was small, requiring Pete and me to stand pressed against each other to allow the door to close. "We have to move quickly, so I'll keep this brief," he said. "What do you know?"

"I assume we are busting a drug smuggling operation," I said. "I know that whoever we are looking for does not value human life. The Rat is dead, and I was nearly killed trying to save him." I removed my sunglasses, exposing what I knew must have been a stomach-turning sight.

Pete swallowed hard and winced quietly as I pushed the sunglasses back onto my swollen face. "The Rat was a government informant. No drugs. We have been investigating a human trafficking operation. Young girls. Bianca Chiriac is the most recent. I have reason to believe she is aboard."

"Let's find her," I said.

"First we'll need to stop the ship from leaving US waters," Pete said as he pulled a phone from his hip pocket. "No battery. I have been aboard since I saw you yesterday at the clambake," he said. "And I have searched the entire aft section of the ship including bilges."

"Need my phone?"

"Just let your people know we are aboard and need backup. Have them call the Coast Guard." Pete pulled a paper from his shirt pocket and unfolded it. It was a diagram of the ship's compartments below the main deck. It included the ventilation and mechanical plans and all doors and access hatches.

I quickly dashed a text off to Deloris, requesting that she get the Coast Guard to intercept *The Princess*, now underway from Rockland. "Done," I said as I felt the slight vibration of a text successfully sent.

Pete pointed at the diagram. "We'll take the engine room by storm, and force the engineer to disable the main propulsion. That will buy us some time to locate Bianca. But this needs to be fast. As soon as they know we are aboard, she's as good as dead. And so are we."

"How many are we up against?" I asked.

"The ship's steward, a couple of foreign workers who are low on the totem pole, and I'm not sure who else. That's the problem. I have no idea who or how many are involved aboard here. But I assume that the girls have been hidden somewhere in the vicinity of the engine room because the rest of the ship has heavy passenger and crew traffic."

"Split up?" I asked.

"I'm afraid so," he said. "I'll take the engine room, and you get into every space you can on the starboard side of the ship looking for our girl. As soon as we are dead in the water, I'll start up the port side." He handed me the paper and added, "I have the layout memorized. Good luck and be careful."

That was the third time someone had advised me to be careful today, I thought as I left the closet and crept through a corridor. I passed through another steel door, closing it behind me. I followed a short set of steps down and into what appeared to be just above the ship's bilge. I walked on a steel grate through a dimly lit area that seemed to be storage for plastic fifty-five-gallon drums. Midway through the corridor, I felt and heard the ship's engines stop and shut down. I knew that Pete had been successful in that part of his plan. At least now, at drift, it would be easier for the Coast Guard to catch up and get aboard.

Seconds later, the lights went out altogether, and the ship became eerily quiet. All I could hear was water sloshing. Pete had managed to shut down all power, including the generators, I thought. Or someone had done so to impede our search. I holstered my gun and fumbled through my bag for a flashlight. Flicking it on, I made my way to the next door which opened to another long corridor. This space was lit up with red bulbs. Bulkheads beneath the bulbs were labeled "Emergency Lights." I stashed my flashlight and continued, removing my sunglasses and keeping my right hand on the starboard bulkhead as I walked as quickly as I dared in the low light.

I thought I heard a very faint tapping. I stopped and listened.

I didn't hear it. I continued. I heard it again, louder this time. I answered the tapping with some of my own, using the butt of my Glock against a steel longitudinal beam. I stopped and listened. The tapping started again, louder and faster. I hurried now forward, in the direction I had been heading, stopping to tap and listen every thirty seconds or so. I followed the tapping to a watertight door with twelve dogged latches, one of which was padlocked.

The tapping was coming from the other side of the door. It had to be Bianca! I worked furiously to open eleven of the latches, twisting with all my might to swing the handles ninety degrees. I drew my Glock and fired a round into the padlock that secured the final latch. The ability to fire open a lock with a single shot is a fallacy promulgated by television. I fired five of the fifteen rounds held in my Glock's magazine directly into the padlock before it was destroyed and fell open in pieces. Holstering my gun, I twisted the final dogged latch and pushed the heavy door open with my shoulder.

The compartment was damp and cold. The only light was that which spilled in from the corridor behind me. A young woman huddled in the far corner, shivering and staring in disbelief. She had a high-heeled shoe in one hand. I assumed she had used the heavy heel to signal against the steel in which she was surrounded. She stood and faced me, trembling and wielding the shoe over her head as if she would use it as a weapon if needed. "Bianca Chiriac?" I asked. "Hancock County Deputy Sheriff Jane Bunker. I'm here to help you."

Bianca did not say a word. She crumbled in the corner and sobbed. I approached to help her to her feet and get her out of the dark, wet hole she had probably been in for the past three days. The remains of pizza crust were scattered around with a few empty water bottles. "Come on. We need to hurry. The FBI is here, and the Coast Guard should arrive soon," I said as I helped Bianca to her feet. I snapped the heels off from both of her shoes, and instructed her to put the now flats on her feet. She did. Just as I turned to exit the holding cell, the door slammed with great force.

Now in pitch darkness, I heard one latch squeak and click into the locked position. When the second latch squeaked, I jumped and started feeling the inside of the door with both hands. It was no use. The inside handles of the dogged latch system had been removed. I listened in horror as all twelve latches swung and clicked. Bianca let out a screaming wail that echoed in the tiny, dark chamber. I tried to quiet her by comforting her. "We'll be fine. The FBI is here and looking for us," I said, hoping that Pete's plan had not been compromised, or worse. I checked my phone and was disappointed that Deloris had not yet responded to my text. As long as we were locked in this compartment, we were safe, I thought as I used the light of my cell phone to find and huddle with Bianca in an attempt to warm her up a bit.

Bianca shuddered with sobs, which eventually subsided to light weeping and sniffling. I dug out my flashlight, switched it on and handed it to her, reasoning that it might provide a tiny bit of comfort. "Are you all right? Did they hurt you?" I asked to start a conversation and try to learn what I could about our captors.

"No," she said. "They can't hurt me. I am too valuable. But the man who tried to save me . . ." Bianca went silent. I assumed she was referring to Franklin Avery and that she had witnessed his demise, or at least been told about it to frighten her into submission. I also assumed that her perceived value to her assailants was less than imprisonment for them, and that they would happily dispose of any evidence if the heat was on. But I did not voice that opinion. I would need Bianca to flesh out some details on her seemingly brief connection to Franklin, but would be patient as the mention of him clearly shook her.

I sent another quick text to Deloris. *Locked in watertight compartment on starboard side of ship. Just forward of drum storage area. Bianca here and ok.* I prayed for a response. Suddenly, I heard the sound of engines starting. When the single light at the top of the compartment came on, I knew that the generators had been started up and all power was back online. I had no idea if this was good or bad news. But it was a relief to not be in total blackness. The light was dim, but allowed me to inspect the compartment. Other than the watertight door, there was what looked like an inspection plate the size of a manhole cover on the ceiling. The plate was held by more bolts than I could count. A rusty steel ladder was welded to the wall, but appeared to have no purpose, as it led nowhere.

Bianca's tears had dried. There was no way of knowing how

long we would have to withstand our present predicament, I thought.

I sensed that the ship was moving forward through the water, but it was difficult to know for sure. We could have still been adrift. I could not distinguish main engine sound from generator sound. "We'll be fine. Why don't you tell me how you got here?" I had already pieced together a plausible theory, but wanted to hear her story and determine whether or not she would be a good witness for the prosecution. She started at the beginning, seemingly relived to be telling rather than enduring all she had suffered.

"I come from Romania. I was granted a J-1 visa to work at the resort in Bar Harbor. I was going to meet a friend from Romania who was working on this ship. I remember being in the taxi. But then I don't know what happened. I woke up on the ship, but not in this place. They put me here because I wouldn't stop screaming for help and fighting."

"It sounds like you were drugged. Did you drink or eat anything in the cab?" I asked.

"Yes. The air conditioner was not working and it was real hot. The woman, I think her name is Dolly, gave me a small bottle of water."

"How many people have you seen since you've been aboard? I need to get a sense of what I'm up against here."

"I only see two men. They come together and give me scraps of food and a bit of water. They give me a bucket to use for a latrine. I am so hungry. I didn't dare eat what they brought."

I usually had pre-packaged peanut butter crackers in my bag.

I rifled through it and found only the thawed bag of peas, which I handed to Bianca. She seemed a bit confused by this strange option. She shrugged, tore the bag open with her teeth, and began popping peas into her mouth rapidly, but one at a time. "Tell me about the man who tried to save you," I said.

"He came to the first place they had me locked in. He heard me pounding, and found me. I told him that I had been kidnapped. He said he would save me. But the men followed him when he came back. They beat him up and took his phone, and said they would kill him. I think they did. Then they moved me to this place and told me that nobody would ever hear me."

"Did they ever mention any other girls?"

"Not to me directly. But they did to each other—like comparing me to the last one and saying things like, 'This one will be worth much more than the redhead,' and stuff like that. And when I was in the first hiding place, I could tell that I was not the only woman who had been held there. It was really dirty." She stopped talking, tipped her head back, and dumped a bunch of peas into her mouth by holding up the bag by the corner and shaking it.

I checked my phone again and was worried that Deloris had not responded. The only thing I was certain of was that Pete would be looking for us. Unless, I thought, he had been caught and dealt with in the same way that Franklin had. Now I was sure the ship was moving. I thought about the worst-case scenario, and quickly dismissed the images that conjured. "Do the men have guns?" I asked.

"Yes. Much bigger than that one," she said as she nodded toward my holster. "I am scared that they will come soon."

Just as I was preparing to soothe her fears with false confidence, I heard a strange noise. It was a gurgling sound. It was constant. I followed it to a round hole in the bulkhead very close to the floor. The hole was six inches in diameter. Ventilation? I wondered. The hole burped and belched. Then, to my horror, water gushed from it. The flow increased quickly, sending me into panic mode.

Within seconds, ice-cold water was numbing my feet. Bianca fell into a state of hysteria. This must be a ballast tank, I thought as I tried to jam my bag into the hole to slow the flow of water that was quickly rising. My bag was not substantial enough. Water was up to my knees, and now over the hole. I stripped to my bra, panties, and gun holster and shoved my clothes into the hole. "Give me your blouse and pants!" I shouted to Bianca who quickly undressed through cries of terror. Together we attempted to shove every article of clothing between us into the hole and keep them there. It was not working. The stream of incoming water was too big and too forceful to hold back with what we had to work with. We were now having to plunge beneath the surface to replace the wad of clothing each time it was spit out. The taste of salt confirmed that we were indeed in a ballast tank. When the water rose to my hips, I knew we had to give it up.

"Get up the ladder!" I commanded. Bianca scrambled up the steel frame. I followed closely behind her, relieved only to be out of the icy water that now rose at a frighteningly rapid pace. I watched as rungs of the ladder below us disappeared under the rising water, one at a time. Bianca and I shared rungs keeping us out of the water until we had reached the top rung and our heads were pressed against the ceiling. We watched our clothes swirl around the surface that crept menacingly closer to us.

When a high heel drifted by, I grabbed it and told Bianca to start pounding. Although she was now shivering and shaking wildly with hypothermia, she did. My cell phone was at the bottom of the tank. I prayed that Deloris had received my texts. I prayed that Pete would open the watertight door, draining the water that threatened to drown us as it continued to fill the compartment.

Now clinging to the top of the ladder, with water up to our chests, I began rapping the ceiling with the butt of my Glock while Bianca tapped with the broken-off heel. I heard two bangs followed by a hollow ringing. Gunshots, I assumed. I had a sick feeling that Pete might have been shot.

Within minutes, I saw a red glow appear on the ceiling at the edge of the inspection plate. Sparks flew and fizzled into the water. Of course the men who worked the engine space would have cutting torches. And they needed to spare Bianca's life in order to collect proceeds from the sale. My life was in jeopardy, no matter how this played out, I knew.

The glow moved around the perimeter of the plate as the water crept up our necks. Bianca and I were as high on the ladder as we could physically get. It was a race: the water against the cutting torch. Water licked my chin as I knew the plate was seconds from falling into the water, exposing us to our captors. I braced myself with my left arm wrapped around the frame of the ladder and pointed my gun toward the plate with my right arm extended and just over the surface of the water. Bianca prayed aloud now.

The plate dropped, just missing my head, sizzled, and disappeared in a fraction of a second. I extended my left arm to straight and stretched my right arm with the Glock in hand toward the hole left by the plate. The first thing I saw was the barrel of a gun. The next thing I saw was a big, dark eye focused behind the gun's open sights trained directly on my head. It was Pete.

THIRTEEN

The acrid smoke cleared through the freshly cut hole as Pete and I locked eyes through gunsights. As soon as Pete could see that only Bianca and I were below, he quickly tucked his gun away and stretched a hand down to assist us out of the water that was still rising. "You first," I said to Bianca, who timidly released her grip on the ladder and allowed Pete to pull her through the hole, whose ragged edge still smoked and sizzled. The water had risen to within an inch of my nostrils. I assumed I had been in the hole for hours, but had no way of knowing that. Sheer terror has a way of twisting the clock. I heard a familiar female voice demanding blankets, and assuring Bianca that she would be all right. It could be a hallucination, I thought, caused by the bump on my head, or hypothermia.

I was surprised yet relieved to learn that the voice was none other than Deloris. I was pulled carefully through the jagged steel opening and into a cabin with four bunks I assumed were crews' quarters, judging by the absence of portholes. The area was crowded with uniformed crewmembers, all gasping in sympathetic and shocked tones at what I knew was quite a sight: two women, scantily clad, soaking wet, and choking on smoke. Blood on my bra indicated that my head was bleeding again.

No words were exchanged until both Bianca and I were wrapped in wool blankets. Before I could ask how she got there, Deloris took charge. "All right, let's get the ladies into a hot shower. And I'll need clothes—anything you have—uniforms or lost-and-found items—whatever. And I want the ship's doctor here, pronto." Two crewmembers responded to her orders quickly. Deloris shooed the others back to their stations, thanking them for their assistance. "Let the passengers know that everything is under control, and that the cruise will be back on track ASAP." I was impressed with Deloris's take-charge conduct.

The Princess of the Seas' first mate and chief engineer both introduced themselves to me. The chief grabbed a radio from his belt and ordered the aft starboard ballast pump shut off just as water began to lap over the torch-cut hole. Both men expressed their shock at what had been going on aboard their ship. "We will make our way back to Rockland and remain there until the FBI clears us to leave," the mate told Pete as Deloris led Bianca and me to the female crew locker room and shower area.

The hot water on the back of my neck revitalized me. My thoughts were clear and focused as I carefully washed the wound over my temple. Events of the past three days fell into place as I lingered under the nearly scalding stream of water. By the time

I exited the shower, Deloris had managed to collect appropriate clothing for both Bianca and me. Once I was dressed, I sat and was debriefed by Deloris.

Deloris had obviously received my texts, and had not responded intentionally. She believed that doing so might put us at greater risk in the event that my phone fell into enemy hands. She had called the Coast Guard, and was told that all vessels were responding to distress calls. When Deloris surmised that multiple fake Mayday calls had been placed, sending all available Coast Guard vessels offshore in response, she sprang into action. She called Cal, my trusted friend and captain, who agreed to transport Deloris and two federal agents working with Pete to intercept *The Princess*. Deloris was able to track our location through my cell phone, she explained. And once on location, the federal agents zeroed in on Pete through a microchip implant. "Not sure where on his anatomy the chip is located, though. I'll leave that up to you," Deloris said in a smart-aleck aside. "The ship's steward was responsible for the fake distress calls intended to tie up all Coast Guard vessels," Deloris continued. "He had a handheld VHF radio at his disposal for use in arranging delivery of supplies from other boats."

"Money is often an evil motivator," I sighed. "I suspected that the steward was guilty of something. Is he in cuffs?" I asked.

"He's in a body bag," Deloris replied coldly. "He had a gun to Pete's head when we climbed aboard—using the rope boarding ladder, I might add. The feds shoot first and ask questions later. The captain is dead, too." That explained the shots I had heard.

"The captain was involved?" I asked.

"Oh yeah. In a big way. I checked the crew list going back five years. And every time this particular captain and steward were aboard this particular cruise, I found reports of missing girls in various ports of call that coincided with their having been there. The icing on the cake was when he pulled a gun on me."

"You shot him?"

"Nope," Deloris confessed. "I have not been issued a fire-arm, remember?" Deloris never missed an opportunity to push for a gun. "Thankfully, Pete's team mowed him down."

"Is there anyone left to prosecute? We need to find the top of the food chain."

"I have been advised that our work here is done. The feds have been on this case for years, and although they appreciate the local assist, you can go back to busting druggies."

This was not a surprise, I thought. But I couldn't simply let it go. "The Rat?" I asked.

"The Wharf Rat was working both sides," Deloris said. "And the bad guys don't play that way." Deloris explained how The Rat had been offered a deal on theft charges to work as an informant for the feds. "The Rat was not aware that Tag Team Taxi had been part of the human trafficking ring, and was care-less. He actually bragged to Dolly that he was working with Pete. That blew Pete's cover and cost The Rat his life." Before I could ask, Deloris continued, "The sheriff has arrested Tag Team

Taxi for targeting, drugging, and transporting girls and possibly the murder of The Rat. It looks like a tire iron was used on him and on you. And we're betting that one of their cars is short one lug wrench."

I grabbed a fresh towel and gingerly dabbed my swollen temple, which was still weeping blood. "So, the cabbies were at the bottom of the chain. But who is at the top?" I asked.

"They are out of our jurisdiction. *The Princess of the Seas* being foreign flagged was key to this ring's operation and success. Most Mainers don't know or care where Bimini is."

"But there was more local involvement," I protested. "What about Larry Vigue?" I asked.

"Not a nice guy," Deloris said. "He delivered drugged girls to the ship, using lobster, pilot, and grocery deliveries to cover his frequent rendezvous. And all he had to do was tell any eyewitnesses the girls were intoxicated. When the boss felt the heat closing in, he ordered Larry dead. They tried to make it look like an accident, as you know."

"Ron Thomas?"

"He wore a white hat," Deloris answered. "Ron had witnessed Larry doing something suspicious, and made the fatal mistake of calling him on it."

"From what Bianca told me, I assume that Franklin Avery was killed for the same reasons," I said. "How many people did they think they could kill before getting caught?"

"We'll never know," said Deloris. "But if you hadn't followed up on the missing persons reports, this human trafficking ring might have succeeded in two more sales of girls. It seems that your persistent presence pushed them to make mistakes. We found another young J-1 worker locked in the steward's state-room. Bound and gagged."

I was fully dressed and debriefed before Bianca pulled her-self from the shower stall, wrapped tightly in towels from head to foot. Bianca took a deep breath. She looked like she needed to say something as she had heard all that was said in the locker room. Deloris and I waited patiently for her to collect her thoughts and verbalize whatever she had on her mind. "That felt good," was all she said.

The ship's medic found us in the locker room and checked us both out. He declared I needed a couple of stiches and sewed me up on the spot as Deloris explained the process and sched-ule moving forward. Bianca agreed to testify and help in any way she could. But she would be leaving for school in Romania in six weeks. Deloris's phone dinged with a text. She read it and announced, "Tag Team Taxi full confession." After digesting that information she added, "All of the key players are dead or confessing. We won't need you to testify, Bianca."

"But we do need to feed you," said Pete Alfond as he knocked and entered holding two cafeteria trays heaped with hot food. He handed Bianca and me each a tray and said, "You are both truly remarkable."

It looked like Thanksgiving dinner, I thought as I feigned interest in eating. Bianca caught my eye, giggled, and said, "Peas." I nodded and shared the private joke as I scooped up a spoonful of the peas and shoved them into my mouth.

Deloris excused herself to call Cal, who was back in Green

Haven and would be worried sick about me, she said. I figured that by the time I got home the story would have been spread to cover the entire town. I knew the sheriff loved the media and would be on the local news tonight. He always explained the fact that he was a ham with the fact that he was an elected official. "There's no such thing as bad press," he would say when Deloris and I chided him for being a media hound. Fine by me, I thought. I never liked attention for simply doing my job. I figured the town fathers would not appreciate the news. If they were worried about the effect of drug busts on tourism, how would they like human trafficking?

When Bianca excused herself to call her roommate, I was left alone with Pete. I was trying to summon the courage to address the elephant when he spoke. "I was going to tell you everything at the party." I didn't know how to respond to that. So I didn't. "Can we start over? I would really like to get to know you. Any chance?"

That, I thought, was genuine. And it certainly deserved an honest answer. "I was intrigued with Pete, pilot boat captain and fisherman extraordinaire, at my service," I quoted his initial self-introduction back to him. "Pete, the FBI agent? No thanks."

After a short pause and slightly shocked look, Pete roared with laughter. He held his belly as his shoulders bounced with each chortle. A tear found the corner of his eye. His laugh was contagious, I thought as I fought the urge to giggle. When he could speak, Pete said, "Well, that was blunt."

"Not everyone appreciates my directness," I said with a chuckle.

"Directness I can handle. It's the message that upsets me." Pete grew serious. "You're special, Jane Bunker. And we deserve a chance. And I can be quite persistent. I will not take 'No thanks' for an answer."

True to form, I had nothing. No joke or quip or retort. I can always manage a wisecrack, I thought. But when bona fide repartee is in order, I fall flat on my face. I racked my weary brain for a single witticism, but nothing came. Why is it, I wondered, that I could hold up my end of wordplay with the Vickersons, but not have the wherewithal for light banter with Pete? I was always quick with a sarcastic comeback to Audrey's sass. But now, when I was most in need, words failed me. I sat and stared in total numbness into Pete's liquid, chocolate eyes that waited patiently for me to speak. Finally, I was plucked from the jaws of humiliation when Bianca and Deloris entered and announced that the launch was alongside to take us ashore. Within the mix of feelings of achievement for a job well done in saving Bianca and a dogged, physical fatigue lay a genuine sigh of relief. I was off the hook with Peter Alfond. For now.

I sat quietly in the launch and watched as the lettering on *The Princess of the Seas'* transom blurred to unreadable. Pete had remained aboard with his FBI counterparts to await the coroner. I never said goodbye or thanks or good riddance, I realized, as I followed Deloris and Bianca from the launch to the float. It was decided that I would transport Deloris and Bianca to the dock where Deloris had left her car when meeting Cal. And Deloris would deliver Bianca back to her job and digs in Bar Harbor. This plan would have me happily home for a late dinner.

I drove in silence as Deloris flicked a pen at a sudoku puzzle and Bianca texted rapidly using Deloris's phone. Deloris made a half-hearted attempt to chat, then quickly retreated to her puzzle. What topic of conversation could possibly stimulate interest following my last forty-eight hours? Weather, scenery, politics, sports? I had no desire to make small talk. I wasn't even mulling anything in my own head. I wasn't planning or scheduling, plotting or solving. I was suffering the symptoms of adrenaline withdrawal that I knew all too well. My adrenal glands had been on overdrive, and now I needed to cope with returning to normalcy. Of course, normal is a relative term.

EPILOGUE

We want to hear every last detail," said Mrs. V as she served up a heaping plate of her latest mussel concoction. "Starting with your date."

"My non-date," I corrected as I swirled the remains of a Scotch and soda around the bottom of my glass. "He stood me up." I understood that my landlords and Wally had heard only rumors of the arrests and deaths that had transpired since our last meal together, and needed the real scoop. Realizing that adding the truth as to why Pete had been a no-show would dampen their immediate dislike of him, I left it out. "But the party was fabulous," I lied to avert the verbalization of the pity I saw in Mrs. V's pursed lips. "Great food, and interesting people."

Seemingly torn between berating Pete and stroking my hand in condolence for the disappointment and humiliation I had suffered at the soiree, Mr. V decided to mix me another drink. Mrs. V, however, was not as willing to let this go. "That rat! You are kidding? Oh, you poor dear," she said with a high degree of sympathy and whining. This was exactly what I had hoped to avoid, I thought as I took a slug of the freshly poured drink. I swallowed hard, both the Scotch and the realization that what I was really sore about was the fact that Pete had not confided in me. Standing me up was understandable and acceptable in light of the reasons why he had done so. But what really hurt was his apparent mistrust and lack of confidence in me as a professional. I thought this perhaps indicated a feeling of superiority over me. And *that* could not be overcome. "Well, that's his loss," Mrs. V concluded when she realized that I was not responding.

"I'm just glad I hadn't invested more emotional energy in Pete Alfond," I said, knowing that no one would ever know the difference. This was the last time I would give Pete any airtime, I vowed to myself. I would not so much as breathe his name ever again. (He barely rated a pronoun.)

All focus shifted to dinner as I savored the first bite. Mussels masala over pan-fried polenta was to die for. I was not confident that mushrooms would work with mussels, but the addition of water chestnuts for texture made the dish. I had to marvel at the energy, love, and effort that went into dinners at the Vs'. At the age of eighty-four, Alice Vickerson had earned the right to boast. As we oohed and aahed with every delicious bite, Mrs. V regaled us with a step-by-step replay of the amazing polenta. She summarized it all with, "And the results speak for themselves!"

The quiet associated with happy diners was broken when Wally spoke up. "Janey lost your shoe, Mrs. V. Like Cinderella."

"Wally!" I laughed. "Don't be a tattletale."

"Are you kidding?" said Mr. V. "Your brother is the only source of information around here. Nice job, Walter." With that Mr. V and Wally shared a fist bump, which oddly surprised me. "I'm sure Prince Charming will come calling with the shoe. But what I'm more interested in is the bump on your head and black eye."

"That's the more interesting story, for sure," I said. "You'll be surprised to know that the lost shoe and smashed skull play out in the same scene." I pushed my empty plate into the middle of the table, making room for me to rest my forearms at my place as I leaned forward in my chair for dramatic effect and affect. "I'll start at the beginning," I said as I felt the intense attention of all three at the table. There was no reason for me to hold back any details, I thought as I realized that sharing the traumatic events of the very recent past would be therapeutic. If I couldn't share my life with my family, I may as well become a hermit, I thought.

Just as I was setting the scene regarding the first missing person report, my phone dinged from within my pocket. I chose to ignore it, wishing that I had been courteous enough to silence the phone prior to dinner. Mrs. V, who was always compelled to announce any activity on my phone, announced, "I think you got a text message, dear."

"That's okay. I'll get it later. Sorry about the interruption."

"But what if it's important?" she argued. "Go ahead and look at it. We can wait."

"Well, I don't want to be rude."

"It's not rude. Go ahead," she urged, crowding the line between inquisitive and intrusive.

"Plus, we are nosy and want to know who's messaging you this time of night," Mr. V chimed in honestly. "What if it's Prince Charming with Alice's shoe?"

"That's unlikely," I muttered. "But okay, excuse me for a minute." I stood, caving to the pressure, and pulled the phone from my hip pocket. I turned my back to the table for the best I could do in the way of privacy with three pairs of eyes riveted on my shoulder blades.

Not taking "No Thanks" for an answer. May I call you tomorrow?

My pulse quickened and I felt my face grow red. "Well, who is it? What's going on? Everything okay?" asked the very impatient Mrs. V.

"Yes," I said. "It's Deloris checking on me," I lied, knowing that the truth would lead to more questions and too much input on how I should respond. "I'll send her back a reply real quick, and be right with you."

All curiosity was in check as I typed and sent, *yes.*